The Unsettling

Stories by Peter Rock

Also by Peter Rock

This Is the Place

Carnival Wolves

The Ambidextrist

The Bewildered

The Unsettling

Stories by Peter Rock

MacAdam/Cage

MacAdam/Cage
155 Sansome Street, Suite 550
San Francisco, CA 94104
www.macadamcage.com

Library of Congress Cataloging-in-Publication Data

Rock, Peter, 1967—
  The unsettling : stories and a novella / by Peter Rock.
    p. cm.
  ISBN 1-59692-171-4 (alk. paper)
  1. Psychological fiction. I. Title.
  PS3568.O327U57 2006
  813'.54—dc22

                                                    2006000361

These stories first appeared, often in slightly different form, in the following publications: "Blooms" in *Tin House*; "Stranger" and "Disentangling" in *Zoetrope: All Story*; "Shaken" in *Spork*; "The Sharpest Knife" in *The Cincinnati Review*; "Thrill" in *Willamette Week*; "Gold Firebird" in *Post Road*; "Lights" in *One Story*; "Signal Mirror" (as "The Unsettling") commissioned by the Salt Lake Acting Company and published in the book from their show "Cabbies, Cowboys and the Tree of the Weeping Virgin"; "The Silent Men" in *Western Humanities Review*; "Disappeared Girls" in *XConnect*; "Pergrine Falcon" in *Index*. Many thanks to the editors.

Manufactured in the United States of America.
10 9 8 7 6 5 4 3 2 1

Book and jacket design by Dorothy Carico Smith.

Life is so incredible. Can you believe it? All these
things we've done, and we're only fourteen years old!

Craig Smith
December 29, 1979 – June 12, 2003

CONTENTS

Blooms

I took a job no one else wanted, and I learned many things I would never have believed. Here's an easy one, to start with: fungus can bloom inside books. Different kinds of molds, mostly, in dark, damp libraries where the air isn't too good. Fungi cannot make their own food; they take what they can from other organic matter. They start on the fabric and cardboard of the books' covers, then feed on the wood pulp in the pages, the vegetable dyes in the ink—kind of like how moss grows on tree trunks, swings from branches.

Samples are taken, and sent to a laboratory, to check if the bloom is virulent. Usually, it's not—it's only penicillin or aspergillus—and then they send in a team to clean it up. This is no job for librarians. They hire other people, whoever they can get. It's not exactly skilled labor.

An injury had forced me from my previous occupation. I'd been working down the shore, on the boardwalk. I wore a suit with three inches of padding, a hockey mask painted with a fanged smile. I leapt around behind fake trees, in front of a canvas backdrop, and people shot paintball guns at me. Ten shots for three dollars—I had targets on my suit, my helmet, a bull's eye on my crotch that everyone found hilarious. I wore two cups, with padding between them. Tough-talking boys couldn't touch me, cursing with their cracked voices, slapping their temporary tattoos; it was their girlfriends—bikini tops, slack expressions, baby fat under their arms—who had the deadly aim. At the end of the day, in the shower, I counted the round bruises on my skin.

One day I was recounting a story to a friend of mine, holding the mask in my hand. He had one of the guns, twirling it around his finger like Jesse James. When it went off, it caught me in the face—sideswiped me, actually, not even as hard as a punch. Dark red paint splattered across my temple, into my ear. I was left with this detached retina, where my vision's crooked and everyone I talk to thinks I'm trying to say something else; it's still shadowy on that side, but some days I believe it's clearing. Some days I'm not so sure.

My boss said he couldn't be held accountable for a time I wasn't working. Playing grab-ass—those were his words. And, of course, with my vision wrecked, my depth perception completely gone, I did not make a very challenging target. I was sore all over. We gave away half the stuffed animals in one afternoon.

Fortunately, none of this impaired me for the new job—the blooms did not move so fast. I answered an ad and was hired over the phone, told where to be the next morning.

They said I'd work on a team; what that meant was one other guy, Marco. He was forty, at least, from South Philly, where he still lived. Older than me, and heavier, with gray flecks in his hair, which was thick on the sides but you could see through it on top, his scalp shining. He had a heavy way of walking, almost sliding his feet. His hands would hang down at his sides, opening and closing with each step. My first impression was that he would never surprise me. Nothing he would do, nothing he would say.

We didn't shake hands when we first met, he just started to show me how things worked. Hair pushed out the collar of his T-shirt, both front and back. He'd done this kind of work before, and he told me there were worse jobs.

I've had them, I said.

He told me he was only working long enough to make enough money to get out of town, and I nodded and said that sounded wise.

I have to get out, he said. The reasons are personal.

We went through a side door, on a kind of loading dock, down a flight of stairs. The books we were dealing with were on two floors—a basement, and then another basement beneath that. There was not one window. Marco had already isolated the area with clear plastic sheeting, hung up the warning signs.

He helped me into my suit, that first day. They were white, made of Tyvek, with a long zipper up the front, and zippers on the sides of the legs. We wore latex gloves, and baggy paper booties we had to replace every time we went outside. The hoods on our heads had clear plastic face panels; we wore battery packs on our belts, a fan with a tube that blew filtered air in front of our faces. It took one morning of breathing my own breath in that hood before I quit smoking. That's one positive thing that came of that job.

The blooms, they were a green fuzzy mold, streaked with black. Fibrous, like nothing you'd want in your lungs. They rested atop books, forced the covers open where they weren't tight in the shelves and squeezing each other. We started out with the vacuums, fitted with HEPA filters that trapped spores. Marco would work one aisle and I'd do the next. The shelves were tall, but sometimes I'd pull out a book and see him there, on the other side, his face close but his expression hidden. We kept moving, slowly and methodically, as if we were underwater.

The days went fluid, each like the one before it, progress marked only by the bookshelves left behind. Sections of maps, then encyclopedias. Novels, even poetry. It was strange to spend so much time so close to a person without being able to talk with them. We went our separate ways at lunch, and the rest of the time we were inside the suits and ventilators. It was all white noise, down there—the fans, the rustle of Tyvek, the sound of pages being flipped under our gloved thumbs.

At least a week passed before we first had lunch together. He asked me to join him. We walked half a block, bought sandwiches from a truck, then headed toward a little park. When the children in the playground saw us coming, they started screaming Astronauts! We always got a kick out of that.

The wooden bench we sat on had been chewed by pit bulls—the owners train them to do it, to strengthen their jaws. Next to the jungle gym, the plastic swings were so gnawed they looked melted. When we bit into our sandwiches, shredded lettuce fell onto the ground, tangled with cigarette butts.

Marco stood and tried to touch his toes. He stretched his arms and grunted. All that work in the damp library tightened his joints.

I wonder, he asked, if you wouldn't mind rubbing my knee a little.

I'd give it a try, I told him.

Not everyone would, he said.

If it helps, I said.

I kind of kneeled down and tried to get a decent hold, through the slippery Tyvek, using both hands.

Marco picked up his sandwich, closed his eyes. He obviously shaved, but there were always these long whiskers along his throat, ones he missed. I rubbed his knee. The sun stayed where it was, straight overhead, stuck there.

You're probably wondering what I'm going to do for you, Marco said.

I told him not really. My knees felt fine.

I live in a rowhouse, Marco said. So I share walls with my neighbors. Thin walls.

A couple lived there, and he'd hear their arguments—threats, recriminations, then the usual coming to terms. Marco would turn up his radio, or go out walking around his neighborhood.

Italians, he said, almost spitting.

I thought you were Italian, I said.

I am, he said.

There was an Indian spice shop near that park, so it always smelled a little foreign. The air was thick. Marco picked his teeth with his fingernail as he spoke.

Pay attention, he said. This won't turn out any way you expect.

I told him I had no expectations.

Sometimes on the mornings after the arguments, Marco would run into the man from next door. You're lucky, the man would say, you were safe—a wall between you and her. Pray for me, these nights! He and Marco would laugh together.

What happened to him? I asked, guessing ahead.

I just stopped hearing him through the wall, Marco said. Stopped seeing him in the front yard. He was gone.

And that was your opening, I said. Don't tell me—she's incredibly beautiful.

Yes, Marco said. But that's not the point.

We took our time in the basements of the library, though we weren't being paid by the hour. It wasn't that I got a lot of thinking done, exactly; it was almost a different plane of some sort, listening to my own breathing, a kind of meditation. Sometimes I even thought of the people who would follow, who would be able to read the books because I'd saved them.

Sometimes people came down the stairs, descended by mistake, and I'd catch glimpses, twice-distorted by my face shield and the clear plastic barriers. The people seemed to have no feet, to move fluidly, as if they were growing their way smoothly upward again, beyond my sight.

Sometimes, on my break, I'd climb those stairs; I'd hold the door slightly open, my ventilator around my neck and the cool air on my sweaty face. I spied into the library, and it was quiet up there, just like it was supposed to be. A green and yellow parakeet hung on to its perch, inside a bamboo cage. I heard the sound of pages turning. If I held the door open a little further, I could see the desk where the librarian sat. She was about my age, with dark black skin, gold eyeglasses; her hair was braided close to her head, in curving lines, the loose ends like ropes whipping her shoulders. Her fingers were thin, her smile wide as she answered someone's question. Whenever I turned away from her and began to descend into the basement, it was as if my body grew heavier with every step. I wanted her to know there were real people underneath her, that I was beneath her every day. I wanted to tell her I'd wiped mold from musical scores and hummed the melody, that I'd read a Russian story about grown men swimming in the rain, another where people could see into the future and still couldn't change it.

If I could tell the librarian one story, it would be this one. And I would tell her only a little at a time, the way Marco told me, until she had to know what would happen next, until she couldn't stand it.

He never used the woman's real name, since he said I was his friend and he was afraid I'd try to track her down, once I'd heard it all, that I'd only get myself in trouble. Louisa—that's the name he chose for her.

Their houses shared a porch, so all Louisa had to do was reach over the railing to ring Marco's doorbell. She wanted to ask him a favor. Groceries. She had the list in her hand, and he took it when she held it out.

It's my eyes, Louisa said. I can't see a thing. She told him that the doctors had found nothing wrong, physically, but that didn't help her.

Marco looked at her eyes, and she didn't seem to see him. Her eyebrows had always been tweezed into a narrow arch; now they were returning, thickening. She stood there, barefoot on the concrete porch, the toenails of her left foot painted red. All the words on the list in Marco's hand tilted, and some stretched off the edge of the paper, cut short. Others were written right on top of each other; he struggled to untangle them.

When he returned from the store, he offered to put the things away for her, and she said she could do it. Stay, she told him. You can talk to me while I do.

She held the door open and then led him, moving deftly around the furniture, hitting the light switch exactly and just for him. Later, he tried it in his own house, his eyes closed. He bruised his shins and tore his fingernails; he cursed and stumbled and wondered if she heard him, if she guessed what he was doing.

In the kitchen, she reached and found the knobs on the cupboards; inside, they were carefully organized, all the cans lined up.

I've got it all figured out, she said. I miss being able to read, but that's about it. I was halfway through a book when it happened.

Marco asked if it happened all at once, and she told him she had one day where everything went dim—that gave her a chance to prepare—and then the next day that was it.

Is it just pitch-black? he said. Or is it like nothing at all? Marco wasn't sure what he meant, exactly. He couldn't stop watching her hands.

Somewhere in-between, she said.

He stayed until all the groceries were put away, and then said he'd be happy to help her again.

I remember what you look like, Louisa said, but do you mind? She reached out, and slowly her soft fingertips moved down his face.

Yes, I said, when he told me that. I knew this was going somewhere.

You know nothing, Marco said.

I learned not to say things like that, eventually; it only made him stop talking—it was as if I'd sullied the way it had been. If I asked, he'd say to wait, to be patient. He could only tell it a little at a time; otherwise, it made him too sad.

The conversation at lunch would turn to other things. We'd walk to the park, stripping off our latex gloves, the sweat between our fingers going cool, the zippers of our suits pulled down and their white arms dragging behind us. The weather turned hot and dark, overcast. Trains came and went, slowly, sat on the tracks behind the playground. We watched the dogs, betting on which owners would pick up after theirs and which would pretend oblivion. Down there they had dogs of all shapes, with their tails lopped off, their ears pinned up. Marco knew the names of all the breeds and what they were for. He'd have his arm across the back of the bench, fingers drumming next to my shoulder. I didn't mind. Once we saw a guy crash his bicycle into a parked car as he tried to look behind him, to check the ass on a girl he'd passed. Marco got a good laugh out of that—a little shift like that would bring him around again.

All right, he'd say, turning toward me. Where did I leave off?

The next time Louisa rang his doorbell, she was holding a book in her hand. She asked what he was doing; when he said nothing, she asked if he wouldn't mind reading to her.

She had already read the first three chapters. It was a novel where all the characters were rabbits, but it was for adults. Thick. Later, he borrowed it, to catch up on the beginning.

Louisa wanted him to read to her in the bedroom, so she could lie down and imagine it all. She set a chair next to the bed, then took off her shoes and stretched out.

This isn't right, she said, after a few pages.

The way I'm reading? Marco said.

She said it was strange, because she couldn't see him. She said that his voice was kind of disembodied, and that distracted her from following what was going on in the story.

Is it all right if I reach out and touch you? she said. While you read?

They tried it for another few pages, but she still couldn't get a sense of him.

What is it? he said.

Your clothes, Louisa said. It might be better if I

didn't have to feel you through them. Is this turning too weird? You don't know what it's like, like this; I start to need different things to feel anything, to understand.

At first it seemed it would be enough to take off his shirt, to strip down to his underwear. Part of it was to test her, maybe, to see if she was having him on somehow, and part of it was that it excited him.

Did she know you were all the way naked? I said, afraid to interrupt.

I believe so, he said.

He had never been involved in anything like that, he told me, never felt that way. He'd been married before, even, and this was different—he felt it in his heart, he said, knowing how ridiculous that sounded. And he never even touched Louisa, not once, yet sometimes, as the weeks passed, he'd wake up in the middle of the night because he'd been laughing in his sleep. He'd just lie there, smiling in the darkness.

Are you happy? Louisa asked him, a little later, that first night.

I guess so, he said.

She told him it seemed like an uneven trade.

Well, he said. I can see. I can read. I can see you.

Are the lights on? she said. Can you see well enough?

Yes, he said, except you're wearing clothes. As soon as he said that, he was sorry, and he wanted to take it back. He wanted to say it was a joke, but it was too late for that. Louisa had already begun to answer.

One piece at a time, she took off her clothing, folded it, and stacked it at the foot of the bed. She lay back, her hand on his leg again. He knew he was not allowed to touch her, just as she could not see him.

Now, read, she said.

And that's how it always was, after that. There was nothing showy about it, as if she was alone, unlacing her shoes, unbuttoning her shirt as he began to read. He turned the lamp up high and moved it closer to her; her shadow twisted low across the opposite wall, attached to his by her hand, checking that he was there. He flexed his bare toes on the cool floorboards.

Louisa's skin was dark and smooth, solid, hiding her bones. She wasn't skinny. Her thighs were heavy, a scar above one knee. Stretching and turning over, she'd laugh and hold a smile, showing her teeth, listening. She had a faded tattoo of a rose on her right hip, and a smaller, clearer one over her right nipple. Perfume rose from her skin as Marco read; sometimes he'd look up into the full-length mirror on the wall, and see her thin waist angling out to her rounded hips, and himself, the book in one hand and a glass of water in the other.

He drank between chapters, rested his voice. He counted the few hairs that circled her nipples, watched how her breasts slid across each other when she turned, enough space between them to hide a flattened hand. The hair under her arms matched that between her legs, where the edges, unshaven, were growing back. Her eyes stared and stared, shining.

Are you happy? she asked him.

He told me that she wore no jewelry at all, that there was nothing on her. Nothing. She and Marco hardly spoke, except for his reading, or deciding on the time they'd next meet. He never asked about her husband, and Louisa never brought it up. He felt there were many silent understandings between them.

Of course it took him weeks to tell me all this, and even in pieces the information was not easy for me to process. It was difficult to shake. Sometimes, even now, I set a glass of water beside me and I hold a book in one hand. I read aloud, my voice echoing off the tight walls of the room I rent, not letting my eyes wander from the page, and I imagine my other hand belongs to Louisa, and that she is listening to me, and that she can't see a thing.

Marco's story was farfetched, but I had never known him to lie. Still, I'd sometimes watch him at work, pausing with a book open in front of him, and I'd wonder if he was coming up with stories to tell me, or searching for something for her, or if he was just staring into the words without reading them, trying to think.

We both slowed as the weeks went on; he slacked off worse than I did, but I didn't mind. Mostly, we spent our time reading. We were using the rubber sponges, then, so there was no longer the vacuums' roar. The reflection of the face shields made it difficult to read; sometimes we let the hoods slump over our backs and wore only the ventilator masks with the HEPA filters, our eyes clear and uncovered. In the books where the fungus had really taken hold, it bled down into the pages in red and purple stains, blurring letters, eating words that we could not recover.

Louisa and Marco did not always meet at the same time. Once she'd called him at three in the morning, saying she couldn't sleep, saying she could hear his footsteps and wouldn't he like to come read? They finished the first novel, then went through another, and another. She liked books about animals, others where women took charge.

One of their understandings was that she had to come for him, and not the other way around; after all, he was doing her a favor. It was on a night when he waited—listening for the doorbell, the phone, her knock on the wall—that he heard the man's voice. Next door, and it was not the voice of Louisa's husband.

Marco was jealous, partly, but he also feared something was wrong. He took a can of corn from his own cupboard, so he could use it as an excuse, say he forgot to give it to her.

He tried the doorknob before the bell, and the door swung open. He stepped inside, the can of corn in his fist, ready to hit someone with it. In the dim living room he moved around the furniture as easily as she had that first day. He'd come to know her house that well.

In the hallway, closer to the bedroom, he listened; something about the man's voice seemed strange, the rhythm too regular and Louisa never interrupting. He stepped to the doorway and looked inside.

She was stretched out on the bed, wearing a long flannel nightgown, her face turned to the ceiling. On the bedside table, a tape recorder was playing, and the man's voice looped out from it, a hiss behind his words.

Marco took another step, into the room, and waited there, silently. He could tell she sensed him, that she knew he was in the room, and the fact that she said nothing made it all worse. As the taped voice looped around, Marco turned and walked back down the hall. He locked the front door and gently pulled it closed.

The next day, she told him the news. Her vision was returning; it was clearer each day. And the reading couldn't be the same if she could see the shape of him, his slumped shadow and the words coming out. Closing her eyes wouldn't work, when she knew she could open them. Awkward—that's the word she used. Soon she'd be able to read, once again, on her own.

When he told me that, I couldn't stop thinking about it. He'd been right—something in me wanted to find her, to hold her down until she saw some sense.

Marco never read to her again. He did find a place, though, where they made those tapes; he went there and volunteered, read a whole book into a microphone. He hoped Louisa might hear his voice, and remember, and have second thoughts. The sadness I felt, hearing this, was like I'd breathed in the spores and they'd thickened in my throat, blooming darkly through my organs, cold, one at a time like the way a blackout spills over sections of a city.

There was a time I believed and hoped that job could continue indefinitely, that I might persuade Marco to stay on, but those blooms are seasonal, mostly. Nothing stands still.

We were finishing up, just wiping down the shelves with the Clorox solution, when he told me the end of the story. In fact, Marco left before the job was finished, without any warning, and I handled the last few days—tearing down the plastic barriers, taking down the signs—by myself. He left that way, I believe, so he wouldn't have to say goodbye.

It wasn't as if he thought things between him and Louisa could have continued—he knew the balance had changed, that they couldn't return—but he expected it all had to go somewhere, that it couldn't just trail off into nothing.

She refused to speak about it. She was cool, not quite unfriendly. She turned down the simplest favors. She said that had been a different time, that they had been different people who needed different things.

He felt that they were the same, inside the changes. He needed her, and he couldn't stand the way she looked at him, every day, watching him with those same eyes as he came home from work with his hood and ventilator bouncing along his back, the arms of the Tyvek suit tied off around his waist. Her gaze rested cold on him, settling so he felt it even after he was inside his house. He sat alone, shivering; it was very, very quiet on the other side of the wall.

If I ever see Marco again, I'll tell him that I know what happened, even if she was ungrateful, even if she never understood.

He healed her.

Stranger

Melissa gets up on her knees, then begins pulling the damp pine needles from the bare skin of her ass and thighs. Dave had put his shirt down, under her, but somehow she'd slid off it. Now he stands ten feet away, peeling the condom loose, tying the open end in a knot.

The whole time he was on top of her, a swarm of tiny insects hanging over his right shoulder, she kept the woods in her peripheral vision. Lying down in the clearing had been her idea; once they'd started, though, she was unable to relax. She expected hunters in wool coats to step out from the trees—her skin trembled, anticipating their cold shadows.

"That was nice," Dave says. "Different." He stands in the sun, naked except for his hiking boots and glasses. He's not yet thirty-five, but there's already gray in the hair on his chest; his legs are too skinny for the thickness of his trunk.

"Yes," she says, stepping into her underwear, her shorts.

"About ready to head back?"

"How much daylight do we have?"

"No idea," he says. "There's the sun." He points at it.

Melissa shivers as she follows him back under the pines, into the shadows. They've traveled all the way across the country for three days of this, and they both pretend to enjoy it more than they do. She's always relieved to pack up on the last day; the rest of the time, she wonders what it would take for something to really go wrong. She knows Dave feels the same way, even as he struts ahead, whistling, the used condom swinging back and forth in his hand.

Stepping into the sun, they start across a meadow. Grasshoppers strike her bare arms and legs, their instantaneous arrivals and departures like tiny electrical shocks; she points out a bare bush, its branches just sticks, the tips of which someone has covered with spent shotgun shells—they look like red and orange fingers, and when the wind blows, it seems many bright hands are either waving her closer or warning her away.

Melissa and Dave climb a small rise and step back onto the rutted dirt road. Holding hands, they start down the road, toward the cabin; soon, they come to where a sign has been nailed straight into a tree. Sap the color of maple syrup bleeds down the bark, dark bugs stuck there. In red paint, crooked letters say, I'LL NEVER DO THAT AGAIN. The area around the sign bears no scars or clues; the sign doesn't even offer an arrow. The first time they passed it, they wondered at the message; now, hours later, they still can't make sense of it.

"I guess this is just a day of signs," Dave says.

"That seems to be the case," she says.

Early that morning, on the highway, they passed a semitrailer, and high above, in the window, the driver had placed a white sign reading, WHY NOT FLIRT? LIFT YOUR SHIRT! Melissa had laughed, and Dave told her to go ahead. She wished he had meant it, but she knew he didn't; he likes to think of himself as smoother than that, the kind of man women appreciate, more sensitive than the men he works with. He is a college football coach—not the head coach, but in charge of the quarterbacks—and it's a rough bunch, men who greet each other by asking how they're hanging and then grabbing to check. *How's your wife and my kids?* they say. At night, Dave often tells her of them, trying to make himself look good. Secretly, she sometimes wishes he were more like them. She wanted to pull up her shirt this morning, flash her breasts through the windshield, make the trucker blow his horn.

~~

The cabin is an A-frame, tall and thin, a cow skull wired

over the doorway, fake Indian symbols painted around it. Melissa has a week's break from dental school, and it's off-season for Dave. He found the cabin in a guide-book—no running water or electricity, owned by the U.S. Forest Service, $15 a night, in the middle of nowhere. He is proud of the bargain. At the airport, they rented a four-wheel-drive truck, then followed the top-ographical maps, struggled along the logging roads. Every time a stone shot up or a branch reached out, Dave pulled over and checked for scratches or dings. She told him to keep driving—either the truck was scratched or it wasn't.

Now he is cooking on the camping stove, cursing it. They're back from the hike, inside the cabin, where all the windows are plastic, scratched with initials, crosshatched; mouse droppings and melted wax cover the shelves and floor. Wooden knobs stick out from walls and rafters, and Dave's hung up everything that could possibly be hung. He's cooking freeze-dried lime-mango chicken. Watching him, Melissa feels an uneasy edge, almost like a headache's coming but not quite arriving, just a dull pain creeping up the back of her skull. Maybe the cabin's not well enough ventilated—the gas lantern's on, as well as the camping stove—but she knows it's not that.

"This food is vacuum-packed," Dave says, reading the label. "Like the meals astronauts eat."

"That's supposed to make us feel how?" she says. "Good? You'd hope we could do a little better, down here with gravity and oxygen and everything."

"You'd think so," he says agreeably. He drops the foil packet into the boiling water, then picks up the camera and begins rewinding the film. Popping the lid off a plastic film canister, he spills cinnamon into the camera, open on his lap. "Damn. My fault. Should have labeled that—stupid way to pack spices." He turns over the camera, shakes it, blows into it.

Melissa reaches to take a notebook from a shelf. Since she married Dave, she thinks, he's become more willing to own up to his mistakes, to show his weaknesses and limitations; he believes this makes her respect him more. If she lets him see her impatience, he'll only laugh, make a joke about her mean streak.

"Maybe we'll eat film in the oatmeal tomorrow morning," he says. "Just kidding. I saved some of the cinnamon."

She opens the notebook, which is full of comments from people who have stayed in the cabin before. The handwriting varies from children's to adults', in black and blue and red ink, Magic Marker.

What a salvation this is. John and Busker (our Alsatian) have gone looking for water for swimming. I can see them, down below. I feel at peace.

Someone backed into the outhouse, but that was B4 we got here. 6" snow + elk down in the flats.

To her, there's something distasteful about the messages, a combination of showing off and the pathetic desire to be remembered, to leave a mark.

Don't you just feel lucky and blessed? Mornings here are so beautiful.

Often at night when I'm in town I can hardly believe this place exists or that there's people in it, like it closes up and folds away when I'm not here. I almost want to come check my special place.

~~

She awakens hours later, upstairs in the cabin, on the air mattress. Their mummy bags are zipped together, Dave's legs pressing hot against hers. Moonlight shines in through a tall, triangular window, the rafters slanting darkly overhead. Dave's hands, on the pillow, smell of cooking gas. Rolling over, she looks closely at his face, the wrinkles at the corners of his eyes, his thick eyebrows, scattered whiskers. She certainly loves him, despite himself; it's easy to love him when he's asleep.

Then she hears something. Outside. Footsteps, on the loose gravel of the drive. They stop, as if to trick her, then begin again, heavy and slow. She tries to see through the window, but the plastic is scratched and cloudy, and the sounds are coming from around the side of the cabin. Now she hears a low moaning, perhaps slurred words.

She pulls herself from the bag without waking Dave and crawls along the wooden floor, to the square hole where the ladder stretches down. She wears a long flannel shirt. The rungs of the ladder are sharp against her bare feet. Downstairs, she ducks at the last moment, just missing the darkly hanging lantern. She opens the door.

It's lighter outside. Standing still, she hears no sound. She steps down from the porch, and then there's a motion, over where the truck is parked. She doesn't move; in her hand, she holds a thick branch, someone's walking stick. She considers waking Dave, but she knows she's the one to handle a situation like this—he would only complicate it.

Whoever is out there is hiding on the other side of the truck, a dark figure visible through the windows. Melissa holds her breath. The light rises from all surfaces; it seems to cast no shadows. The air is cool, the smell of the pines sharper, yet fainter, without the sun to warm the needles. At first, only the head sticks out, then the two sharp bumps of shoulders. Melissa steps closer, to get a clearer view. The cow turns its neck, rubs its jaw back and forth on the hood of the truck. It wheezes, stomps its hoof.

Melissa holds out her hand as if she has something to offer, as if she is no threat, and the cow seems to be frozen there, waiting for her. They are only ten feet apart when it jerks its head away and shuffles into the trees, hardly lifting its feet, kicking gravel as it goes.

The light is thick and soft around Melissa, and there's the faint sound of something like dark wings in the night, the nervous twitching of nocturnal creatures. In the morning she'll try to explain this to Dave. She promises herself she won't write about it in the notebook.

~~

She has slept at least another hour when the knocking begins, someone rapping at the door, pausing, then beginning again. She shakes Dave until his eyes come open.

"It's your turn," she says.

"What?"

"Something's outside."

The knocking resumes, now more impatient.

"That's not a cow," she says.

"What are you talking about?" Dave sits up, hits his head on a rafter. "Damn." He rubs above his ear, kicks his legs free from the sleeping bag.

From downstairs comes the sound of the door swinging open, its bottom rasping along the floor, then uneven footsteps, something kicked against a wall.

"Hello?" It's a woman's voice, straight through the floor beneath them, less than three feet away.

"Hello," Dave says.

"We got a little problem up the road."

Melissa wants to sleep. The sound of the voice— shrill, demanding, wide awake—irritates her.

"We could use a little help. My husband's hurt, and

it's not so easy for me to move him around."

"Did you call someone?" Dave says.

"I'm calling you. How would I call anyone? I don't know where you're from, but out here when a person asks for help it's because they need it."

In the silence, Melissa watches Dave think; he's trying to decide what to do, and she can tell he feels her watching him. He wants to make the right decision.

"Am I going to have to come up there?" the woman says.

~~

The woman drives, the truck jostling and creaking through the ruts. Dave sits next to her, watching the single headlight's illumination. They've passed the painted sign twice, and he suspects they're circling, backtracking, that the woman is in some kind of shock. She wears a red bandanna around her head. The skin on her face looks weathered in the dim light, her eyes small and round. She told him her name is Nancy; she's been silent since, driving, her long, thin fingers tight around the steering wheel. He feels her looking at him, but every time he turns toward her she's squinting through the windshield. He wonders what kind of problem it was— he'd assumed it was a car accident, but here she is with the vehicle.

"Was your husband conscious when you left him?"

"He was."

Dave holds the small, plastic emergency first-aid kit on his lap; when he bought it, three weeks ago, Melissa said it was a waste of money. She had stayed behind at the cabin, though Nancy seemed certain that they'd both be needed. Dave assured her it would be all right. He could feel Melissa turning stubborn.

"Getting close," Nancy says, leaning forward against the wheel.

In the dashboard, the glass is broken, and the speedometer doesn't even have a needle. There's a dark, rectangular cave of wires where the radio had been. The truck rises over a gentle curve and then two headlights shine, off to the left, hidden back in the trees. Nancy slows and eases the truck over a small ditch, onto a hidden road; they keep on moving, slowly, under the trees, as if the single headlight nudges the trunks aside to make room.

"Fool," she says, squinting. She parks and leaves the truck running, twenty feet from the pair of headlights.

A man steps out of the trees, into the lights. He is tall, with a thick, dark beard, a tangle of hair around his head. He wears a flannel shirt, suspenders. He's already talking, his hands up to slow her, when Nancy opens the door.

"I kept the lights on, like you said to, and he just walked into them and stood there, five minutes, staring at me, just asking me to put him down."

"Quiet," Nancy says.

"Is there an accident here?" Dave says. He sees the blood on the man's hands.

"You stay in the truck," Nancy says, slamming the door.

He watches through the windshield as the two of them walk a short distance away. What he took for headlights, he realizes, are actually two round halogen lamps, propped up on stones, a few feet apart; there's no other vehicle. It's clear that Nancy and the man are arguing, but he can't hear them. The man is pointing at the truck, back at the road, and Nancy's pointing into the woods. Turning, Dave looks in that direction, behind him, where the lamps are shining. Something large and red is hanging there, from the branch of a tree. It's a body, a bloody body. He narrows his eyes, trying to focus. It's some kind of animal, he decides. A deer, antlers almost resting on the ground, front hooves stretching down; the skin has been peeled off the flanks and hangs, doubled over the shoulders.

He's still looking back when the truck's door opens.

"Get out," Nancy says.

~~

Dave stands holding the first-aid kit, watching the truck drive away. Behind him, the man watches, too, holding a rifle in one hand and a long knife in the other. He must be over six and a half feet tall, pushing three hundred pounds, at least forty years old.

"I guess she went after Melissa," Dave says. "And they'll come back."

The man doesn't answer.

"We don't really have much with us—you could even take the truck, you know," Dave says. "It's rented. We got all the insurance on it and everything."

Above, between the trees, stars shine down. The two lamps still blare into the trunks and branches, lighting the red carcass of the deer. The man clears his throat, but doesn't say anything. After a moment, he takes a few steps and stands next to a plastic storage locker that must have fit in the back of the pickup; he hits it with the butt of the rifle and it echoes.

"Sit here," he says. "I'm not going to tie you up, because if you took off running, that would be a stupid decision. Where'd you go? Know what I mean?"

Dave sits on the locker, waiting, thinking of the map. The nearest town is forty miles away, farther. Now the man returns to his skinning; he leans the rifle against a tree, pulls the skin out with his left hand, and cuts it free with the knife. The deer twists only a little, over-powered by death.

"My name's Dave."

The man turns slowly, steps halfway back, closing the distance between them. There's blood on the knife, dark on his hands.

"You can call me, let's see—how about Henry?"

"You know," Dave says, "you should have had me go along, talk to Melissa. That probably would've made it easier."

Henry is skinning again. His boots are huge, camouflage.

This is real, Dave is thinking. *This is actually happening.* He can already hear himself telling the story, and he almost wants it to turn stranger, so people will be more impressed. It is already hard enough to believe; it's difficult to take it seriously without panicking. His only thoughts are all the sayings that hang on the walls in the locker room: DO BETTER THAN YOUR BEST. TO ASSUME THE WORST IS TO MAKE IT HAPPEN. He tells himself not to get on Henry's bad side, but Henry seems calm enough. There's something about him—despite his size, despite the gun and knife—that seems harmless. Not harmless, exactly, just not harmful. Dave's known lots of boys with huge bodies that were afraid to use them, afraid to hurt someone. He's learned you can only teach meanness so far.

~~

When Henry is finished, he takes the skin in both hands and throws it deeper into the woods. He returns, the rifle pointed at the ground.

"You going to tan that hide?" Dave says.

"I doubt that very much."

"You think something's gone wrong? Seems like

she's been gone a while."

"Maybe, it might be better," Henry says, "if we don't talk specifically about this situation here." He walks over to the lamps and begins to adjust them.

"Right." Dave sits back, letting the silence grow, trying to imagine himself in another place. He thinks of Melissa, of what she is doing now, and of the hike they took this afternoon. Setting out, he'd begun picking up all the old cans and bottles they came across; soon he had too many to carry, and had to give it up. Melissa said a team of scouts should handle that, and when he tried to correct her, he couldn't remember if it was called a pack or troop. She said it might do him some good to litter once in a while. She said if she had a gun she'd shoot rows of bottles, leave shards of glass all across the wilderness. She likes to provoke him.

"What are you thinking about?" Henry says.

"Hiking," Dave says. "This is our first anniversary, my wife and mine."

"Congratulations." Henry shrugs his shoulders, as if that won't change the way things will go.

"You ever seen that sign out there?" Dave points toward the road. "The one in red paint?"

"Haven't seen it."

"The one that says, 'I'll never do that again.' We were wondering what that could be about."

"I don't know this area real well," Henry says. "What's your answer?"

"We couldn't figure it."

"I mean, what would you never do again?"

"I don't know."

"What about coming out here, to that cabin? Would you do that again?"

"Thought we weren't talking about this situation," Dave says. He checks his wrist; he'd taken off his watch and left it in the cabin, next to the sleeping bag. It must be past midnight now, and getting colder. The lamps shine on the carcass, but they don't reach far, the darkness tight in every direction. The trees lean a little, shifting their branches in a wind he can't feel.

"I'll never get drunk with the guys I work with again," he says. "That I wouldn't do. I'm a football coach, just to give you some background." He almost says how his job depends on the performance of one nineteen-year-old kid, one quarterback, but the sad truth in that joke always keeps people from laughing. Dave looks up; Henry's still standing there, waiting for him to continue.

"This was after a big game, one we won, so we went out to celebrate. Just drinking and drinking, everyone challenging each other. Finally, I was about to pass out, but every time I fell asleep they'd put smelling salts under my nose. And they'd make me do another shot, promise it was the last one."

Talking helps him feel better, keeps his mind busy. And it's best to build up a kind of friendliness; that way, later, Henry might not want to do anything to hurt him.

Dave's worried about Melissa, but he won't let himself slip into negative thinking. She can take care of herself, after all, she's the sensible one; he thinks of her short black hair, her temper, the muscles in her calves. She's the one who quiets talkers at movies, who straightens out the overcharging electric company, who stands up to drunks. She's studying to be a dentist, and she actually enjoys the anatomy they do on cadavers—cutting back the skin to show the jaw, the gums, opening the throat to see what it holds. None of that bothers her. She can handle a night like this.

"So did they ever let you sleep?" Henry says.

"Yeah, they did. Only once I was asleep, they wrote all over my body, in permanent marker. All kinds of curse words, drawings. Stripes on my dick, everything. Had a green mustache for weeks."

Henry laughs, which is a good sign. He offers a can of chewing tobacco, then takes a dip for himself when Dave refuses.

"Hell," Henry says, "I'll never give her my pistol again, knowing she has it now, her frame of mind. That I'd never do again."

~~

Dave has a bad feeling when Henry takes out the camouflage suit—it seems a sign that action is about to be taken, that the night is turning. Henry says it's just that it's getting cold. Before he touches the suit, he has Dave pour water over his hands, to rinse off the blood; his fingers are thick and crooked, hands twice the size of Dave's.

He tells about the suit as he pulls it on. The inner layer is like rubber, and charcoal in the fabric eliminates human scent before it's released into the air.

"An animal can walk right up to you," he says. "Won't smell you at all." When he pulls off his boots, his feet are bare.

Dave listens. His breath is white, rising. He wonders if he could outrun Henry, take off while Henry struggles to get the suit over his thighs. The rifle's still in Henry's hand, though, and it's true Dave wouldn't know where to run, that even if he escaped there would still be Melissa.

"Total Illusion 3-D Camo," Henry says. "Makes me invisible. This outer suit is made of a special, silent kind of material; these polyester leaves, sewn on here, flutter and break up your outline, so you blend into the forest." He pulls on the gloves, claps them together, then the mask, which is a kind of hood with only two small eye-holes, strips of leaves between them. In the lamplight, he looks like a walking tree, a man overcome by vegetation. He doesn't sound human, either; his voice is muffled.

"That's something, all right," Dave says.

Henry pulls up the mask, so it rests atop his hair and makes him even taller, two headed. Reaching into the plastic locker, he hands a sleeping bag, also camouflage, to Dave.

"Unzip it," he says. "Wrap it around yourself."

And then he sets to collecting wood, piling up kindling. He won't let Dave search for the wood, but allows him to arrange it, to push the dried leaves underneath. Soon, the fire is taking hold. Dave and Henry sit on either side of it, watching each other above the flames, both stealing expectant glances toward the road.

"Another thing I'd never do," Henry says. "One time, a couple years back, winter, a child went missing, you know, and they got everyone they could to go out searching. Five days on my snowmobile, colder than anything." He stands, adds a chunk of wood, spits into the flames.

This time, when he offers the snuff, Dave takes a pinch; some of the younger coaches use it, but he never does. Dentists hate it, but he's only trying to connect with Henry. Melissa will understand that, if she'll just get here. He spits, tries to adjust the grains of tobacco with the tip of his tongue. In the heat above the flames, Henry's two heads melt and twist, stretching even higher and then coming back together. Dave wonders if he put on the suit just to show it off; though Henry is probably older than he is, it doesn't feel that way. And he feels a kind of empathy, also—Henry is waiting for Nancy, and he can't do anything about it but wait. Nothing's moving as smoothly as Henry expected.

"Did they ever find the child?" Dave says. "Did you?"

"No." Henry scratches his beard; the soles of his shoes shine in the firelight. "You ever hear of wolf children?" he says. "Like the ones raised by animals?"

"I don't think so."

"Sometimes wolves will dig a burrow for a lost child," Henry says, "line it with leaves, sleep in a circle around it to keep it warm. I saw a whole television program about it, these kids. They run around on all fours, sniff everything, lap water out of a bowl. Hardly feel the cold. Skin of their hands and knees gets all thick and horny and they run straight up mountains. Can see better in the night than the day."

Dave listens. Swiveling, he looks behind him. He doesn't believe a word of it, but the possibility of these children makes the space under the trees turn darker.

"They have these children on the show?" he says. "They have pictures, or what?"

"Drawings, I guess. Mostly this was a hundred years ago or more."

"Of course it was," Dave says, laughing, then thinks he should have held his tongue. He spits, the tobacco gritty in his teeth, foul in the back of his throat.

"There was more open space, then," Henry says. "Thing is, when they got caught, they could hardly ever learn to talk or to sleep in a bed or anything." The mask is still resting atop his head, a little crooked, the eyeholes empty and dark. "I just wondered," he says, "if they might have been better off left where they were."

"Hold on," Dave says. "I'm just trying to follow you, here. Are you saying you'd never search for a lost child again, or that this lost child got taken in by wolves, or what?"

"I don't know what I'm saying," Henry says. He smiles, his teeth surrounded by beard. "Maybe if they're not caught for a couple years, then you should let them go. I don't know. Maybe I just wanted to tell about the show I saw."

~~

The combination of hunger, lack of sleep, and the chew—along with the warm beer Henry found in the locker—has left Dave dizzy, almost giddy. He forgets himself, starts in on the questions again.

"You two together?" he says.

"What do you mean?"

"You married or anything?"

Henry doesn't answer, and Dave nods in agreement, as if he should have known better. He pulls the sleeping bag more tightly around his shoulders, his feet almost in the fire.

"Makes sense to me," he says. "You see all these rich folks coming in, sport-utility vehicles and whatever, out here where they don't know anything. Can't blame you. I'd be tempted, too, if I was in your place."

"Makes sense to you, does it? You have no idea. You

think this is about money?" Henry smiles his smile, crushes the beer can in his huge hand, throws it into the fire. The aluminum buckles in the flames, turns black. The thick, white bed of ashes rises and falls, breathing, sometimes revealing the hot coals beneath. A log collapses. Sparks shoot upward, burn themselves to cinders.

"I got something to tell you," Henry says, "just for you to know. This afternoon we were watching everything. We were standing in the trees. We saw the two of you, how you put your shirt under her, and we heard the noises you made, her legs in the air, your bony ass going."

Dave doesn't say anything; he almost hopes Henry will continue, tell him what he and Melissa looked like, pressed together in that clearing, under the sun and sky.

"Maybe we shouldn't have watched," Henry says. "Probably I wouldn't have, if I knew you then. We never would have thought of it, if we didn't come across you."

One headlight shines, out on the road. It comes closer, searching for them; they can hear the tires as the truck passes by; the two red taillights slide away, blinking out.

"What's she doing?" Henry says. "She knows the way."

The headlight reappears, and the truck passes by, slowly, back the other way. Henry stands and checks the halogen lamps, which are still burning brightly, aimed at the road.

Five minutes later, the truck returns, and veers into the trees, toward them, the one headlight winking as the wheels roll down through the ditch, up the other side. It doesn't come any closer.

"Maybe she broke down," Dave says.

"No. I can hear the engine. Listen."

"Think she wants you to go out there?"

"Maybe both of us," Henry says. "I can't leave you here."

"What am I going to do? Run? All I want is to give you whatever you want, whatever that is, and then I want to be together with my wife."

"Quiet."

"If she wanted us both," Dave says, "she'd just drive in here again."

Henry stands for another five minutes, silent, then sticks a finger in his mouth and throws his dip of chew into the fire. Sliding the lid from the plastic locker, he takes out a thick metal flashlight. He pulls the mask back down over his head, and once again he seems made of leaves.

"Stay here," he says, his voice muffled. He almost leaves the rifle behind, then remembers it, and walks away, crossing the beams of the halogen lamps. Fake leaves span the space between his legs, flutter along his shoulders.

Dave hesitates for only a moment, then stands and backs away, kicking the sleeping bag toward the fire. Underneath the branches of the trees, he bumps into someone, an arm reaching to hold him; it's the deer carcass, a hoof wrapped around his waist. He shakes it off, steps away, and almost immediately trips over the bloody hide; on his feet again, he stumbles, hands out in front of him, slapping tree trunks as he moves between them. He can't hear Henry because of the silent fabric, can't smell him for the charcoal suit, but the beam of the flashlight is clear and true, and no one needs camouflage in the dark. The truck idles, the driver's door open and the ceiling light on, the whole thing glowing like it's at the bottom of the ocean. Through the bright windows it's clear that the cab is empty; perhaps someone is lying in the bed of the truck, or hidden in the dark trees surrounding it. Dave is flat on his stomach, his urge to shout overcome by his desire to let it happen, to watch.

Still moving closer, Henry strays into, then out of the headlight's beam.

"Hello?" he says. "Hello?"

His voice is caught in the mask, turned back on itself. Standing still, he aims the flashlight at the ground, then slowly switches it off. He's realized where he is and what has happened, and he knows that it's now too late to become invisible.

At the first gunshot, birds rise and clatter through the branches above. Sticks rattle down. Animals startle and slip through the underbrush.

There's only the sound of the truck after the second shot, the engine roughly idling. Dave, pressing himself harder into the ground, tastes the dirt on his lips; he can feel the wild children close around him—quick, seeing in the darkness, sensing that he is no threat.

A dark shape moves beneath the truck, an arm reaching through the open door and into the light. It's Henry, his long body sliding up, low, flat on the seat now so he can't be seen through the windshield. Dave holds his breath, watching, hoping Henry will make it.

He does not hear the shift, but slowly the truck begins to ease backward, sticks cracking beneath the tires. Another shot, a bullet tearing into metal, and Henry sits up straight, the truck accelerating. It side-swipes a tree, and a brake light shatters. The open door wrenches back and is torn off, left behind. The whole thing lunges over the ditch, onto the road. The headlight stares through dust.

Tires spinning, finding the ruts, the truck slams forward. The cab is alight, and Henry is visible, inside, still hooded, sliding away with the sound of gravel, gone.

A thick silence rises, multiplying in the darkness, the stars held out by the trees overhead. Then Melissa's voice sounds, startling him, closer than he expected.

"David?" she says. "Are you here?"

Shaken

for Motoko Vining

Asada locks his car and turns away, leaving it parked on the shoulder of the highway. He crosses the low ditch and begins climbing upward, following a stream. It's early autumn; these days, the sun stays low and cool, rolling along the horizon for hours. Most of the leaves on the ground are last year's—dried and bleached out, the same dull white as bones.

Walking under the trees, he breathes in, then exhales, the air cool in his throat. He has a sweater tied around his waist, a canteen on his hip, an energy bar in his pocket. In his hands, he carries only his fishing pole.

A year ago was the first, the only time that he's been to this place. An engineer where he works told him it resembled Japan, and that drew Asada here, stirred his curiosity. His family had moved to the States when he was fourteen, and now he is forty-four; while he doesn't recognize the similarity in this landscape, he hopes it might startle memories from inside him. He has put off his return all spring, all summer. He had to come before his hesitation stretched out into the first snowfall, before the trip was delayed into next year.

His breathing is already coming faster; he slows, but does not stop. This slope climbs for miles, even beyond the timberline, far beyond his destination. He is hiking to where an old stone mill, gutted and abandoned, sits beside the stream, where the remnants of a dam still collect a shallow pool. The stillness there is only disturbed by the gentle slapping of leaves; aspens circle the water.

The year before, standing beside the pool, he had seen what he believed was a shadow on the stone wall of the mill. It folded, though, then spread, and he could not see what might have cast it. Climbing along the wall, twisting higher, the shadow moved as if it held weight and was expanding, growing arms and legs. Asada's chest had gone cold. He had fled down the mountainside, stumbling, not looking back. This time, he won't run. He'll stay. He has not been surprised for a very long time, and he feels a desire to be shaken.

The bank is rough and torn where, months ago, the swollen stream ran. He crosses the stream, trying to follow the clearest path, and fish dart from stone to stone, abandoning the shadows along the edges. Bending, he tightens the laces of his leather boat shoes, the most casual footwear he owns. He wonders if this would be easier with hiking boots, and whether people often hike alone. Perhaps it's usually done in groups, or in couples. He tries to imagine a woman walking beside him.

There is a movement in his peripheral vision, to his right. A deer, standing only twenty feet away, raises its head and stares. It's a doe, slightly darker than the leaves on the ground, ears out like funnels, light showing through them so Asada can see the red veins forking there. He can smell her, also, sweet and rank, tight in his nostrils. Lifting his fishing pole, he points it like a gun; the cork grip presses against his cheek as he sights down the round, metal ferrules, straight at the deer. She only snorts at him, unimpressed. She walks away slowly, her white tail switching back and forth.

Asada also walks on, in the other direction. He is disappointed in the deer for not running, and in himself, somehow, for not making her afraid. This is not a marked trail; he is probably the only person for miles. He wonders how she became so accustomed to people.

Again, as he climbs, he thinks of women. At the computer company where he works, there are several he's friendly with, yet the ones he's pursued have rarely wanted to know him better. White women realize he's not as exotic as he looks, while Japanese women consider him slow to assimilate, to adapt to life in the States. None of these women work in his department, so they cannot understand, cannot know how it affects a person, translating technical correspondence. He uses Japanese words that most Japanese would not know, English words that Americans would never encounter. Together, these two groups of words are like a third language—one beset by redundancy, with two words for every single thing, with almost no one to share it.

Tree branches cross like latticework overhead. He holds his fishing pole in front of him, clearing spiderwebs. Today, he doesn't mind being by himself. He doesn't want to explain his expectations to anyone and, besides, he feels things are more likely to happen if he's alone. The bushes thicken. Parting them with his hands, he looks down just in time to avoid stepping on a dead bird. A crow or raven, its black feathers still shiny while its dull eyes stare. Asada holds his breath. After a moment, he hears a car on the highway, distant now, somewhere below. He leaves the dead bird behind.

He has been walking under the trees, in the shadows, for over an hour when he steps into the clearing. The side of the mill facing the pool is lit by the sun. The white stone wall looks cold and bright; the three windows— two low, one above—are squares of darkness. For a moment, it seems that the mill has moved closer to the water, and then he realizes it's the breadth of the pool that's changed.

The pool is all reflections. The tips of the aspens bend inward, stretching there. Birds dart low across the surface, doubling in the water, folding their wings to plummet, opening them to rise. Asada stands near the low dam, where all the earth has been washed from between the white stones. He looks into the mottled gray trunks of the aspens, at their bright yellow leaves in the sun. Behind the mill, a broken fence stretches, wooden rails down in some places; farther along, a whole section has collapsed.

He notices that there's no lure on the end of his line, not even a hook. It doesn't matter. He casts out his bare leader and the pool ripples and settles. Little trout rise, curious, holding themselves steady in the clear water. He watches until they lose interest, and then he reels in the line. A breeze rolls down the mountain and the aspens' leaves slap and clatter. Asada shivers, sweat drying inside his clothes. His legs and feet are sore from the hike.

Then it begins. Ten feet from where he stands, where the pool drops off into slightly deeper water and he can no longer see the bottom. It's as if something is rising from below—an indistinct shape, its edges finding clarity, different shades verging on colors. A round face, almost, a darker body, flickering, trailing off. Asada's heart accelerates, his scalp tightens. A cloud's reflection slides across the pool, blurring the surface, and the image does not return. He looks up, then, toward the mill—it seems a dark shape moves in one of the low windows, as if someone was standing there and has slipped behind the wall, beyond where he can see.

Asada unties the sweater from his waist and sets it

on the ground, in case he has to move quickly. He reminds himself that he is more curious than afraid. Attempting to appear calm, he again casts out his line; this time, the trout don't even bother to pretend they're interested. He looks away from the pool, squinting into the aspens, the shadows between them. What he thought were natural marks are actually letters, he realizes, initials and words that people have carved into the trunks. Between the stones at his feet, he now notices cigarette butts; they don't appear to be especially old.

The second time the figure rises, the reflection is in a different place—across the pool, nearer the opposite bank, surfacing between the trunks of trees. Asada looks away, at the mill. The lower windows are empty. He looks up, to the window above.

It is the figure of a woman, standing thin and dark. Steady, unmoving, hands held out in front. It is difficult to make out the face's expression, to tell if the features are Asian or otherwise. The long hair is tangled, hanging across the face. The dress is loose, or perhaps it's a kimono; it hangs as if wet. The figure appears to have just climbed out of the water.

And then the window is empty. Asada almost calls out, but he does not. There are rules, he feels; calling out might simplify the situation, and that is not what he desires. Waiting, trying to remain patient, he wonders if someone standing in the trees, somewhere farther up the slope, might cast their image into the pool so it was reflected upward, so it appeared in the window. No, he decides—if that were the case, the figure would have been upside down.

Asada sets his fishing pole on the ground. Wading, tripping through the bushes, breaking low branches in his hands, he heads around the back of the mill. The wooden door has a lock attached to it, but the hasp has been torn from the wall. The bottom of the door is sunken into the ground; he manages to bend the top enough to wedge his way through.

There is no one else inside. Above, there is the sky, no roof at all. There is no remnant of a second floor, either—not even a ledge beneath the upper window, twenty feet above. No place anyone could stand. Asada steps over crushed, faded beer cans, over the ashes of an old fire. A trickle of water enters under one wall, slips away beneath another. Standing at one of the low windows, he looks out across the pond, to where his fishing pole rests, next to his sweater, which is folded on the white stones. He bends his neck and looks up the smooth wall, at the high window. If he wants the figure to return, he decides, it would be best to return outside, to stand where he had been, to concentrate on the pool's reflections. He crosses to the door and forces his way back through.

The air has turned cooler. He puts on his sweater, eats the energy bar, drinks water from his canteen. He holds his fishing pole like a sword, slicing it through the air. Now it is dusk, and the spaces between the aspens are difficult to see; above, the yellow leaves are pale, unlit. Shadows extend darkly across the pond, threatening to seal off all reflection. He wants there to be every chance, but soon he will be unable to see; he'll have to follow the stream through the darkness, its sound, all the way down to where his car waits.

The black shape comes through the water like a seal, cutting smoothly beneath and not quite breaking the surface. No reflections remain, only shadows. Asada looks upward, toward the mill. The figure has returned, and the face is now more distinct; the hair is thrown back, the features clearly Asian. The arms are still held out. The edges of the shoulders begin to shiver, as if the solidity cannot be maintained, as if the whole thing might dissipate, blow away.

And then it begins to climb through the window. Asada expects it to leap into the pool from that height, but it does not. And it does not swing a leg over the sill, but slides through headfirst. As it comes, it changes, turning fluid, seeping beyond itself. Shadowy, it twists like smoke, rolling down the stone wall, leaving wet marks in its wake, loosing tentacles and spinning them back to the center. At the bottom, the mass unfolds, never settling; it slides across the ground, into the thick bushes.

Asada stands, holding his breath. He will not turn his back. He will not run. His ribs flex inside his chest, their cage rattling its hinges. His senses of taste and smell, his touch and hearing and sight, they are all whittled sharp.

In a moment, the head rises above the line of bushes, on the other side of the pool, just visible against the dusk. Wavering, becoming solid, the body appears in sections, as if ascending a hidden flight of stairs. Then, feet still hidden in the underbrush, the figure starts up the slope. The legs seem to move slowly, yet the body slides smoothly along, its speed increasing. As it heads into the trees, the shadows thicken behind it.

Asada steps quickly, his feet kicking the white stones so they skitter across each other and splash into the pool. When he reaches the aspens, he hesitates, then begins running between them, up the slope, in the direction the figure disappeared. His fishing pole rattles through low branches, snaps in half across a tree trunk; he stumbles, drops it, the line tangling and snapping, the whole thing dragging behind him and finally letting go.

He arrives in a clearing, the ground still slanted, where trees have fallen. Rotten and hollowed trunks cross each other; dried grass pokes up between them. Asada feels that he is close. He breathes deeply, bending over, his hands on his knees. And then, inside a round knothole of one of the fallen trees, he sees what looks like fabric. Dark and wrinkled, yet not a shadow.

He steps closer, and pushes his finger gently through the knothole. As soon as he touches the cloth, a high-pitched screaming sounds from the fallen tree. Asada stumbles backward, falling to the ground. The quiet returns, and yet, through it, there is the faint sound of scratching, of movements within the log. Asada stands, and moves carefully to the hollow end. He squints against the falling darkness.

In a moment, a tangle of black hair begins to emerge. It is a girl, he realizes, a young woman. Loose bark falls from her hair; there's dirt smudged on the pale skin of her face. Her features are delicate, beautiful. Slowly, she crawls from the log and stands, five feet from Asada. Her kimono is soaking wet, and so long it hides her feet. She brushes her hair from her face with long, pale fingers, and tries to smile; her expression is frightened.

"Tadasu-san," she says, her voice low and melodious. "Watashi ga dareka wakaranai no ne?"

"No, I don't recognize you," he says.

"Tadasu-san ga nihon wo detekara sanju-nen mo tatsu mono ne."

"Thirty years?" Asada hesitates, realizing that he is answering her in English. It is the language that comes first to him; she seems to understand.

"Why did you run away?" he says. "Who are you?"

"Sugu ni koe wo kakerare nakkatta," she says. "Tadasu-san ni watashi no iukoto ga wakatte moraenai to omotta no."

"You were right," he says. "I don't understand."

"Yumi yo," she says. "Itoko no."

"Why did you come to me?" he says, but she does

not answer him, not right away. Instead, she begins to tell him her story. It has been thirty years since he's seen his cousin, Yumi, and then she was a baby. That was in Japan; she stayed behind, and she is still there, she tells him now. Her body is there, but it is in a place where no one will ever find it. It is in a forest, far from any town, where no one would expect her to be. She rests in a shallow ravine, and leaves have settled on her, icy flood-waters have washed her clean. Over a year has passed since she died. Silt has thickened around her; roots have taken hold, grown straight through her. It is wonderful.

As she talks, Asada watches her carefully, trying to understand. Her voice is like a song, surrounding him, like nothing he's ever heard. He wants to reach out and touch her, but he doesn't dare; he fears she'll sink into the ground, or rise and dissipate through the trees' branches. When he'd stuck his finger through the knot-hole, her body felt solid. Pieces of bark still hang from her hair.

She is saying that no one in Japan knows that she is missing. She had fallen out of contact with her family— she is ashamed to tell him the details, not that they matter. She is happy now.

"Why did you come to me?" he says again.

"Anata ga watashi ni tottemo aitagatteta kara," she says.

Asada believes this—she has shown herself to him because he had wanted to see her, had needed it, more than anyone else. And he does not pull away when Yumi steps closer. As she leans against him, there is no sound, no change in sensation. The only light is from the moon. Asada turns a slow circle, his eyes searching in every direction. His arms close around himself. He is alone.

The Sharpest Knife

We were pulling out of the hotel's driveway, still not moving very fast, when we saw the old man. He stood on the shoulder of the highway, tall and thin, in a red and black mackinaw, a wide-brimmed straw hat. His nose was hooked, his face gaunt, and his close-set eyes stared straight through the windshield as if he were memorizing our faces—Hannah's beautiful, pale skin and my studied avoidance of his gaze—as we passed.

"Have there always been so many hitchhikers around here?" I asked. We had been passing them all day—couples, solitary figures, travelers with frame packs and wet dogs, all forlorn on the outskirts of those small southwest Washington towns.

In the rearview mirror, the man grew smaller; he'd turned to watch us; we went around a bend and I could no longer see him. We were heading into the next town,

Stevenson, to get some dinner.

"Hitchhikers? Not that I remember." Hannah brushed her short, black hair from her forehead.

She'd grown up in that area, in a town called Carson. Her family owned the rickety old hotel, the natural hot springs where people came to be restored by the mineral waters. These waters had not been sufficient for her father, who had throat cancer—he'd recently come home from the hospital to die, which was the reason for our visit. We'd planned to stay for a couple days and it had already been a long week, just waiting for something to happen. The prospect of death did not seem at all natural or expected, in that house; Hannah's parents had always preferred to keep everything as static as possible.

That morning, Hannah's mother had told us to stop hanging around like we were impatient to get to the funeral, to go on a hike or something. We'd set out hoping to make it to Lava Canyon, on the south slope of Mount Saint Helens, but the weather had turned to snow and sleet. We were forced underground, literally, into a lava tube called Ape Cave. For almost two hours, we blundered along, one flickering flashlight between us. We stumbled and cursed, and when we came upon other hikers, their headlamps and lanterns blinding us, we smiled and acted as if we were having a wonderful time. We'd been married for two years, at that point—this was back when we lived in Seattle, about six years ago.

That evening, after the short drive to Stevenson, a cold wind blew off the Columbia. The river was close, but out of sight. We parked and hurried toward a brewpub that didn't allow smoking, yet had pretensions toward authenticity. License plates, many of them from Alaska and Canada, covered the walls. We were seated, and ordered, and unfolded our napkins on our laps, trying to settle. Hannah seemed more subdued than usual, worn out, but I knew better than to remark that she looked tired.

"I feel like I could fall asleep right here," I said. "That hot water."

"It's the minerals," she said.

We had returned to the hotel for a soak, after our adventure in Ape Cave. The men's and women's bathhouses were separate, with rows of white porcelain tubs, and also cots, for after the soak, when the attendant wrapped me in hot towels.

"Did you like it?" Hannah said.

"I guess so," I said. "I didn't realize everyone would be out in the open like that. All those doughy guys with tattoos, checking me out. Every time I glanced up, they looked away. The macho thing was to get in the 'cold tub,' you know, at the end, and whenever someone did that, everyone watched him. And then that hippy with the soft voice, the attendant—"

"Walter."

"Yes, Walter; he leaned close over my tub and whispered that I could drink the hot water, but that it might have a laxative effect, after four cups."

"And are you finding that to be true?" At last, Hannah smiled, gesturing to the bathrooms behind me.

And yet her smile did not quite put me at ease, because during my story I had realized that the man we'd passed on the highway, the old hitchhiker, was eating dinner in the restaurant, seated at the bar. His hat was off, now, and his head was shaven close, a whorl of white whiskers on his skull. He kept turning to check on us, his white beard flashing in my peripheral vision. A tall dark beer sat in front of him, and he ate a hamburger, holding it firmly with two hands, his sharp elbows out to the sides like wings. He'd gotten his food before we had, which suggested that he might have arrived before we did.

"Did you want to talk about your dad?" I said.

"No," Hannah said. "What's there to say?"

Not long after our food arrived, the old man at the bar stood and stepped in our direction. I expected that he was heading to the restrooms; I did not look up as he approached, yet when I expected him to pass he slowed and stopped at our table, looming silently over us. He held a toothpick between his gnarled thumb and fore-finger, rolling it. His heavy, brown leather boots were cracked and oiled. I looked at Hannah's face; she was watching mine. Just as I was about to speak, as I looked up to offer an apology, to try a joke about picking up hitchhikers, I saw that his attention was fixed on her.

"You cut off all your long hair," he said.

She hardly looked at him. She stabbed at her blackened catfish with her fork.

"Hannah," he said, "everything that happened happened almost twenty years ago. I had hoped you had forgiven me by now. I guess not."

His voice dropped in and out of a whisper as he spoke. Hannah didn't look up or answer him, and after a moment he turned and walked away, out the door.

"Who was that?" I said.

"A local character," she said. "Don't pay him any attention—no one ever has."

That's all we said about it. We had coffee, paid our bill, and slowly put on our coats again, not eager to return to the hotel and the situation with Hannah's father.

Right at the edge of Stevenson, our headlights caught the old man's figure, lit against the dark trees, his thumb out and his hat brim like a halo circling his face, wrinkles lined with black shadows.

"Just pick him up, then," Hannah said.

I pulled over, and he turned and unhurriedly walked toward our car, as if he'd expected us to stop.

"Appreciate it." He opened the back door and pushed our hiking boots to one side. He sat directly behind me, closed the door, and then I heard the click of his seatbelt and we were off again.

"This is my husband," Hannah said. "And this is Mr. Phelps." She did not turn to look at him as she spoke; she faced forward, as if her attention kept us on the road. Her hands twisted in her lap, fingers pulling on each other.

"You must be a pretty seasoned hitchhiker, Mr. Phelps."

I twisted my neck around to direct my comment, but the man did not answer. The sharp pine trees ran thick on either side of the highway; they seemed to lean in, creating a kind of tunnel. The radio had been on and I'd switched it off; now, in the silence, I wished that we had some music, some other voices. The old man cleared his throat, behind me. I could feel his bony old knees in the small of my back.

"I understand that your father has not been well," he said.

"He's dying," Hannah said. "He won't recover."

"Well, he's been an excellent neighbor, your father. Our relations have warmed somewhat, over the years."

"Pull over," she said.

"What?" I said.

"Next to this mailbox," she said. "Mr. Phelps will be getting out right here."

He climbed from our car without another word, shambled away without a wave as he disappeared down an overgrown driveway. I watched Hannah's expression relax.

"Well," I said; as a silence settled, I decided not to say anything more.

We were staying in the hotel, out of the way of Hannah's parents. Their house, a smaller, sturdier building, was nearer the river, its windows dark as we drove past—which was a relief, since it meant we didn't have to stop and visit with them, say goodnight.

The parking lot held only three or four cars. The hotel was mostly empty and the baths were closed, the attendants and masseuses all gone home. The clerk at the front desk stood at the sight of Hannah, hung up the phone as we walked silently past and up the stairs to our room on the second floor. All the rooms shared a common bathroom, at the end of the hallway. The floorboards creaked, and the doorknobs were all loose, the locks and keys ill-matched.

Hannah and I undressed without looking at each other. I saw us both, tired and in our own thoughts, caught in the cloudy mirror in that instant before I hit the switch and the lights went out. When I sat on the edge of the bed, the box spring sagged so that Hannah rolled into me. She'd told me that part of the charm was that everything was rundown, that no furniture had ever been replaced.

Making room, she rolled away, and I got between the sheets, under the thin blanket. We turned over, then over again; the box spring squeaked; I doubted we'd ever get comfortable.

"I know you want me to tell you," she said. "I know you want me to talk about it."

"Only if you want to," I said. "He's your father."

"No," she said. "Not that. About what happened with Mr. Phelps."

"Who?"

"It was twenty years ago," she said, "but it was the biggest thing that had happened to me, the most drama we'd had around here. It probably made me who I am more than anything. I just never told you about it."

"What did he do to you?" I said.

"Hold on," she said. "Slow down. Listen."

I waited. The window over the head of the bed had no curtain, and my eyes were adjusting to the moonlight. If I turned my head, I could see the smooth silhouette of Hannah's face. I had long suspected there was something, some dark story from her girlhood that would help me understand, that might explain her long silences, her unpredictable moods.

"Do you remember how it used to be," she said, "in the fall, at the beginning of school, how exciting it was to get new clothes?"

"Shoes," I said.

"And school supplies," she said. "This was when I was eight, the first year I was allowed notebooks with lines. My first spiral notebook. It was yellow."

In that half-darkness, that strange light, Hannah's voice seemed to shift and twist. It became more tentative, more singsong, like a little girl's voice.

"It was the whiteness of the pages," she said, "one hundred and fifty sheets. The next morning, before breakfast, I sat alone in my room, on my bed, and began to count them all. And it wasn't very far in, on the eleventh page, that I found it. Messy writing, in red pen—"

"Someone must have written in it, in the store," I said, "before you bought it."

"That's what I thought, at first—but what was more important was what it said."

I waited. The faint shadows of trees stretched across the ceiling, through the window.

"Don't you want to know?" she said.

"Yes," I said.

"It said, 'Cabinets, dressers, and doors enjoy being opened and closed; little girls, the way they walk is sharper than the sharpest knife.'"

"Did you show anyone?" I said.

"My parents? No—it was a secret, my secret. It delighted me."

"What do cabinets and knives have to do with little girls?" I said.

"That morning," she said, "I went through all the pages, and they, the rest of them, were all blank. White, with lines. I carried that notebook at all times, close to me. No one else touched it. And a few days later, when I checked, there was more writing. The same scribbling red pen."

"What did it say?"

"I can't remember, not exactly. Except that it had something to do with ghosts." Her warm leg touched mine, beneath the covers, and pulled away again. "And everything," she said, "everything started to feel a little different to me, after that."

"Were you afraid?" I said.

"No, not at all. I wasn't afraid, I just looked at everything differently, because it was like a ghost was writing in my yellow notebook, or like the words just appeared, the ink seeping into the paper while the cover was closed tight, while I held it in my hands."

"So there were more words?" I said.

"Yes," she said. "It went on until Christmas, almost, and sometimes they came slower, sometimes faster, like some kind of riddle."

"And you never told anyone?"

"It was my notebook," she said. "The words were for me."

A phone rang, somewhere far away, perhaps in the lobby, and eventually trailed off. The wind rose, ruffling through the trees along the river. I waited, uncertain whether Hannah was still awake. I couldn't tell if she was waiting for me to ask for more, or if asking would cause her to stop talking altogether.

"My parents caught him," she said, still in the little girl voice, her whisper even softer. "I woke up and they were in the door of my bedroom, the light on. Mr.

Phelps was sitting on the floor, next to my bed, a red pen in his hand, the notebook open on his lap. He wasn't wearing shoes. The window behind him was open."

"Had he touched you?" I said.

"There was a moment, there," she said, "of silence, that moment when the light had just been switched on and everyone was startled and couldn't see well, and then the shouting began. My mother and father, shouting. Mr. Phelps never said a thing. He slowly closed the notebook and set it down, stood, and walked past my parents. They didn't touch him, but they followed him, still shouting. I could hear them go down the stairs, out across the yard—"

"What happened to him?" I said, afraid to interrupt.

"The way he did it was he climbed a tree," she said, "then took off his shoes and walked across the roof to my bedroom window—that's how they caught him, they finally heard him—and then he'd write in my notebook."

"Why?" I said.

"They asked me and asked me and asked me what had happened," she said, "what I knew, but I didn't tell about the notebook, and that was the only thing I knew anything about."

"But did anything happen?"

"What?" she said. "I just told you what happened."

I had a lot of questions, of course, but knew that asking them wouldn't be the likeliest way to get answers. Out in the hallway, I thought I heard footsteps; we were supposedly the only occupied room on the second floor. I turned over, the sharp coils of the mattress cutting into my shoulder.

"Hannah?" I said.

She was asleep, or simply not answering. I rolled onto my back again, staring at the plaster of the ceiling, the water stains like little men being struck by the lightning of the cracks. The cloudy mirror reflected the moonlight. I'd left my watch on the dresser, and couldn't tell if a lot of time was passing. Lying there, I believed I could hear the trickle of the hot water, snaking in the pipes, all through the property and rising, steaming, from the ground. I imagined animals—foxes, deer, raccoon—bending to drink before pulling back in surprise, their lips burned.

I put my feet on the floor, stood, and quietly crossed the room. I was only going to check the time, but when I reached the dresser my hand did not pick up my watch; instead, it grasped the doorknob, turned it. I stepped into the hallway and closed the door behind me.

The bathroom was at the end of the hallway, and had a dusty curtain in place of a door. The sink was bolted to the wall, its faucet running, unable to be completely shut off. The vinyl flooring, stained and torn, revealed its many layers. The window above the toilet had no pane in it, and a magazine rested open on the sill.

It was a copy of *Oui*, a magazine I had glimpsed a few lucky times in my boyhood, that I hadn't seen on a newsstand in a long time. In fact, this copy was over twenty years old, from 1977, its advertisements for turntables with stereo sound, Volkswagen Sciroccos, English Leather cologne. The best photos of the pictorials had been carefully torn out and pocketed by adolescent boys or sleepless husbands like myself; in those images that remained, the women, in bedrooms and next to swimming pools, liked to hold their breasts up in front of them. They had more pubic hair, back then, than I believed women grew. In one photograph, a woman with a thick torso and peroxided hair waded into the ocean, her dark nipples pointing at the horizon; beneath her, it said, *The only time she's not bored is when she's alone.*

The magazine wasn't enough to distract me, not for long. I set it down, exactly as I'd found it, and pushed my way through the curtain, back into the hallway. Before I reached our room, I suddenly turned and began to descend the stairs. I tried to balance along the edge, rather than in the middle of each step, to minimize the creaking.

The dark lobby was empty, abandoned. The air, because of the mineral springs, smelled faintly sulfuric, and the darkness seemed to amplify this. Outside, through the screen door, moonlight fell softly across the gravel parking lot. I considered testing the swinging doors to my left; if they were open, I could slip into the hot bath, then the cold, back and forth until the pull of my skin was worn out—and yet I knew that this, like the magazine, would fail to keep my mind off Hannah's story.

Her parents' house was only a hundred yards from the hotel, set down close to the river. Following the narrow path, I realized that I wore only boxer shorts, but I kept walking. My bare feet were sore from stumbling through the cave all morning.

The back door was open, the kitchen silent. I stood next to the sink and held my breath; there was no sound at all. The stairs here, carpeted, did not creak. On the landing, I passed Hannah's parents' room, their door closed. I pushed gently on the door to Hannah's old room. It smoothly swung open.

A rectangle of moonlight stretched cold across the floor, thrown through the window. I stepped close, to look out, to check the shingles beneath the window, the steepness of the roof. There was no tree that I could see; it must have been cut down. I turned, my eyes adjusting. The room had been maintained as a kind of shrine to Hannah's girlhood—the shadowy horse figurines, the posters of Leif Garrett and Shaun Cassidy, the softball trophies. A bookcase held a long line of Nancy Drew, and books about animals. On the bottom shelf, pinched between the spines of the taller books, I saw the glint of metal, the wire spiral of the notebook.

I dropped to my knees, I snagged it with my finger, tilted it free. Even in that darkness, the yellow cover flashed. I began to open it, to check, and then, suddenly, the light switched on. I heard the sound, my eyes flashed, and there was Hannah's mother in a white nightgown, all her gray hair sticking out one side of her head.

"What are you doing here?" she said. "It's after two in the morning." Standing there, she looked both frail and furious, her fingers clenched into fists.

"Sorry," I said, standing, one hand down to cover the fly of my boxers. "Hannah needed something from in here." I held up the notebook. "I said I'd come get it."

"It couldn't wait until morning? Honestly. This is not the time. I mean, her father—"

"You know Hannah," I said. "Goodnight." I stepped around her, toward the stairs.

Passing through the kitchen again, I heard Hannah's father cough, from his bedroom. It was a thick, ugly sound, followed by spitting. He died before noon the next day, and that drama overwhelmed all else. Hannah's notebook, and my midnight foray to procure it, were forgotten, or at least never mentioned.

I did not tell Hannah that I went and found her notebook. I still have not told her, these six years later. Scarcely a week goes by when I don't take it out and secretly study it.

There are six, or five and a half, entries, spaced throughout the yellow notebook. The first one is the one Hannah told me about, that night; her memory of it had been perfect—*Cabinets, drawers and doors enjoy being opened and closed; little girls, the way they walk is sharper than the sharpest knife.* Below this sentence is a drawing, done by Hannah, I presume, an attempt to respond to the words. It is a crayon drawing of a girl with knives where her legs should be; she is walking with a red smile like a hook on the profile of her face, her black ponytail swinging behind her in an S. The knives' wooden handles attach at her hips. Their sharp tips stab into the ground.

The yellow of the notebook has dulled and darkened, over time; in some places, the color has been worn away by the pressure of other books in the bookcase, the sliding in and out. The writing is all in red pen; it strays across the lines, the spaces between the words uneven; sometimes words are written over the top of each other. One could almost deduce that all this was written in a hurried excitement, in darkness, with a sleeping girl breathing quietly beside you.

The second passage reads, *Ghosts are able to watch our dreams, while we are sleeping; this is how they recognize the people who need them, the ones to show themselves to.* Beneath this, Hannah traced her own hand, in pencil. With red pen, I've traced my hand on the same page; the tips of my fingers brush the words; her girlhood hand fits entirely inside my adult one.

I would like to try, if one day I am a good enough writer, to continue the passages, to finish the story. To write one story for every passage, or link them together, to illustrate them with words.

The other entries do not have drawings. The third one reads as if it's from a dictionary: *A stranglehold is a hold that stops the opponent's breath. Complete and exclusive control (over a person, situation, etc.); an idea or belief may exert a stranglehold.* The fourth: *Our thoughts are what cause our bodies to change. A narrow mind has a broad tongue.* I find these endlessly fascinating, provocative and mysterious, as I do the fifth, which I believe is an excerpt from Emerson, borrowed from an essay: *A man of rude health and flowing spirits has the faculty of rapid domestication.*

The very last passage ends abruptly, which fits perfectly with Hannah's story, for where it ends marks where Mr. Phelps was interrupted. This, more than the others, promised to be a kind of story. In its entirety, it reads: *One day a man was driving past a place where a woman was living. She went to meet him, and bit him to death. The man had a friend who was in search of him. After he had traveled about, searching for his lost friend, he came to the place where*

I wonder what would have been the end of this story, and search for its source, and guess at what might have come next. I don't know if Mr. Phelps knew, if he meant for it all to fit together. Did he foresee the ending, or have a plan? What was he thinking in those late nights, the cool air easing through the window, the beautiful young girl peacefully sleeping?

Sometimes I'll take a day off work without warning

anyone, without telling. I'll drive out to the coast, or wander through the city, ride the buses across the neighborhoods. I imagine, on these days, that I'm a different person. Last Friday I drove out along the gorge, along the Columbia River; I was headed toward Mount Hood, ostensibly, but it's no mystery that for a long time I had been planning to return to Carson. It's an easy drive from Portland, where I live now.

Hannah's mother sold the hot springs, right after her husband's death, and the new owners had reportedly begun a new development, taken steps toward modernization. As I drove, I noticed that the whole town had shifted, in fact, and was comporting itself differently. Signs for yoga and espresso lined the highway.

The hot springs themselves had a new sign, with an OPEN SOON banner draped across it. I drove on the new white gravel, down amid the contractors' pickups, and circled the edges of the construction site, where the new hotel was going up, along the river. The old hotel no longer existed; it, and Hannah's childhood home, had been razed, taken away. As I passed, I could see the pale marks where they'd been, the lost footprints of foundations.

A man in orange coveralls waved at me, but I didn't stop. I climbed the driveway, back onto the highway. I did not go far on the blacktop; I turned in at the driveway, next to the mailbox that said PHELPS. The overgrown trees and bushes slid along the sides and roof of my car as if I were passing through a carwash.

The peeling white paint glared in the late afternoon sun, making it difficult to look directly at the house. It leaned slightly, standing two stories, an addition cantilevered off one side. There were no vehicles, anywhere—which made sense, considering his hitchhiking. When I parked and climbed out, slamming my door, inhaling the faint hint of sulfur in my nostrils, no barking dog ran out to challenge me. Nothing changed.

The front door's brass knocker was shaped like a fist. I knocked, then heard footsteps, slowly approaching. It was not Mr. Phelps, however, who swung the door open; it was an old woman, her white hair pulled back into a thin braid, her smile a question. She was as tall as I am, and this startled me, took me slightly aback.

"I was hoping to speak with your husband," I said.

I told her my name, that I had driven from Portland. She asked me to come inside, to sit down.

"Coffee? Have a seat," she said, and disappeared through a doorway.

The front room smelled of sawdust, and was spare and neat, with lace doilies on the side tables. A spiraling rag rug stretched wider than the floor, its edges bent up on the walls. One door led to the kitchen, another to a stairway, a third onto what appeared to be a bedroom. What was most remarkable in the room were the complicated plastic cages and tunnels, orange and yellow tubes that snaked all along the walls, even up above the doors. Furry shadows, rodents, scurried along, their claws faintly scratching inside. I sat down, surrounded, just as Mrs. Phelps returned.

She settled in a rocking chair, across from me, the milk in the glass she held the same color as her hair.

"Calcium," she said, when she saw me noticing. "My husband, you should know, passed away two years ago. We were married fifty years, almost exactly."

"I'm sorry," I said. "And congratulations."

Embarrassed, I lifted the chipped china cup she'd given me, sipped at the coffee. It was lukewarm, burnt and full of grounds, as if it had been on the stove all day. I spit it back, quietly, and looked past her, through the doorway that led into the bedroom. I could see overflowing bookcases and, on the floor, two large, leather boots. Their laces scribbled out across the floor, their tongues jutted upward.

"Those are some gerbils," I said. "'Habitrail'—is that what those cages are called? I remember them—"

"Hamsters," she said. "So what is your business?"

I began to explain to her about my job. She interrupted me, clarified that she meant to ask why I had come seeking Mr. Phelps.

"I met your husband, once," I said. "Picked him up hitchhiking. This was with my wife, Hannah. She used to be your neighbor—"

"They didn't even say goodbye," Mrs. Phelps said. "Just sold the place and disappeared without a goodbye." She took a drink of milk, her swallowing audible. "We were neighbors, with your wife and her parents," she said, "for a very long time."

For some reason, sitting there, talking to Mrs. Phelps, I did not correct her, or myself. Hannah and I are no longer married, though it is not exactly relevant to the story I am telling. I had called her my wife in order to establish my right to be there; once I'd said it, going back and explaining would have been unnecessarily complicated and uncomfortable.

"What I came about," I said. "I think it really would have interested Mr. Phelps."

"Nothing really interests Mr. Phelps anymore," she said.

"It's about the notebook," I said.

"The notebook," she said, nodding.

"From when Hannah was a girl," I said. "I have that notebook."

"Did you bring it with you?"

"I've often wondered," I said, "what Mr. Phelps was thinking, what was his intention."

"Those were different times," she said.

"Did he discuss it with you?" I said.

"Not at the time," she said. "After everything blew up, he did. It wasn't a complicated thing—it was only that people overreacted about it. It was just tied into his way of seeing things, reading people." Pausing, she rubbed her hands together with a dry, papery sound. "He always said, you know, that he could tell things about her, your wife, simply by the way she walked to the school bus, when she was a girl. He said he was doing her a favor, with the notebook."

"How's that?" I said.

"Already, when she was so young, he could tell that she was becoming a person who could find no pleasure in what she didn't understand, whose world would only turn narrower and narrower and narrower."

As Mrs. Phelps spoke, she drew up her hands, palms facing each other and slid them out, toward me, bringing them together in a point. Behind me, I heard the scratch of the hamsters' claws, saw their dark shapes in my peripheral vision.

"Like a stranglehold," I said.

"Pardon me?"

"That's along the lines of what I wanted to know," I said. "What you just said."

She smiled, thin lips tight over her teeth. "Would your experience of your wife," she said, "bear out his suspicions?"

"I don't know," I said. "Hannah's a complicated person."

"Well," Mrs. Phelps said, finishing off her milk, "maybe his instruction did some good, then."

"Maybe."

"That would have made him happy," she said. "To hear it, that he'd had a positive influence on a young person."

Claws scrabbled, one hamster chasing another over

the doorway, down a chute; sawdust flew as they shot across a plastic chamber, into another tunnel.

"Did you ever have children of your own?" I said.

"Never," she said. "How about you?"

"No." I stood. "Not yet, anyway."

I sat outside in my car for quite a while before starting the engine. Watching the Phelps's house—the light in the kitchen, the old woman's shadow cast around—I was hoping for something else, something more. Another light, suddenly turned on, in a room upstairs, or perhaps a lanky old figure shambling from the shadows, come home from hitchhiking.

Nothing moved, nothing changed. Right before I drove away, though, heading back to Portland, I noticed a pile of wood, stacked on the far side of the house. I had somehow missed it, before; now it was dusk, and the glare had eased. Squinting in the half-light, I decided that the wood was not merely scrap, that it was actually paneling, dark siding, and window frames. It appeared to be the remains of Hannah's childhood home, collected, piled all together. It was as if the entire house might be reconstructed, and the events it once framed might be repeated, practiced and adjusted. As if everything—with Mr. Phelps, with Hannah, and with me—might then have a different, happier ending.

Thrill

Ahn has never liked the thrill rides; being in the grip of
a machine does not appeal to him. Now, with the baby,
there's reason to let his wife, Sumiko, ride by herself. It
gives her pleasure.

The baby is just over a year old, and heavy, in the
carrier on Ahn's back. They wait next to the Screaming
Eagle, a huge wheel with seats on the inside that hangs
from a towering metal arm that swings back and forth
as it rotates. The ride has not yet started; first, the riders
have to take off their shoes. Sumiko waves, her legs dangling from the seat, her bare feet swinging. She is surrounded by overweight teenage girls in midriff-baring
shirts, boys with arms already raised, not holding on,
eager to demonstrate their bravery.

Ahn and Sumiko's house is half a mile away, and
sometimes at night they can hear the amusement park

through their bedroom window; voices rise and fall in waves of fearful delight, then dissipate through the trees' leaves. Now, the Screaming Eagle trembles to life and the music cranks up. Ahn feels the baby's heat on his back, the sticky fingers on his neck, pulling at his hair, stuck in his ears. Sumiko is screaming with the rest, a blur, indistinguishable as she's flung about, overhead.

Ahn steps back, looks away to the Tilt-A-Whirl, the arcade and ball-tosses, the Ferris wheel—and then, at the concession stand, he sees the girl. He has not seen her for over a year, and had not expected, nor hoped, to see her again. She is working at the concession stand, handing out corn dogs, twisting cotton candy onto cardboard sticks. Has she seen him? It's important that she does not. Ahn steps behind one of the ride's metal supports; he can still, leaning out slightly, watch her. The girl is a young woman, really, twenty or so, smiling at a customer. She's cut her hair shorter and dyed the bangs darker, red, but her face is the same. It is a face he will never forget.

The first time was almost two years ago, a rainy night. He and Sumiko had just moved to Portland from San Diego, had traded sun for rain. It was a night like many nights; Sumiko had gotten home late, taken a shower, and came to dinner in her white bathrobe. They'd been eating in the living room, just simple udon, and out the window, behind Sumiko, it had appeared to Ahn that one of the white pickets of the fence was broken, its sharp tip missing. He stood, and stepped closer to the window. The fence was fine; he had been mistaken—it was that there was a hand resting on the picket, obscuring its white edge, and the hand was attached to a slender arm, and a body, and a face, a girl's face in the bushes, looking at the house. The girl stood twenty feet away, on the sidewalk. Ahn didn't say anything. He did not stare, did not betray that he had noticed; he could see his own calm expression in the window, reflected back at him.

The girl returned. She came once a week, twice a month—there was no regularity, no reason. Once dusk set in, Ahn was always checking, in his peripheral vision, to see if she were watching him. He had been down, depressed in those days, still working at home, diagramming products that were never produced, and Sumiko usually worked late at her firm.

Alone at night, he would read the newspaper, drink a cup of tea, toast a piece of bread, vacuum the floor. Every simple thing held a thrill. He never looked directly at the girl; he never mentioned anything to Sumiko. He liked how he could see his own reflection in the window, and how the girl's face—white and round, patiently watching—was sometimes caught within the edges of his body.

Ahn took off his shirt, one night, and then his undershirt. Naked to the waist, he strode forcefully back and forth across the living room; for almost ten minutes, he swung his arms, pushed out his chest; heat radiated from his skin. His fingers trembled with the buttons when he put the shirt back on. Sumiko came home, soon after, and asked him what he'd been doing; she said something about him seemed changed. Smiling, she unbuttoned his shirt, unbuckled his belt. She pulled her dress over her head, her black hair sliding smoothly through the hole in its neck. She led him to the couch, and when she straddled him the lights were on, the curtains open.

Ahn sometimes wondered how much the girl could know—did she realize that his family was originally from Korea, that he was born in San Diego, that Sumiko's family was Japanese-American? Did she know their names? Had she guessed that Sumiko was three years older? What was important, what was clear by her watching, was that she found them remarkable.

So much heat was lost through windows, Sumiko often said, in those days, and he told her he liked the heavy curtains open. He did not tell her why, and she did not ask. As her pregnancy progressed, he sometimes reached out to slow her, turned her profile to the window. He placed his hands under her robe, on the round warmth of her stomach, as if to say, *This is what we have done.*

The first night Sumiko brought the baby home from the hospital, Ahn held him up to the window, showing him the crescent moon. He was allowing the girl to admire the perfect shape of the baby's head, his perfectly symmetrical ears.

Ahn loved it without effort, being a father. It surprised him that he did not resist the diaper changing, the sour milk smell in the sheets, the sleeplessness. Late one night, he had lain awake next to Sumiko as she nursed the baby. They'd been back from the hospital for only two days. Watching, Ahn thought of secrets—how he believed they were permissible, even necessary, how they should only be kept for so long. He told Sumiko, then, about the girl who watched their house, about the first night and the later ones, about the time on the couch, their two bodies framed in the lighted window. Sumiko listened. Startled and interested, yet in a muted way that made him uncertain if she had heard him correctly. And then she lay the baby down, buttoned her nightgown and closed her eyes, asleep.

The following morning he decided not to mention the girl again unless Sumiko did. It could have been that it bothered her, and she was letting it settle, or that she had dismissed it all as unimportant, inconsequential, or even that she understood. Still, in the evening Sumiko tensed when passing the windows, moved with increased hesitation.

At dinner, the third night after he'd told, Ahn could see the girl's white face over Sumiko's shoulder, past the reflection of Sumiko's shiny black hair with its straight white part.

Sumiko noticed him looking past her. Slowly, she set down her silverware, took her napkin from her lap. She stood, and untied the sash of her robe. For a moment, faintly smiling, she looked across the table at him.

Then she turned and stepped away from the table, close to the window, almost touching the pane. She shrugged her shoulders and let the robe slide down her arms, so it fell softly around her feet. In the window's reflection, Ahn watched his wife. The white of her bra, her underwear, stood out, startling against her darker skin. Hands on her hips, she hooked her thumbs under the fabric of her underwear and pushed it down, exposing her caesarian incision. The black threads of the stitches rose and fell, like handwriting, a scribbled word. A faint smile on her face, Sumiko slowly raised her right hand and waved through the window.

Gold Firebird

Harnessing the sun, the gold Pontiac Firebird careened across the wide desert mirages. It surfaced, distinct and glinting, and disappeared once again. Then, shimmering, it rose and veered and finally jerked to an impatient stop alongside the pumps of an isolated service station.

Kent heard the bell, the signal of the car's arrival, tires across the hoses stretched out there, fifty feet from where he stood in the open bay, under a Cutlass up on the lift. He hit the car's underside with a bent wrench he kept on hand for just that purpose, then stepped out of the shadow, through the open garage door.

He felt the blacktop through the soles of his boots. It was a dry hundred and five, at least, but he was used to it. Squinting at the familiar, smooth shape of the Firebird, he half-believed he was mistaken, seeing it shine, there. The driver, a woman, was the only person in the car. He could not see well, his vision obscured by the pumps; it seemed she was turning to reach into the back seat, then pulling a shirt over her head. Setting down the wrench, Kent raked his dirty fingers through his tangled gray hair. The pumps were self-serve, so sometimes he'd go days between actual conversations.

Now the Firebird, in the shadow of the overhang, was not so bright. He walked toward it, away from the building, nothing but desert baking in every direction. Heat made the air down low thicken and buckle, unreliable. All this he'd grown used to, out here, halfway between Reno and Vegas. Beatty was the nearest town, though few would count it.

"That car!" he shouted, approaching. "What is it, a '75?"

The young woman was sitting in the Firebird with the door open, her feet out on the pavement so all he could see were her cowboy boots—black and white, heavily tooled, the heels worn down. Then, through the windshield, her wraparound sunglasses and ragged, dirty blond hair.

"Must be a '75 or '6," he said, his voice lower now. "What with those headlights; those changed, around then."

When she stood up and slammed the door, he saw that she was wearing a thin yellow dress—a sheathe or shift, he wasn't good with words—and in a sudden silhouette he noticed her thin, bowed legs. She looked to be in her twenties, only perhaps as old as the car she drove, and she was slightly taller than Kent. She half-smiled as she stepped past him, toward the office.

"Restroom keys're hanging on the wall," he said. Watching her, he wondered if she'd been driving across the desert wearing nothing but sunglasses and cowboy boots; he imagined that sight, to see it through the windshield, oncoming, then gone before you'd even realize. By the time you recognized what you'd seen, miles would have stretched between you.

He had not been mistaken. It was a Firebird Esprit 400, all smooth lines, slippery, a rolling promise. Four hundred cubic inches, four-barrel carb—he knew it well. Circling the car, he jerked tumbleweeds from the grille, poked at the moths and desert hoppers with the squeegee now in his hand, noted the jackrabbit fur along the front bumper. He started in on the windshield, top to bottom, bug-spattered and sand-pitted; first he saw into the back seat, piled high with unfolded clothing, and then the television, sitting in the front passenger seat, its screen raked around to face the driver's side, its cord snaking toward the cigarette lighter. Three books, their covers bleached, lay on the dashboard. He felt a stab at the familiar sight of the thickest one, the Bicentennial Edition of the Guinness Book of Records; the middle one was a Choose-Your-Own-Adventure, the title too pale to read; the last was called *Stories About Not Being Afraid of Ghosts*. The author's name looked Oriental.

Kent moved around the car. The paint was dull, but nonetheless gold, undeniably so. The big engine ticked, cooling. Rust speckled the chrome strips, but that was only visible up close. This was a vehicle, not merely transportation.

Something sticky had set along the driver's side and around the back window, making the glass hard to see through. He scrubbed at it, wet his squeegee again, scraped along the edges. He knew she was returning because the office door, opening, let out a sliver of radio music—some overproduced country and western—and then the knock of her cowboy boots' heels approached. When the knocking stopped, he turned. She stood there, ten feet away, watching him, a stick of beef jerky in her hand.

"Where you headed?" he said.

Taking off her sunglasses, squinting, she looked up and down the highway. No one was coming; no one would come. He feared she'd pay him and just take off, but she seemed to be in no hurry.

"I see you got a TV set up in there," he said. "You get any reception?"

"I'm just driving," she said. "Not going anywhere. It makes the driving go faster."

"You watch while you drive?"

"Cruise control," she said. "Sometimes I read, too, so it's like doing three things at once. Or more, depending what I'm thinking about."

Her voice was high-pitched, wavering, and he realized that her silence before was only the gradual surfacing from driving alone. She didn't mind talking. She had time.

"All the engines now are just aluminum," he said. "They sound different; you can't feel them rumble in your spine, like this one here."

"I watch videos," she said.

Shifting, he looked over the front seat and saw the VCR nestled in the passenger's foot space, half-buried under videotapes. He kept scrubbing at the sticky rear window.

"*Rockford Files*, mostly," she was saying. "Old episodes. Whole seasons' worth."

"This is the same car Jim Rockford drove," he said. "I guess you know that."

"I always did kind of want a Trans Am," she said. "Instead, I mean."

"I once owned this same car," he said. "Same color, even."

"And what happened?"

"It just got taken away."

"Bank?"

"I don't know," he said. "No, not the bank. My wife. Haven't seen either one of them for twenty-five years."

The young woman did not express sympathy, or say anything at all. She stood there in that thin yellow dress, the sunglasses, the cowboy boots. Her hair still looked blown sideways, and there was no wind. She tore the beef jerky in half, one end in her teeth, her hand pulling down, her neck straining. She watched him watch her do this.

"I left a dollar on the counter," she said, chewing and swallowing. "It was the last one."

He pictured the jar of jerky, full this morning.

"Last dollar, I meant," she said, watching him think.

"The gas," he said.

"Exactly. I'll have to pay you some other way—like washing dishes at a restaurant, that old thing."

He looked past her, to the garage's open bay, the Cutlass up on the lift. She turned, following his gaze.

"Know anything about replacing struts?" he said.

"A little," she said. "Probably not as much as you do."

"So what are you suggesting?" he said.

"Don't you have any ideas?" She did not smile when she said this, only seemed disappointed at his lack of imagination.

Turning back to the Firebird, he saw for the first time that the left rear panel was bent, Bondo-ed. He scrubbed again at the sticky window; the heat of the car was suddenly getting to him.

"Stubborn," he said. "What could this be?"

"Piss," she said.

"What?" Startled, he stepped back.

"Don't be such a prude," she said, closer now, laughing low. "I hate to stop, you know, unless I'm out of gas. So I have a cup I use, a jar with a lid. And when it's full I just empty it out the window, start filling it again." She shrugged, her thin, bare arms sliding up her sides. "No big deal."

"I'm not a prude," he said. "No one ever called me that."

"How about a massage, then?" she said.

"Pardon me?"

"For the gas."

He dropped the squeegee back in its bucket of dirty water. "Fourteen bucks," he said, coughing, pointing at the numbers on the pump. "I've been taken for more. Maybe you'll pass through again."

"Never," she said.

He felt the pressure of all the deserted miles around them as he watched her say this. Behind her was the station—his station, and his home, his room upstairs. A pyramid of Pennzoil cans, dents turned back, stood against the wall. Their yellow matched her dress.

"When you say 'massage,'" he said. "What do you mean?"

She smiled, at last. "Aha," she said. "No, it's not that, whatever you're thinking, the old Nevada massage. When I say 'massage,' I mean you not moving at all, not trying to touch me with your hands or anything else.

"I wasn't thinking anything," he said.

"I'm licensed," she said. Holding up her hands, she flexed her thin fingers. The short nails were painted black.

She followed him to the station, and stepped through the office door when he held it open. The Judds were on the radio, singing "Mama, He's Crazy."

"This song works since they're mother and daughter," Kent explained. "Naomi's the mother, the hot-looker, but Wynonna's got the voice. Listen to that growl, there."

"I prefer to work in silence." The young woman stepped to the radio and switched it off.

"People tell me I ramble more, lately," he said. "I can talk and talk, like I didn't used to—sometimes I'll start and people will wander away from me. I can't help it. Maybe it makes me more honest, though?"

She just looked around the small, cluttered room— at the half-finished crossword puzzles, the grease-smeared telephone, the schematic diagrams of engines, hydraulics, electrical systems.

"I prefer jazz," he said. "It works better in the desert than you'd think."

"I'll need you laid out flat," she said.

He leaned against the dusty blinds so they clattered. He pointed to a door in the corner.

"I got a bed," he said. "In my room, upstairs."

"You live here?"

"I own it."

"Bed's too soft," she said. "Gives way too much. I use more of a table. Let's clear this desk off, here."

They did so, piling receipts and papers on the chair,

along the counters. When he began to lie down, though, she stopped him.

"I can't work through your clothes."

"What? You want me to strip down?"

"No," she said, her hands up to slow him. "No, no. Just up top; I need your back bare."

He unzipped his coveralls to his waist, shucked out of the arms, pulled his T-shirt over his head. He lay himself down on his stomach, the dusty desktop against his skin.

"You're in pretty good shape," she said, "for someone your age."

"You don't know how old I am."

"How long you been out here?" she said.

"Since '76."

"Bicentennial."

"Exactly."

"So," she said. "Twenty-five years."

She jerked off his work boots, one at a time, so his kneecaps jumped on the desktop.

"I'm not sixty," he said. "If that's what you were thinking."

Her cool palms came down first, smooth, circling from his waist, up to his shoulders, startling and then slowly familiar. He opened his eyes and saw only the dirty vinyl floor. He closed them again.

"Shh," she said. "Don't talk. Relax."

She continued, taking handfuls of his flesh, fingers

spiderwalking down from his shoulders to his waist. Then she pounded with her fingertips, then used them as pincers, and then came karate chops, then the warm smooth palms again. She leaned gently against him, only that thin fabric between the warmth of their bodies. Her fingers clattered across the back of his ribcage, solid, and pressed into muscles, finding electricity, unsnarling knots. How long since a woman had touched him like this, how long since he'd allowed it? Alice, it had to be Alice. His wife. All those years and everything gone wrong, the photographs and then the disagreement that led to the leaving.

Alice—he remembered one time on the shoulder of a night highway, her spread out on the hood of that very car, the Firebird, a night when they could not wait the half hour it would take to get home. Now the fingers worked down the tendons of his right arm, across his wrist, spreading his palm, pulling on each of his fingers, stretching his thumb, then returning—wrist, elbow, shoulder, clavicle, and down the other side. The air conditioner chuffed and shivered, then cycled trembling to a stop. There was no sound except his breathing, and hers. No wind outside, nothing for miles as he recalled another time, off a hiking trail, the voices of other people suddenly so close as Alice rose, astride him, jolting him into the sharp twigs beneath his bare back, the sharp stones he could hardly feel.

"Roll onto your side," she said.

He did so, turning toward her, resting on his hip and shoulder. She stepped back. He looked up at her face and she looked back at him; she didn't pretend not to notice his erection. Despite his bunched up coveralls, it was apparent, tenting out the fabric, pointing right at her.

"Maybe we should take a little break," she said.

"How's that?" he said, startled, not sure how he wanted to understand her.

"Why don't you go into the other room and take care of that situation," she said. "Then come back in and I'll be able to finish the massage."

Her tone was so matter-of-fact that he could not deny its logic. He swung his legs around, over the edge of the desk and sat there, thinking how to get down, to walk without hurting himself or looking ridiculous. Clasping the gathered material of his coveralls at his waist, he shuffled, hunching toward the door to the stairs—no, it would be too hot up there—and, still keeping his back to her, through the door with the EMPLOYEES ONLY sign, into the garage. He took only one step and stood there, the door closing behind him, between them.

He let go of his coveralls; they fell down to his knees. He pushed down his underwear and took hold of his cock, trying to remember the feel of her skin, but his fingers were far too rough and it was difficult to make himself believe. Standing there, eyes closed tightly, he tried to imagine her grasping the hem of that yellow dress

and pulling it over her head like liquid slipping away
from her skin so she stood there bowlegged in her
cowboy boots, squinting in the sun, standing next to the
gold Firebird, the same car that Alice had taken, and
now he thought of Alice, spread-eagled across the hood,
and he remembered how she loved to gun that big
engine, the tires she went through, the whooshing
sound of the gas sucked down as the carburetor's second
set of throats opened. *Machine eats landscape*, she would
say, her thin arms out straight, fingers tight around the
steering wheel.

That's how she'd driven away from him, after the
argument about the photographs. He'd always had control of his body, he told her, always kept it under control;
his mind wandered, but whose didn't? He played in
bands, back then, different outfits in San Francisco, and
in that world there were always women getting in your
mind. He liked, he likes, the shapes of different bodies,
the mysteries, the places hair grows or doesn't, the wrinkles and scars. That's natural. And now all those events
were twenty-five years back, the Bicentennial, the last
time he can remember so many American flags everywhere. Why wouldn't she believe him? Why did her mis-
trust seem to have some basis to him? He hardly knew a
thing anymore—these days, people flew airplanes into
buildings—except for how he felt back then, watching
her drive away.

He opened his eyes. His memory had taken him; he

had forgotten what he was doing; his coveralls were at his ankles, his underwear at his knees. His hands held each other, rather than getting to business, and down below he was flaccid, loose, all forgotten. Bending, zipping, he fumbled to the window, checked and saw the gold Firebird, still there, dull in shadow, tumbleweeds collecting in the barbed wire across the highway. One blew free, in that moment, and skittered along the hot pavement, through the open garage door, and bounced off the back wall, under the Cutlass, which was still suspended.

Kent looked over the dirty rags, the wrenches hanging on their pegboard, the crooked black pillars of worn tires. Shuffling in his stocking feet, he opened the door and stepped back into the office.

She was not there. He checked another window—the Firebird sat motionless, empty. Would he have heard her footsteps on the stairs, if she'd gone up to his room, if she'd stretched out on his bed? His bed gave way too much, she needed a table, but how would it be to simply lie down beside her, the length of her inadvertently touching his side in the heat? He kicked his feet into his boots, didn't bother lacing them.

The stairs creaked. The air thickened as he climbed through it. She was not there, the room empty—the sagging mattress, the jazz magazines and warped records, the broken television with its bent antenna and half-assed tinfoil, the dull-bladed fan in the window, the heat. Through the sand-scratched glass he saw the white desert stretching away. Nothing but hot clumps of sage, pathetic Joshua trees.

And yet something was different; something was wrong. Out behind the station, a hundred feet away, a black square marked the desert floor. Not just a square, not a lost sign or piece of metal or scrap of black plastic bag—it was, he knew, a hole. The trapdoor of the dugout was slapped open. That's where she'd gotten to. He wheeled from the room, kicked down the stairs.

The dugout was nothing more than an underground space, a kind of room with dirt walls and floor, the earth held overhead by stout wooden pillars, the sunken roof covered by dirt. Back when the station was a house, the dugout had been for storage, a cool place against the desert; in fact, jars of preserves and pickles remained from that time, stacked dusty next to his cleanser, toilet paper and other supplies.

He hurried across the heat, stopping at the open trapdoor. Looking down, he couldn't see a thing; perhaps a hint of light, a glow on the ladder's lower rungs? He imagined her hiding back in the station, just waiting for him to descend so she could run out and lock him under. He looked all around, turning a slow circle, then laughed at himself. What good would that do her?

"Hello?" he called down, crouching, hands around his mouth. The dark hole swallowed his voice, answered with silence.

His back to the hole, he stepped onto the ladder. He descended slowly, unable to see behind him, his eyes focused on his hands, which grasped the splintery rungs and became harder to see.

She was here. He turned to face her, in the light of one candle. Her shadow slipped out behind her, legs bent where the floor met the wall. The pockets of her dress were jammed full, weighted down with cans and jars. In her hand, she held his trumpet.

"How long have you been driving?" he said. He'd meant to ask why she'd come down here, how she'd found it, but this other question came out. She just smiled, not answering, not at all nervous.

"Take whatever you want," he said. "Anything."

They stood ten feet apart, on opposite edges of the candlelight. Had there been candles down here? Had she brought it along? Now she glanced away, confident for a young woman alone with a strange man, underground, perhaps a hundred miles from the nearest person and no promise, then, that that person would care. He had not even told her his name, had he? And yet he did not know hers, either. Suddenly he realized he should not have followed her down here, that nothing good could come of it. He bent his neck and looked up, at the blinding square of blue, above and behind him; a black crow slid across it, then angled back, slashing across the line of its first pass to make an X, returning as if it wanted a second look.

"You play?" she said, slightly lifting the trumpet; the candle's flame doubled in the brass.

"Well, yes." He looked back at her, his eyes still blind from the sky, the crow.

"Down here in the dark?"

"Yes," he said. "I like the silence between the notes. The lack of echo, you know? And in the dark I can imagine, pretend I'm anywhere, like I don't know where I am."

"I see what you mean," she said, now setting the trumpet down on a shelf. "Sometimes closing your eyes is close, but never quite. You really want to turn yourself inward. Inside out, almost."

"Listen," he said. "Really—take whatever you want. I'm sympathetic with your situation, whatever it is."

"No," she said. "We're not even, yet. Not square. Not even close."

"Pardon me?"

"How about—" The pale skin of her face flickered with the candle's flame. "—instead of the rest of the massage, I tell you a story? It's a good one."

"We could go back to the station," he said. "No reason to stay down here. I'll buy you a Coke. Anything."

"I haven't always been driving around like this," she said, as if not hearing his offer.

"I didn't expect you had been."

"I was married," she said. "Well, technically I guess I still am married. A married woman. A wife."

This last word was cut short, as if she were smiling an ironic smile he could not quite see.

"We bought a chest of drawers," she said. "A dresser. An antique. My husband and I bought it, secondhand. At a garage sale. An estate sale, actually, a dead person's empty house in a little town. Six drawers, heavy, dark and varnished. It rattled when we carried it, and I remember thinking that there must be something inside, the clatter when we wedged it into the car, driving with the trunk tied down and yawning."

He watched her as she spoke, as well as he could, her hand at her mouth, perhaps her fingers wetted as she reached out to touch him or to put out the candle's flame, to pinch it out. He could almost hear the sizzle, the hiss, but that wasn't it, either. She bent her elbow and it was as if a wire or transparent line stretched to the trap door, which slapped shut without warning, with a hollow sound, raining loose dirt over his head. The candle blew out.

"The wind up there," she said.

In this new darkness it was as if the space had bent inward, the black air itself twisted and tightened and still. This, he realized, was how it always was, when no one was here, all day and night, no difference between the two; he imagined snakes, tortoises burrowing beneath the desert floor, the space suddenly opening up on them as they tumbled into this darkness. He shivered. Any rattler here would be slow and cool. Torpid.

"For months and months," she said, "I forgot that sound, that rattle. Half a year, maybe, of taking out my bras and underwear, wearing and washing and folding and replacing them, before I felt the small thing that had been left behind, rolling there in the back of the drawer. Do you know what it was?"

"The candle," he said. "The door—"

"A roll of film," she said.

"Wait—"

"Thirty-five millimeter," she said. "Undeveloped, all wound and hidden inside itself, waiting all that time."

The black air smelled of damp dirt. He heard the squeak, the slide of her fingers on the brass of the trumpet again. Was she closer to him? Was that her breath, the warm shiver of air on his face? She was whispering; they both had been, for quite some time; there was no reason to whisper.

"It wasn't waiting," he said, trying to raise his voice. "Film doesn't wait."

"That's exactly what *he* said—that was the seed of the disagreement, its beginning. He said to throw it out, the film, and I wanted to see what pictures might be in there. What would you say?"

"Well," he said. "They were somebody else's, and probably there was nothing. Costs money, too."

"What?" she said. "Six, seven dollars? That's nothing to pay, to turn a mystery; besides, we bought them all with the chest of drawers. We owned them."

"So they were a dead person's pictures?"

"Maybe," she said, "maybe not. Don't you want to know what they were of?"

As she paused, in the lost underground silence he thought he heard the sound of an engine, four hundred cubic inches growling to life and slowly fading, sliding away. His mind flashed on the gold Firebird, and in that flash he saw Jim Rockford pull one of his patented J-turns—reversing at high speed, jamming on the emergency brake, skidding one-eighty degrees, speeding off in the other direction—and also saw that that was the same way that women left. And yet he was mistaken, this was some sort of mirage, for he was still here, underground, and she was right here, silent, awaiting his answer.

"There's no reason to pry like that," he said. "You should have thrown it away."

"I've heard this before," she said.

"Maybe you were mistaken," he said. "Maybe the roll of film got put in the drawer, slipped in after you bought the thing."

"I took them to the drugstore," she said. "And the next week when I picked them up I could not wait. I sat there in my car in that parking lot and went through them, one at a time, all twenty-four photographs. They were pictures of my husband, every one of them—"

"Like I said," he said. "Could have slipped in—"

"Only they were not times," she said, "not places I remembered; they were shots of him standing in bedrooms with beaches visible through open windows behind him, in a field of wheat, in a waterfall with a wild smile on his face, his bathing suit balled up in one hand. And it was really his expression in these photos—that dreamy smile I'd never seen before, never saw him so happy. What's the word? Blissful."

"Hold on," he said.

"No," she said, "you wait. Because an even stranger thing was that in every picture there was the hint of an arm circling his waist, or a pale, blurry figure behind him, or a slender leg half in the frame. Women? At first I wondered about other women—he was not younger in the pictures, and he wore clothes I knew well, and there was even that period of the mustache experiment. The photos were from times I was around. Our times. And he didn't seem to be smiling at anyone, or even aware that his picture was being taken."

"Ghosts," he said.

"Exactly," she said.

"On the film, I mean," he said. "That's all. A problem with the processing—"

"He tried to say that," she said. "He tried to explain. He couldn't explain. He seemed as perplexed as I was, and I did believe him—at first I thought I could even forgive him, that we could keep on."

"A developing mistake," he said. "A mistake turned everything inside out between us. I can't believe that, still, won't accept it."

"Ghosts," she said.

"They were not ghosts," he said. "And they weren't women, either. Or maybe they were ghosts, if that's what ghosts are. I recognized the times and places, I did, but that did not mean they were actually times and places where I had been. They were pictures of daydreams, I guess, times when I was not where I was, exactly, moments where I was thinking of other women. Imagining them. That's all."

"It made me so uneasy," she said.

"Who could do that?" he said.

"I realized," she said, "that the film made visible what was always there, that those ghosts were always around him, part of him, between us."

He imagined himself turning and climbing, felt the splintery rungs of the ladder in his hands, the press of hot, sage-fresh air slicing down as he lifted the trap door, the intense sharp brightness and the disequilibrium it could bring—the stumbling, the surfacing bends. Yet the darkness did not thin. They could have been any-where, in a city, at the bottom of an ocean, any year or month or time of day, their faces, ages, and names unsteady as they talked, lashing the moments.

"He wanted to know," she said, "just what I was blaming him for, but it wasn't like that—there was no judgment, it was just facts, ghosts, the photographs still stacked in my glove compartment—"

"That gold Firebird," he said, "she didn't care about

sense, anymore, the way she saw me, it was only me talking my way in deeper, trying to explain myself when being myself started it all. Who else could I be? It's our bodies that can be blamed, not thinking, not thoughts. I don't even know where that comes from."

"Once you know something about a person," she said, "you can't not know it."

"It's not a thing you can run from."

"You have to run," she said.

"A person," he said, "a person can come to see that what you do is circle, that you're circling back to where you started, where you left, however it is now."

"In a way," she said, "I felt those cold arms around me. I still do. Driving can't shake them, but maybe the motion keeps them from settling, taking me down."

"Wait," he said. "Wait, wait, wait. That's all. I don't know how, or who could take a picture like that. They were places I hadn't been, times that never exactly were."

"It was those ghosts around him that held me away," she said. "They eased the temperature and shivered my skin and would not let me rest. They wouldn't let the doors lock, and they made the highways shine. They packed the car and turned the key."

Lights

after Chekhov

The dog was barking excitedly outside. Through the window, in the porch light, the three men could see him—his front legs stretched out straight, his thin whip of a tail curved over his back. His name was Orca and, like most mongrels in New Mexico, he had a short, stiff coat of mixed black and tan, long legs, triangles of ears, and a thin snout. He was barking at the black, empty windows of the houses up and down the street; he paused, his mouth settling into a kind of smile, and then started again.

"He's just lonely, out there," Alex said. "He's always been nervous; I got him at a shelter, you know." Standing, he opened the door, and the barking stopped. Orca turned and lurched toward his master, his whole body wagging. Alex stepped out into the yard and bent his tall frame almost double; the fabric of his work pants strained as he began scratching at the base of the dog's tail.

"Good boy, you! Oh, you're a character! Char-ac-ter! Who do you love, now? Who gives you attention? Oh, my Orca, my whale-boy!"

His voice changed, becoming ridiculous and more highly pitched, as he spoke to the dog. Vincent, now standing in the doorway, was slightly embarrassed by the older man. It was especially bad tonight, since they had a visitor.

"Yes, yes, yes!" Alex was saying, scratching, his thick body bent so his bald spot flashed. Then he looked up, to where the two men stood, watching him from the open doorway.

"He never barks when anyone's here," Alex said, "and he only barks when it's nothing."

"Ghosts," Vincent said. He turned to the other man. "Did you say your name was Jones?"

"Jonas," the man said.

All three of them had not had to get up, to check on the dog, but there they were, standing in the faint light, the darkness all around. Between them, they had already drunk a six-pack of warm beer. Now, when Alex proposed a stroll to the top of the embankment, to get some air, Vincent and Jonas agreed.

The closest houses had walls of fresh stucco; down the block, they were wrapped in white Tyvek and glowed faintly, with no glass in the windows; the houses at the corner were barely framed up, their walls only skeletons. All of these houses were empty—hollowed out, in a way—with no furniture, no electricity or plumbing. In another two months they'd be full, families everywhere, children playing in these streets. Alex was the head contractor for the development, and Vincent—thirty years younger, on summer vacation from college—was his assistant. Both men stole glances at Jonas as they walked, to see if he was impressed or would comment on their work. His expression was hard to read, the darkness compounded by the thick, dark beard that covered his face.

Around them, all was still and silent. Orca did not stray far ahead. The stars above seemed to be even more distant than most nights. The cool air smelled of sage, sawdust. To one side stood the Porta-Potty; on the other, the shadowy crane and bulldozer, the dump truck that had broken down that afternoon.

"Useless," Vincent said, as if to wound it.

The three men climbed the embankment, leaning over, their hands on their knees in the steepest sections. At the top, they turned and faced the city, the lights of Albuquerque.

There was the curving line of the Rio Grande, the dark silhouette of Sandia Peak, across the valley, but mostly it was the lights—yellow and orange, green and blue, streetlamps close together, like eyes, and the pale squares of windows where people were up late, unable to sleep. All together, glittering, the lights outshone the stars, following the valley's undulations so that, at moments, the land seemed to move slightly, as if breathing in slow and gentle swells.

The distant lights made the air feel colder. The only sound was Orca's panting, then the liquid hiss as Jonas turned his back to relieve himself. Headlights came and went. Strip malls repeated, every couple miles. The thickness of the lights only began to fray and scatter at the edges of the city, where the sprawl was still in motion. Behind the embankment where the men stood, empty desert stretched.

"Some hill," Jonas said, zipping up.

"We built it," Vincent said. "Mostly. It used to be only about half this tall."

"That's right," Alex said. "We're making the way, taming the wilderness. Think of all the people coming after us—"

"We'll be long gone when those people get here," Vincent said. "It's kind of pointless, when you think about it. Once there were Mexicans and Indians out there, and we plowed them under. Not that I feel bad about it. That's the way it is. There's hardly any trace of them, nothing, and it'll be the same way with us."

"Now where's all this coming from?" Alex said.

"It's terrible," Vincent said, pointing out the few dark buildings at the city's center, the lights like a halo, creeping outward. "Things just fall away behind. Thoughts, whatever. We just keep moving away from wherever we've been. We can't help it, even if it is sort of pathetic, you know? It's not like there's improvement—"

"That's a poisonous way to think!" Alex said, interrupting him. "You're twenty years old and you haven't done anything. Thinking like that, you never will."

Vincent didn't seem to hear Alex's words. He turned instead toward Jonas.

"Can you see the lights of the carnival?"

"No," Jonas said, his voice soft. "We haven't set much up, yet. The lights aren't on, or you'd see the Ferris wheel for sure."

"Well, I've had about enough of this. Let's go back." Vincent led the way as the three men—half-stepping and half-sliding, laughing, not quite falling—descended the embankment.

Jonas had arrived an hour after dark, a map in one hand and a case of beer in the other. He was lost, he said; he'd just come into town with a carnival, where he worked setting up the rides. Wearing patched jeans and a plaid flannel shirt, brand-new yellow running shoes, he'd seemed perfectly sober, merely embarrassed. He'd stood there, short and skinny, with dark, shining eyes; his beard made his head seem larger than it probably was. Jonas could not remember any streetlights or landmarks, and so much of Albuquerque looked so similar. It made sense that he was lost, since the curving streets of this development were not yet on any map. Alex had laughed at this predicament, and decided it would be best and easiest to find the carnival in the morning.

Now, two hours after this decision, they returned past the empty houses. Orca ran ahead and returned, checking that the men were following, then disappeared into the darkness again. At the house, he collapsed on his wool blanket, folded on the porch.

"Home again, home again," Alex said, holding the door open. Just inside, two square coolers rested; taking out three beers, he handed one to Vincent, one to Jonas. "Colder now," he said.

"You sleep here every night?" Jonas said. A white piece of thread was stuck in his beard, under his mouth.

"We start early," Alex said. "And neither of us lives too close. The rest of the crew—they're all Mexicans— they don't live so far away."

"Cuts down on theft and vandalism, too," Vincent said. "Us being out here. Vagrants like to sleep in the houses, you know?"

"Makes sense," Jonas said, smiling, looking around the room.

This was the development's model house, the one they showed off to prospective buyers. The couch was hard, just wrapped Styrofoam, and the television and computer were made of plastic, hollow and light and fake. Everything was uncomfortable, only for appearance, except the card table with the plans spread across it, the folding chair where Alex sat down.

"Of course," he said, "sometimes those 'vagrants' are

Vincent himself, with those girls of his, wherever he finds them."

"Shut up," Vincent said. He unlaced his boots, then stripped to his boxer shorts. Kneeling, he blew some more air into his inflatable mattress, struggled with the valve. Almost toppling his pile of books, he slid into his sleeping bag and reclined, facing Alex, who was obviously enjoying playing the host. Often, Vincent felt crowded by Alex. His sunburnt, fleshy face, everything about him thick, capable of doing nothing—talking, eating, sleeping, breathing—quietly. With that reddish hair all over his body, and the shapeless clothes mended by his wife, who supposedly liked to fall asleep with her head resting on his chest.

And now Alex smacked his lips and sighed with exaggerated relish; he turned the beer can as if to read the label, then nodded and held it out as a kind of toast to Jonas, who sat on the floor with his back against the wall, his head next to the sill of the window. Jonas toasted back, then nodded to Vincent, also. Vincent lifted his can off the floor, but didn't drink. He was exhausted, yet he felt slightly uneasy about sleeping while Jonas was still in the house, awake.

Standing, sliding his feet—his boots now unlaced—Alex crossed to the cooler, extracted three more beers, and distributed them.

"Even colder, now," he said. "Delicious."

"I'm not half done with mine," Vincent said.

"Free beer tastes best," Jonas said. "Not that I stole it."

"I know what you mean," Alex said, sitting down again. And he did know; looking across at Jonas, he knew that they understood each other. They each recognized, in the other, a fellow working man. Alex wondered, though, what Jonas made of Vincent. Vincent, with his affected little beard, like a dark spade on his chin, with his arrogance and book-learning, his authentic Carhartt work clothing, his two-hundred-dollar boots. Vincent didn't work hard, but he made few mistakes. He took himself too seriously; his only joke was to jerk out the tape, from the measure he wore on his belt. 'Man,' he'd say, his hand above his head, three feet of that yellow, metal strip stretched out, 'Man is the measure of all things.' Then he'd let the end go, and the tape, rattling away, would disappear, winding itself up. Now Alex watched Vincent drink the beer, swallowing with a sharp sort of wince. It irritated him.

"Listen." Alex looked down at them from his chair, his voice lower and his boots off, as if now the evening would begin. "When I was a young man—not unlike Vincent, here, though of course I never matriculated at a university—I was beset by ideas, too. I was almost poisoned to death. It was all kinds of New Age notions, and Carlos Castaneda, mixed in with a book of ancient philosophy I found on a bus. 'Lightning guides all things'— that was one of my favorites."

"Carlos who?" Vincent said. "I mean, there's a difference between New Age and philosophy."

"It's all part of the same problem," Alex said. "Listen. You have to understand that this was the late '70s, early '80s. I wore turquoise bracelets and a necklace. Silver rings on my fingers, even on my thumbs. Of course, where I was coming from was only as I understood Castaneda, which likely wasn't very well—just that the everyday world couldn't be allowed to have power over me, that it was only appearance and that all it took was a person to be aware of that fact, to see past it. That sort of thing."

"And what did you see?" Vincent said.

"That's exactly the point—I mean, I think there was supposed to be something like luminous filaments of energy, extending into the cosmos, but it wasn't really that I wanted to see anything. On the contrary—what I wanted was an excuse to be irresponsible. Why believe in anything if it's all only appearance? Why do anything at all, take anything seriously?" Alex had set down his beer, to gesticulate with both hands. "It was extremely comfortable," he said. "I was a terrible person."

"Now I find that hard to believe," Vincent said, pretending to be indignant, one finger in the air. "No one says that about my boss!"

"What do you mean, 'terrible'?" Jonas said.

"I mean, I thought I was living on a different plane, but I was just disconnected from everything, everyone. I'm just saying that's a long way from my life, now, the work we're doing here."

"How so?" Vincent said. "This doesn't change anything. These houses will fall apart, and the people will die, and all their thinking will be forgotten; all this here will be dark and abandoned, two hundred years from now—five hundred miles from here, though, some fools will be building some kind of geodesic domes, drinking cheap beer with some random traveler, talking when they should be sleeping."

"Random traveler?" Jonas said.

"That's just his slang," Alex said. "He doesn't mean anything by that."

"I wasn't taking offense." Jonas turned toward Vincent, then looked up at Alex. "So, you said you were a terrible person, before. Give us an example. Something you did."

Alex shifted, and the chair's legs creaked. He took a long swig of beer, then squinted at the ceiling as if inspecting the spackling.

"Let's see," he said. "I think I can remember a time."

"Oh, man," Vincent said. "It's after midnight."

"I was twenty-four, if that," Alex said, "and I'd gone out to spend a week in this little resort town. A buddy of mine had a vacation place out there, and I was going to do some work in exchange for the time. This was up north of Santa Fe, not far from Taos, actually a town where I'd spent a few years when I was growing up. I'd rather not tell you the name—it doesn't matter."

"Mysterious," Vincent said.

"Roll me a beer," Alex said. "Get one for yourself. You might learn something here, if you listen." He stopped the can with his foot, then set it on the table to settle. "Anyway," he said. "It was the end of the day, and I was sitting on this old wooden porch, leaning back in a broken-down wicker chair, thinking. The town was near a natural hot springs—that was its main attraction, and I could see the clouds of steam rising, half a mile away, across the desert. The sun was taking its time setting; its weak glare, the glow of the sand, hid the bleached bones, the prickly pear and cacti, all the flea-bitten jackrabbits I knew were out there. It was like I could reach out and tear that scene away and see what was behind it, if I wanted to, if I felt like it.

"All around me on the wooden pillars and handrails of the porch, people had carved their names, and dates, and other facts and opinions. Taking out my penknife, I began carving my own name—halfway through, though, I was overcome by self-disgust, at my desire to leave such a worthless mark in a world that was, after all, only surface, only appearance. I threw the knife aside, stomped down the steps, and began walking across the desert, toward the few buildings of the town.

"There were still people walking the streets at the end of the day—heading home, dealing with errands. I sat down on the wooden steps of a convenience store, drumming out a rhythm with a little metal flashlight I carried. I just watched the people pass, feeling above it all in my sandals with the tire-tread soles, some kind of hemp bracelet around my ankle. Mostly, I was watching the women who passed me, assessing their builds and the ways they moved, imagining how it might be to have hold of one of them. Despite all my jewelry and philosophy, I wasn't high-minded at all, when it came to women. And I wasn't just looking, I was considering the chance of a situation that could last me a few days, that could easily be left behind. The more depraved the better." Alex shrugged and smiled. "Even Vincent here, after all, is not above a little trolling, on weekends, bringing back some girl with rings in her nose to explore these empty houses. He finds them in the strip malls, I think."

Vincent snorted, but didn't answer.

"Anyway, I was sitting there when I heard the clatter of a bicycle chain. I looked up, and this woman was coasting toward me—strong-looking, about my age, with a clear, wide face. She wore overalls, her hair tied up in an orange bandanna. I watched her come to a stop, then kick her stand down; when she started for the store, I acted as if I was in the way, and slid aside to let her pass. She looked down at where she was stepping, but did not meet my eyes, or apologize for making me move.

"As soon as I heard the door close behind me, I stood and took a couple steps closer to her bicycle. It was an old one-speed, with wide handlebars that held a wicker basket. A note had been taped, on the seat; in thick, black ink, it said: *Oh! If this seat could talk!!* I found that very encouraging, to say the least. I rested my hand on the seat, imagining for a moment, and then hurried back to my station on the steps.

"When she came out of the store, I shifted a little, at the last moment, so her calf brushed my side. She didn't say a thing. Instead, she lifted her bag of groceries into her bicycle's basket and let out a sigh. There was something in the sound of that sigh—it was then that I knew I had a chance.

"'Excuse me,' I said. 'Do any of these stores stay open twenty-four hours?'

"'No,' she said, finally turning. 'This is just a little town.'

"She glanced at me, then looked again; there was a change in her expression, a new curiosity. Her eyes wide, smiling, she took a step closer and stared right into my face.

"'You're Alexander Sutherland, aren't you?' she said.

"There was a gap between her front teeth; her smile made me want to lean closer, to see inside. It was only through this smile that I recognized her—she was a girl I'd known many years before, in high school. Her name was Katherine, but we all called her Kitty. Back then, she'd been a little lazy, catlike and aloof. Her thick hair always so full of static." Alex slapped his leg and laughed. "Many of us wanted to stroke her, and I not the least! I'd sent notes to her that she never answered. I'd followed her home from school, but never dared to get close.

"She'd moved away suddenly, in the middle of tenth grade, and now, fifteen years later, I'd found her again. Sitting on the steps, I stared into the space between her overalls and her body, the air caught around her, more than enough room for me to slip my hands inside, to feel the padded bones of her hips. She wasn't heavy, just solid. She had always been taller than we were—girls often are, at that age—and the woman standing before me was still my size, at least. She appeared to have been transformed, to have become so strong and yet, perhaps, to have also become easier to get hold of? If not for her smile, I wouldn't have recognized her. I stood, and we were the same height. Immediately, I had the desire to stretch out with her, our bodies touching from feet to forehead. I had never had a woman who was my size.

"She told me how glad she was that I was a carpenter—that's what I called myself, back then—and that I was still in touch with everything. That's the way she put it. 'You work with your hands,' she said. 'That's so rare, these days.' Her voice was full of wonder and pride, like I'd exceeded her highest expectations. 'How good that is,' she said, over and over. She didn't want to talk about herself, she just wanted to hear about me; still, I saw the diamond on her finger. She was engaged, and lived in that town with her fiancé, who was a banker and worked thirty miles away, in Santa Fe. I took this news as a very good sign. The situation was perfect, compelling, as if created just for me.

"Hold on," Alex suddenly said, standing, interrupting his own story. "I got to shake the dew off the lily. Could use the fresh air."

"Yes, the air," Vincent said. He turned toward Jonas, who still sat slumped against the wall, his expression blank. "You can go out the windows, too, just so you don't dribble on the sills."

"The air," Alex said, opening the door. "And the stars." They listened to his fading steps, and then Vincent spoke again, his voice lower.

"He's not bad. He likes to talk—that's all. During the day he can talk normally—at night, sometimes, and especially with an audience, he just gets out of control."

"I understand," Jonas said. "I don't mind at all."

"It's just the way he goes on, the words he uses. When he gets like this, he never wants anything, he 'desires' it. He doesn't go after anything, he 'pursues' it. The language—I don't know where he comes up with this shit. Not to mention how this story could've been over fifteen minutes ago."

"So you've heard it before?"

"No, but it's all the same."

They went silent at the sound of Alex's heavy footsteps on the porch.

"So," he said, closing the door, resuming his story even before he'd sat down again. "We began to walk together, with no agreed-upon destination or purpose. She held her bicycle out to her right, and I was on her left. We were talking about me, and my past, and what I hoped to do next. I asked about the sign on her bicycle's seat, and she laughed it off. She had a certain bold sadness about her, I noticed; her smile seemed more of a challenging than a happy one.

"As we walked, I tried to work in fragments of philosophy I'd read somewhere, to pass them off as my thoughts. 'Some people,' I said, 'don't notice what they do when they're awake, just as we forget what we dream about. There's a crack between the two worlds, a place they overlap—it opens and closes like a door in the wind.' I took her silence to mean that she was impressed, that she was considering the depth of my insights.

"It was dusk when we started walking, our shadows long and faint. The desert stretched out, the sand ridged like the surface of the ocean, in gentle waves. The wind, dry and gritty, cooled off and gusted, now and then, causing us to squint and jostle each other. By the time we reached her house, an old brick building, darkness had fallen, and all the shadows were gone.

'Won't you come in for a cup of tea?' she said. 'I'm all alone.' She said her fiancé came home late, that sometimes he even slept on a couch in his office. She said it would be nice to have some company, that the nights could be very boring.

"I held open the gate, and she pushed her bicycle

through the opening. I watched the tendons in her neck, the sharp corners of her shoulder blades, thinking that she could hold me as tightly as I could hold her. I was happy, relieved that she was to be married, since that made everything easier, made it all temporary. And I was happy that her fiancé was not home, yet I still had doubts of my success—just because of who she was and how it had been when we were children.

"Her house had once been a store, long before, and there was still a long wooden counter, cubbyholes for mail. A staircase led straight up to the second floor. The first floor was subdivided into small rooms by walls of fresh sheetrock. She led me through one of these rooms—past toys, and a baby swing that hung from an exposed beam—and into another.

"'You have children?' I said. The possibility didn't bother me, of course. It only made the situation richer.

"'No,' she said.

"'Are you expecting one?'

"'No,' she said. 'Caffeinated or not?'

"'What?' I said, confused for a moment. 'Do you have any herb tea?'

"Lipton's was all she had. We settled into two leather easy chairs, surrounded by expensive-looking, dark furniture—she'd told me her fiancé was from the East Coast, and the furniture looked that way. I watched as she lit a candle, then turned out the lamp. The candlelight flickered across the width of her face, the curve of her brow, that smile, her sharp and generous mouth.

"'Are you comfortable?' she said. 'Is there anything else I can do for you?'

"'Yes,' I said. 'Is it all right if I call you Kitty, like we used to do?'

"'All right,' she said, looking surprised, yet pleased. 'I haven't heard that in a long time.'

"'Do you remember the notes I used to write you?' I asked.

"'No,' she said. 'I do remember thinking that you might like me.'

"I told her that that should have been obvious, and she told me she guessed it hadn't been. She pulled the bandanna from her head; her dark hair was still thick, but now it reached only to her shoulders. And then she started in on my way of life, again—how it was earthier, more natural, how I seemed so 'centered.'

"I sipped at the hot tea, listening, trying not to unsubtly betray my desire to ask her to stand up, so I could unhook the straps of her overalls, so they would fall down around her feet. I could almost hear the heavy sound they'd make as they hit the floor. 'You may think my life is closer to the earth,' I said, 'but it's still lonely, just as superficial as anything. For instance, the people I know, my friends—I mean, they're just searching. Going to sweat lodges and Indian powwows, making all their pets eat vegetarian. There's no structure, you know? If I dance with a girl at a party—even if I sleep with one, forgive me—I always feel her looking over my shoulder, to the next man and past him, even. It's desperate.'

"Kitty did not agree with me, nor did she argue—either reaction would have brought her closer to doing the things I desired. She only sighed, and looked into the bottom of her teacup, and stared out the window, as if to reassure herself that nothing had changed since she'd last checked, moments before."

Outside, Orca let out a couple tentative coughs, then a howl, and then he was scratching at the door, his nails scrabbling along the bottom, shaking the knob.

Alex broke off his story, at the sound; a look of surprising tenderness rose in his face. Standing, he crossed the room in three long steps, jerked the door wide open, and held it there. Orca whined; his tail swept from side to side. When Alex stepped onto the porch, Orca turned and leapt off it. The big man followed, leaving the door open. For a few minutes, Vincent and Jonas could hear his voice—high-pitched, spiraling, completely unlike the one he'd been using to tell the story—and his heavy footsteps, his panting and wheezing as he ran around the yard.

"Oh, yes! Orca! My silly friend in the full-body beard!"

Eventually, Alex returned, hitching up his pants, a little out of breath. Closing the door, he pulled three fresh beers from the cooler, handed them around, then sat down in his chair.

"Here's to our canine friends," he said, taking a drink. "Boy, this is even colder. Each can tastes better than the last."

"It's the ice that does that," Vincent said, a book open in front of him on the floor. For the past half hour, he'd been pretending to read a chapter on fiber optics.

"To our canine friends," Jonas said, holding up his can.

"Beer," Alex said. "She offered me a beer. It was Tecate, and we drank it out of the cans. She squeezed a wedge of lime and the juice caught me right in the eye. Next, she moved her chair closer to mine, so the armrests bumped together; we faced the same way, toward the window.

"'I see you,' she said, 'and I remember back to when I was a girl, and I imagine all the different paths, all the different places I could have chosen, even all the people I could've ended up with.'

"The candlelight was dim, so we could see out, onto a long wedge of desert. As we sat there, the moon slowly rose, its strange light making the sands burn blue. Long black shadows gradually shortened, pulled closer to whatever cast them. Time passed. Another beer was opened. Kitty's face looked younger, more like I remembered it, and she began speaking in a way that pleased me, in directions I encouraged. She was talking, I believe, about how blind people were compensated with enhanced hearing. Why, she wondered, were not lonely people given greater powers of love? I told her I didn't follow her logic—that that was like saying the blind should develop enhanced sight, because they were unable to see. I said that loneliness and love were two sides of the same thing. Opposites.

"Somewhere during that conversation, I realized that my hand was touching Kitty's; I didn't know who had made this move, but we both pulled away, as if the touch had just become apparent. How long had our hands rested like that? I could not tell. I felt that we'd been drawing closer over the course of these hours, very tentatively—then moving away, reconsidering, and drawing closer again.

"It was after ten o'clock, and I pretended I had better get going, acted as if I wanted to leave; then I allowed myself to slip into telling another long story."

"'Just one more beer,' Kitty said. 'It's bad luck not to finish a six-pack, when we're this close.'

"Out the window, suddenly, there were headlights. They wheeled past, around behind the house; in a moment, I heard the mechanical clunk of a garage door opener, and then a car's engine, shutting down, doors opening and closing. Voices.

"I tried to prepare my face, to adopt an expression of cordial and innocent pleasure, one that would assure him of my good intentions, that would make it clear I'd been on the point of departing.

"The fiancé's voice rose as he came closer. 'I over-come the likes of this every single day!' he was saying.

'Are you serious?' There was only a split second as he passed the open doorway; I barely saw his short, dark hair, his suit, his red tie whipped over his shoulder. He was holding a cell phone to his face, talking into it. 'Absolutely not!' he said, his voice high and sharp. 'That's not even a question I'd asked. You know me better than that. Don't say you don't. Don't.'"

"Oh, man." Vincent closed his book with a loud slap and rolled over onto his back, rubbing his eyes. "You want me to believe they had cell phones, back then?"

"Vincent!" Alex said. "You're listening? I thought maybe you'd fallen asleep."

"How could I?"

"Well, you're right—that was the first cell phone I'd ever seen, and it made a deep impression on me." Alex paused, and drank from his can of beer. "The fiancé was alone," he continued, "I'd just believed he wasn't, because of the talking. I just sat there, listening to the sound of his hard-soled shoes climb the stairs, and then his footsteps pacing on the floor above our heads. I was watching Kitty, her reaction to his entrance, the sound of his voice. Her face paled. She seemed embarrassed, though I was not sure if it was of him or of me—of my presence, there.

"It seemed possible that I might be spared the awkwardness of an introduction, so I stood and began taking leave, serious this time. Kitty was in as much of a hurry as I; she walked me out, across the porch and the front yard, to the gate, where we paused. I remember the faint creak of that gate's hinge as we leaned against it, wavering, uncertain whether to open or close. Neither of us spoke, at first. I took the metal flashlight from my pocket and, nervously, I twisted its head, so the light flickered on and off. Something in me wanted to see the pain in Kitty's face, to look for silent tears. The light was as unsteady as her expression.

"'Do you think you could really care for me?' she said, whispering. 'Do you really think so?'

"And at last I felt the metal hasps of her overalls, against my chest, and I lay my hands inside the denim so I could feel the curve low in her back, and the heat of her skin, her thick waist, and how ready she was for me, how serious. I leaned in, but she was not expecting it; my lips met her teeth, which was even better.

"'Please don't,' she said, weakly pulling away.

"'Come with me,' I said. 'Just for a little while. Half an hour. We'll go out in the desert.'

"'I can't,' she said. 'Tomorrow. Come for me, tomorrow. Before noon, so I won't have to wait.'

"'Before noon,' I said, nodding.

"'Until tomorrow.' Kitty kissed my cheek and, turning, disappeared into the house. Through the window, I could see the candlelight, her faint shadow sliding along the walls. I recognized the sadness in her life, and also that none of my schemes would make her happier, in the end. Not at all.

"I wanted to get away from there as quickly as possible, back to the place where I was staying. I wasn't sure of the direction, but I knew it couldn't be far, since the town was a mile across, if that. Hurrying, I walked under the black windows of empty houses and abandoned buildings. There was not a soul on the streets, which strayed from asphalt to gravel and back again. The wings of birds in the sagebrush stirred at my passing. I felt wounded by my failure, angry that Kitty's relationship with her fiancé was not better. And as I drifted along the edge of the desert, under the moon, the expanse seemed like a projection of my mind, of the way I was feeling, a bottomless and frustrated ocean; I imagined a sharpness beneath that smooth, still surface—blind fish and sand sharks moving through that denseness, whales flexing the slow, powerful flukes of their tails. The air felt warmer, suddenly, more humid, and then I heard what I thought was a voice, a woman's voice, crying out—"

"Perfect," Vincent said, the word drawn out as if he were talking in his sleep. "And it was her—Kitty!—and you finally got those overalls off her, finally, and the two of you did it—in and out of the hot springs, in seventeen positions, and you realized that you were in love, and she ended up marrying you, instead, and, whoa! Now she's your wife—"

"Not even close," Alex said. "And it's not as if I'm even talking to you. Let me finish, here."

"Where are you coming up with this shit about the

whales and the sand sharks? Up by Taos? Get to the point!"

"Hold on," Jonas said, slowly getting to his feet. "Is there a bathroom in here, a sink? I just want to wash my face, you know?"

"The water just got hooked up." Vincent pointed down the hallway, a flashlight in his hand. "Take this— I'm not sure there's any bulbs in the fixtures, back there."

Jonas nodded and took the flashlight, then crossed the room and stepped into the hallway.

"Hey," he said, leaning back, reappearing. "Keep talking, with the story. Loud enough so I can hear you back here." He gave a half-wave, then moved out of sight, again.

"Eventually," Alex said, "I found the place I was staying. As soon as I got there, I madly started finishing all the carpentry work I'd started, putting my tools away without even cleaning them. My hands were shaky, and I didn't know why."

As Alex spoke, while Jonas was still in the bathroom, Vincent slid from his sleeping bag and quietly crossed the room. He took a pencil, then wrote on the corner of the blueprint that was unrolled across the top of the table: *I'm afraid of him ? What does he want?*

Taking the pencil, Alex replied—*RIDICULOUS! STUPID*—without slowing his monologue.

"I drank a bottle of red wine that night," he said, "and I worked with minimal light—I couldn't remember whether I'd told Kitty where I was staying, and I was afraid she'd come after me, any lighted window a beacon that would call her. I packed up everything, then fell asleep, despite myself. I needed those hours of rest…"

"You just love to talk," Vincent said, hissing as he tore the corner from the blueprint, balled it up in his fist, and retreated across the room. "You can't even tell what's going on here."

"…I awakened with a headache, feeling anything but fresh. Bent over double, trying to make myself smaller, harder to see, I got everything in my car. I drove out of town with a hat pulled down tight on my head, scrunching so my sight line just cleared the dashboard. I was nervous because, in the daylight, I didn't know which house was Kitty's; I feared she might be walking the streets, carrying a pack or suitcase, searching for me.

"At last I was out on the highway. Speeding. The sun had just risen; the shadows in the desert were long, and I could see the shadow of my own head, framed by the window, sliding along the lane next to me, on the asphalt. I sighed, and the sound surprised me. My thoughts circled around and around. When I closed my eyes I saw her sad smile, the space between her teeth. My hand, where she had first touched me, felt tender, faintly sore. 'What is wrong with me?' I wondered. I tried to remind myself that it was all only surface, appearances, but this provided no easy relief, for once. I pulled over to the side of the road and tried to sort myself out. I wondered: 'Am I in love?'"

"Of course you were!" Vincent said, clapping his hands in exasperation.

"Of course I wasn't, but I didn't know that at the time. I didn't know what I knew, I was too afraid to find out, but now I see that wasn't it at all—"

Alex went silent as Jonas returned to the room, handed the flashlight to Vincent, and sat back down on the floor, next to the window, with his back against the wall. Something—neither Alex nor Vincent could tell what—was different about Jonas. It was uncanny; he seemed to be, at once, the same person and not the same person at all. This Jonas seemed smaller, younger, and slightly more vulnerable. Perhaps the more sinister Jonas was still in the bathroom, or perhaps that Jonas had been entirely summoned by Vincent's suspicion.

"Go on," Jonas said to Alex. "Continue."

Standing, Alex got himself a beer, and one for Jonas. He took the warm, unopened can from in front of Vincent and, without comment, traded it for a cold one.

"That morning," he said, sitting again, his face turning serious, "parked on the side of that highway, I almost turned around, thinking I should go back and apologize, but I didn't. I was too weak for that." He opened the beer, sucking away the foam before it could overflow. "What had happened was I'd run into someone, I'd been confronted by someone who was ready to believe, to connect somehow, and all I wanted was to get in her pants."

"Overalls," Vincent said.

"I was afraid," Alex said. "Even if I couldn't understand it at the time. I felt the fact that she'd exposed me, but I didn't really understand it." He paused. In the silence, he stood and sat down again, unbuttoning his shirt at the neck. He noticed that Vincent's eyes were jerking sideways, that Vincent was subtly nodding his head, slapping his own cheeks. Finally, Alex understood the signal—Jonas had shaved off his beard; that was it; his cheeks were thin, raw and pale. His head was half the size it had been.

"She exposed me," Alex repeated. "That was that."

"And that's it?" Vincent said. "That convinces me of exactly nothing."

"Did I start that story to convince you of anything? After all, that was my point—you can't know things without experience."

"You started the story because you said you'd been a terrible person," Jonas said. "I expect we all have our stories like that."

The sound of crickets rose up, suddenly, then died away, as if a swarm had blown by on a gust of wind.

"People feel things," Alex said. He finished off the beer, crushed the can in his hand, and dropped it rattling to the floor. His voice was quieter than it had been all night. "It's as simple as that. Connections can be made, and those feelings matter, even if they slacken, even if they're mistaken."

"I can't believe I gave you three hours of my sleep for this sermon," Vincent said. He noisily turned over, the nylon of his sleeping bag whispering around him. "Good night," he said, facing the wall.

Alex looked at Vincent, then over to Jonas, who seemed to be asleep with his eyes open, his legs out straight on the floor, his yellow running shoes pointed at the corners where the walls met the ceiling.

"I'd like to stretch my legs," Alex said. "One more time. Who wants to join me?"

Vincent didn't even answer, pretending to already be asleep. Jonas stood, slowly, reached his arms above his head, and twisted his neck one way, then the other. He held the door open for Alex, and followed him outside, where Orca was already running ahead, leading the way.

The two men hardly spoke. There was only the sound of their footsteps in the gravel, tiny landslides spilling behind them as they began to climb the embankment. They climbed more slowly, this time; even Orca had less energy. Pausing to catch his breath, Alex noticed how Jonas's cheeks shone in the moonlight, his skin a pale, translucent blue. Orca waited, now, panting at the top.

"We've tired you out with our chatter," Alex said. "I apologize. We're not used to company."

"I've had a good time," Jonas said. "Interesting."

Almost no one was out driving. It was too late.

There were fewer lights, yet they made that up in brightness. They reached out for the night sky, straining outward.

"Sure is something," Alex said.

He checked sideways, to see Jonas's agreement, and in that moment the black sky behind Jonas sliced open, in sections, and slowly folded around him. First his feet were taken, so he seemed to be levitating, and then both arms at once, and finally his head, until he had completely disappeared. Alex looked away, at the lights, settled and breathing, down in the valley. When he looked to his side, once again, Jonas was standing there, calmly, exactly as he had been before.

"Tell me the truth," Alex said. "Were you really lost, tonight? Do you actually work for a carnival?"

Jonas kicked a stone and it rolled down the face of the embankment, a rip in the moonlight. "We put up the rides," he finally said, "and then we take them down."

As a silence gathered, Alex waved his arms toward the lights. "Our only pleasure out here is drinking, telling stories—"

"We come in and out of towns so fast," Jonas said, as if not listening. "As fast as a wrench can take a nut off a bolt. Like in your story. I understand."

"Pardon me?"

"It's easy to be a terrible person," Jonas said, "to do anything, if you're always leaving a place the next morning." He shook his head. "Everyone I work with, the things they do, sometimes. Myself, even—"

"I hardly understand anything, these nights," Alex said. "All I know for certain, right now, is that I miss my wife. It's like I feel it all at once. This is the last night I stay out here, no matter how convenient it is. My wife, she knows me. This is no way to live. Did I tell you I have two children, two little girls?"

The men stood silently for a few more minutes, each thinking his own thoughts, looking out over the city. Then they stumbled back down the slope, past the empty houses. Orca stayed closer, now, his tail limp, his head held low.

"It's late," Jonas said. "It must be. I don't have a watch; I didn't hardly notice, because I was listening."

"Once we get inside," Alex said, "I want you to take my cot. As a favor to me. Lots of nights, I don't sleep, I have so much work to do. And don't fuss about it— you'll only wake Vincent."

"I'll be fine on the floor," Jonas said, but once they were inside, he did not argue.

Alex unfolded the cot, the blanket, and helped get Jonas settled. He dimmed the lamp, then sat down at the table. Taking out his wallet, he extracted three photographs and set them in front of him, their three faces looking up into his. Patrice, Margaret, Rachel. His elbows wide on the table, his head in his hands, he stared back at these bright faces, and sighed. They were his lightning. When that door swung open—between

waking life and dreams, between appearance and whatever might be beyond it—these three were there, on
both sides, looking out at and into him.

~~

Just before sunrise, Vincent was awakened by Orca's
barking. He opened his eyes and saw the cot, standing
empty in the middle of the room, the blanket neatly
folded atop it. Alex lay flat on his back, on the floor,
snoring loudly with his mouth open, his shoes off, only
covered by his jacket.

Vincent felt uneasy, unlike himself; his skin was hot,
tight from lack of sleep, and he couldn't quite focus his
anticipations, recall his suspicions. He fought free from
his sleeping bag as if it were trying to smother him, then
stood and ran barefoot, out onto the porch. It was only
Hector and the rest of them, the pickup's bed so full of
men that the wheel wells almost touched the tires in
back. The men yelled something at Vincent, something
about being ready to work; despite studying it at school,
he could rarely understand their Spanish.

The air was blinding, the sunlight slanting harshly
down, the new day all around him. Black spots floated
before his eyes, then vanished. Turning, he headed back
into the house, almost tripped over Alex, and ran down
the hallway, past the empty kitchen, to the bathroom
door. Vincent paused, held his breath, then pushed it

open. This room, too, was empty. All that remained were the dark whiskers, thick in the sink, settled like a bird's nest around the drain.

Signal Mirror

for Taylor Reed

If people in Midvale had hackles on the backs of their legs, hackles that raised at the hint of danger, that's the way it was when Derek appeared. His jeans slung low, and one of those tools on his belt that can be a pliers and a knife or whatever you need—it was clear from the beginning that he could handle any broken thing. He was bigger than Midvale, bigger even than Salt Lake City, and no one liked him because he was exactly what we needed.

How did I meet him? It was at one of those yard sales where the same junk's wheeled out of someone's garage every weekend, and I overheard a man's voice saying, All I want is some of those pants with the double-thick knees and ass, you know? And then he turned, and pretended to want the salt and pepper shakers—clear glass, shaped like eggs—that I was holding.

Right away, he admitted it was a trick, to get me talking to him, and pretty soon I was, and we were talking. We stepped away from the sale and sat down on the curb, our feet in the gutter. He wore black cowboy boots, the pointed toes shining; he smiled wide, so the corners of his lips almost touched his sharp sideburns. He wore green plastic sunglasses that attached inside his regular ones; they cut the bridge of his nose in a straight, dark line. He spit tobacco juice between his black boots, and told me everyone needed just one decent vice. He told me his joke about the old lady and the escalator and the healing magnets in her shoes.

It all started with Derek, and that's how it will end. It's just this middle time between him that we have to live through.

When will I come back to Utah? Sometimes I feel I'm already there, or at least my return has started already and my thoughts are there, ahead of me. When my body comes, you'll see me, here where you've been surrounded by my thoughts, breathing them in and out. And when my body arrives, where will my thoughts be, then? Circling. I'll take them inside and grow strong and calm, my heart dialed low and ready.

People come and go—resurrection's not too strong a word. I mean, I want to come back. I'm a descendent of settlers, handcart pioneers. I tutored other students in high school, for Honor Society; even the slow girls complained about Midvale, but I never felt I needed a bigger place.

Watch and listen: I am not the girl you see standing here. I mean, I am this girl, but I am actually somewhere else. This voice is not coming from where you think. I will try to explain.

Where am I? I live in Las Vegas. Right away, your mind is already heading in the wrong direction, toward the lights of the Strip. No, this is out on the eight-lane boulevards with the same chain stores repeating every four blocks, boulevards where there are still dirt alleys between them, where horses stand in broken-down corrals and ragged roosters crow every hour except dawn.

The construction workers never stop, plowing into the desert. There's another apartment complex beyond our pool, almost finished, and another, beyond that, that's just getting framed up. I share my apartment with a girl I work with, and no one's ever lived in it before.

So it's not the Vegas you're thinking of. And it's all hantavirus down here—you catch a mouse in a trap, you got to spray it with Lysol and let it sit a while. Once I got a garter snake, still alive, in a mousetrap—remind me to tell you that one, later.

I don't even work in those outskirts. I'm way out farther in the desert. I carry gallons of watered-down Kool-Aid, and I go barefoot everywhere, now, so there's a ridge on the bottom of my feet, running along the side, that makes them look like a sandal's sole. The desert forces you to do more with less, to be ready. I carry a condom, in case I need an emergency canteen—it's amazing, how much water they'll hold. Aboriginal Living Skills, is what I call it. Scorpion stings, snakebite, whatever. I go native, braiding up my hair in two, the ends tied with rawhide shoelaces. I wear one turquoise bracelet and one of colored plastic beads, held together by elastic. I wear the straw sombrero that belonged to Derek, that I took from his place after everything happened.

Derek will know me, even if I look different, even if my hands and feet are rougher than back when we'd drive up one of the canyons, when we'd hike a little way off the road. He had a portable hammock that folded up tight to fit in his pocket, and he'd tie the fancy knots he knew, string it up between trees. We'd lie there, pressed together side by side—shoulder to shoulder, hip to hip—staring up through the branches at the constellations neither of us could name.

We were easy with each other, just being together. Sometimes I even took a little dip, turning my head to spit between the knotted ropes. Derek left sex things up to me, and we never went far. That wasn't the point. He kept his pants on, but he'd take his shirt off, on the warm nights. When he stood up, in the moonlight, I could see the diamond pattern the ropes had pressed into his back.

It was beautiful in the canyons, and we couldn't lie

together like that at my house, because of my parents, and at Derek's apartment the air was bitter, it made my eyes tear up and my nose run. That place—just a mattress on the floor, and the only table covered with Drano and pieces of steel wool, Sudafed tablets, matchbooks. The counters of the kitchenette were covered in camping stoves and hot plates, rubber tubing and glass jars. Derek told me he was a pharmacist. Combustible, he used to say, looking around that room, snapping his fingers just once. He told me Midvale was full of pharmacists. The pills he made, he put them in plastic bags, or bottles with the old prescriptions torn off. He'd make a lot, then give them to me, to hold until he needed them, to sell them to people. There wasn't room at his place to keep them.

Some of those pills, the last batch, are the ones I have now, the ones I'm working my way through. I never told Derek when I started taking them; I knew he wouldn't miss a few, and they helped connect me to him, helped me when sometimes he started talking fast.

What did he talk about? All kinds of things. He told me he'd lived in Reno and Spokane and San Francisco. He said he knew places, there, where they held fights between people and monkeys, that he'd seen it in basements; the gorillas stank, and the orangutans were the dirtiest fighters, and a man with a tranquilizer gun was always ready. This was secret, Derek said, illegal. He said that wrestling worked better than trying to box, but he never fought, he only bet.

The one time we went to Salt Lake City together, we went to the zoo. In the ape building, the gorillas hung back, then raced forward and banged their whole bodies against the thick windows, so close to us. I jumped back five feet, but the glass was made to hold. The gorillas stood close and stared at Derek, their eyes mean and steady. He just laughed.

I know some people think it says something, how animals react to a person, that it tells you something, but those gorillas were tainted by living there, breathing the same air as all you people in Utah, afraid of anyone who is strong and different.

I know something about all this, how animals react. Like I was saying before, I work with tortoises, out in the desert. And as the city expands, the construction workers excavate; they dig up the burrows, and put the tortoises aside. Their shells are as wide across as dinner plates, and they have sharp little beaks and claws, shiny eyes, their slow eyelids like thin fingernails. They get taken to the holding area, and that's where we pick them up.

We try to figure how to relocate them—how much they move in a day, how much space they need. We epoxy radio receiver to their shells, and we file notches on the edges, for identification, and I hold my receiver overhead, arcing it through the air, careful that the signal's not bouncing off a rock and the tortoise is actually behind me. In the morning before the sun comes up, I'm already out here; I pound on the ground, I scratch the sand with a stick, and the tortoise will come out to forage. How do they react to me, and what does that tell you? I don't know; I'm trying to learn from them. Far away, miles away, cars float above the highway as the heat comes on. I work alone, but at the end of the day we signal to each other with special mirrors—they have a hole in the middle to squint through, to aim it, so you can flash right on each other.

There was a time when Derek and I didn't need mirrors, not even a phone, or a pencil and paper, or hardly even a mouth shaping a word. He once told me that if you take these pills long enough, enough of them, they start to slow you down, to have the opposite effect. They make you calm. I'm not there yet—I'm still jagged and quick, ahead of myself.

Out in the desert, I drink the Kool-Aid, swallow the pills. I follow the tortoises, and in one minute—no, ten seconds—I can imagine, even preprogram, their every movement. They can outlive a person; they cannot be perturbed. Did I tell you already how I sometimes find them dead, upside down, or about the coyotes' bite marks on their shells? I think I already said that. The point is that they are stubborn and sure. They have that slow, purposeful walk, those dried folds of skin in their underarms, those pitiful tails. They just drag themselves along for twenty feet, then go under a bush, then set out again, then go underground when the sun gets to be too much. They couldn't even imagine Las Vegas with its lights and its four rush hours a day and every kind of store open 24-7.

Back in Midvale, there's nothing open all night, almost, only the 7-Eleven and the Maverik. The Maverik—that's where the shape of everything started to change.

It was the middle of the afternoon, bright sun outside. Derek and I had walked over to get ice-cream sandwiches, and once we were inside we split up a little, went down different aisles. All the colors of the shelves were straining at me, almost buzzing, and so I looked away; I saw Derek's face looking down, floating above me. There was a television screen, bolted to the ceiling, showing the picture from a security camera, and his face was inside it—he wasn't really watching me, it just looked that way, and he wasn't staring at the camera, either. He was daydreaming, his expression sweet and distant.

And then he looked away, and I kept watching him, when he didn't know I was. He was near the wiper blades, and the insulated mugs; I couldn't tell what it was, but then he took something from the shelf and slipped it down the front of his pants.

When we met at the counter, he paid for the ice-cream sandwiches—maybe that was the trick, paying for something so it wouldn't seem like he was stealing something else, and it must have worked, because when we went outside, walking away, no one followed us.

I wanted to ask Derek what he'd stolen, but I also wanted him to show me without my asking. I was thinking it was a surprise for me, maybe. And somehow, not even talking, we ended up right in the middle of a crowd of people, a place where some kind of accident had happened. I didn't see blood around, or any crashed cars, or tree branches overhead. In the middle of these people, where we ended up, was a blue blanket, resting atop the shape of a body. No one was saying anything.

Without warning, then, Derek kneeled down and pulled back the blanket, uncovering the dead woman's face. Her eyes and mouth were open. She had short, brown hair, and dark freckles across her nose, and tiny silver earrings in her ears. She looked surprised. And then Derek put something—I couldn't tell what, but I knew it was the stolen thing—next to her head, and then the voices started rising, and there were hands on Derek, and on my shoulder. We got loose, shook our way free, and came out on the other side of the people.

Right after that, we were in the mall, standing in front of a window where, inside, a machine with two metal arms was stretching and folding taffy like it could never stop. My body felt uneasy, like cold water was racing all along my skin. I couldn't tell if I was blinking my eyes.

Stay here, Derek said, then headed for the men's room. But once he was gone, I saw someone waving at me, down one of the side hallways between the stores. A woman, holding open one of those doors where only workers go.

I didn't walk all the way, just took a couple steps in that direction, to get a better look at her. She held a yellow plastic shopping bag in one hand. Her dark hair was short, but her earrings were different—long, dangling—and she had lost the freckles across her nose; still, I thought I recognized her. I stepped closer.

I need your help, she said.

Are you alive? I asked her.

I'm in trouble, she said. Oh, it could get lots worse. She was glancing her eyes all around me; she smelled like every perfume at the sample counter. I couldn't be certain. I wanted to believe it was her.

Yes, I said. Derek can help you, again. Even more.

Just you, she said. Come in here. She closed the swinging door and we were alone, whispering in the dim hallway. We began to walk deeper, further from the stores and Derek, past an open door that showed only a bucket and mop. The way she was talking—the things she said, and how she seemed to know me—made me believe.

What is your deal? I was saying. Do you feel like I do?

I knew you were the one, she said. I can't go through a regular exit. Here, boost me.

She handed me the yellow bag—it wasn't heavy, but it was full; I knew it held the blue blanket that had covered her, and the stolen thing that had brought her back—and locked her fingers together, to show me what to do. There was a window above our heads. She took back the bag before I could look inside.

Her shoe was in my hand, then, her knee in my breast, and I heard the plastic bag sliding and scraping through. Her foot pulled away, her leg bending.

Thank you, my friend, she said, and then she was gone. I didn't hear her land on the other side, as if she went up, and not down.

I couldn't reach the window, alone, I couldn't see through it. No one saw me or cared when I came out of that hallway, back into the mall. Derek wasn't by the taffy machine, or the bathroom, or anywhere. I went outside, into the parking lot, around the corner; I could see the wall, and that window, but the woman was gone.

I started walking away from all that. Derek's place was not far; I hardly paid attention, I knew the way so perfectly. When I got there, though, once again, I found myself in the middle of a situation, and I was surrounded by people.

For a moment I thought I'd walked backward, in time and space both, and this crowd was the same people, and I almost looked for her body before remembering that she had risen up, that she had disappeared through the window.

People were saying the house was empty when it happened, and that it wasn't just a fire, but some kind of explosion. All kinds of police cars and fire trucks were arriving, pulling over curbs, onto lawns. Red lights skipped through trees and across the fronts of houses, sliding over peoples' faces. Everyone and everything was rushing at me, it felt like, like I was the lowest possible point anywhere.

In the roof above Derek's apartment, there was a round, blackened hole. I started to call his name, then stopped myself. I made my expression like everyone else's, standing around me, and then I slowly walked away.

Not long after, the bishop from my ward wanted me to go on a mission; that's the answer God has for every troubled girl. Instead, I found this job, working for the government, and this desert seemed far enough away from my troubles to satisfy everyone.

Yes, I am not the girl you see standing here, and this voice is not coming from where you think. I am angling my signal mirror toward you, over the land and the mountains; maybe I arrive at the speed of light, maybe the image and sound are delayed by half a day. When you see a flash, a reflection shining and sliding and scattered along a brick wall, along a sidewalk, along the wall of your house, that is me.

If you lean close to that small shining place, you can see and hear me. Think of me as a kind of angel. I am talking to you from the desert, I am signaling for Derek. I'll feel it when he sees me, and my face will hang above him, like his did in the Maverik, and we'll begin to talk.

Maybe he's already returned. Maybe he's among you, and you've seen him. He could have shaved his sideburns, his arm might be in a sling, but you'll recognize him, just from what I've told you.

These days my thinking is so fast, spooling ahead, waiting for me in the future, with Derek, drawn back to me—that's the time when the last pill is gone and we've become the calmest, calmest people. We'll sway in the hammock, and we'll walk the streets, holding hands. It will spook people, when they see us coming. The only words you'll use to describe us are calm and serene and love.

The Silent Men

The last diners left the restaurant around midnight, and it was usually after one o'clock before Kristine, a waitress, headed home. Some nights she caught a cab, but it was better to walk, to unwind the pressures—the timing, the money changing hands, all the expectations and personalities—so that she would be able to sleep. Tonight, as she walked past the Liberty Bell, down through Old City, she could hear trucks rattling off the Ben Franklin Bridge, crossing the Delaware, and distant sirens, ignored car alarms. The darkness made the hot, thick air feel dirty.

Her apartment was on the fourth floor, and there was no elevator. She took off her shoes before climbing the stairs. When she unlocked the door, there was no one inside to meet her; there were no messages on the machine. She started to fill the bathtub before she turned on the lights, before she sifted through the credit card offers that constituted her mail. She poured herself a glass of wine, wished she'd thought to bum a cigarette from someone before she'd left work, and stood in the living room for a moment, listening to the water splashing in the bathroom. The empty echo of her apartment, the cleanswept and shining hardwood floors, pleased her.

In the bathroom, she unbuttoned and shed her clothes, which smelled of perspiration and food, every meal she'd served that night. The water almost scalded her; she slipped in an inch at a time, finally dunking her head so her black hair eased, smoothing the tightness from her scalp. And then, through the thickness of the water, she heard the faint ringing, the cordless phone left on the counter, next to the sink. Surfacing, she dried her hand on the towel behind her head, stretched out her arm.

"I'm calling about the poster," a voice said.

"The dogs?" Kristine said.

"I got this number from the poster."

A man's voice, she thought, raspy and slow. She had hung the posters, with the help of her friend Seiko, all over town—a xeroxed photo of Uno and Rastus, sitting on the couch with her between them. TWO LOST DOGS, it read, and their names, and her name, her phone number. She had considered adding REWARD, but somehow that felt too desperate.

"Odd, how they both ran off at once," the voice was saying.

"Have you seen them?" Kristine said.

"Would they have run off, together? It's kind of romantic."

"I don't know," she said. "They never really got along that well."

"But the fact that it's more than one missing might lead you to believe that something entirely different has happened, like someone could have taken them."

"Maybe."

"Do you think maybe dogs are always filling in for something, that people own them to fill some lack they feel?"

"What do you know about my dogs?"

"What would a person want with someone else's dogs? It's curious, I agree. They're not show dogs, are they? Could it be for breeding?"

"They're both fixed," Kristine said.

"What?"

"Neutered. They can't breed."

Kristine began to wonder if the voice might belong to a woman. It seemed possible, the pitch modulating from word to word. In the kitchen, her refrigerator shocked itself to life, then made a sound like a dog lapping water. She almost expected the jangle of collars, the clicking of nails.

"Is that a bandage on the big dog's tail?" the voice said. "How did he get that? I'm not saying you're to blame."

"He knocked it on things," Kristine said. "That's all.

Wagging it. You didn't tell me your name, did you?"

"I was merely calling about the poster."

"But not about my dogs."

"Was there anything else wrong with them?" the voice said. "Did they suffer any other maladies?"

"Maladies?" Kristine said. "Rastus had distemper, once."

"Is that physical or behavioral?"

"Both, I guess. He was cured."

"That's good. That's fortunate when something doesn't linger. And, you know, you shouldn't consider it some kind of judgment that they left you."

"Of course I don't. What do you know about my dogs?"

"Only what you've told me, what I've learned from this poster. They're lost. You, though; I do feel I know something about you."

"How's that?"

"Your face in the photograph, of course, how lonely it is."

"My face?"

"Not as if something tragic happened to you," the voice said. "More like nothing much has happened. Is that saying too much? Because I've known loneliness before, I've been lonely myself. I turned that around. I stopped reaching out and started making people reach out for me. And you were lonely even back when you had the dogs, in this picture; I can see it."

All of Kristine's toenails were painted dark red. As she listened, she turned the spigot with her toes, felt the hot water bleeding through the warm, seeping along her body. Her legs were sturdy; not fat, not muscular. Short, but in proportion to her body. Her hips flared out, solid, and her waist belled in. Her breasts were heavy, buoyant now, half beneath the surface of the water. Kristine liked the way she looked, compact yet not petite.

The line had gone quiet, the voice silent.

"Are you still there?" Kristine said.

"I've been thinking a lot about you, actually, and these dogs of yours. That's why I brought the poster home with me. That's why I called. Goodnight."

Kristine dropped the phone onto the bathmat, then eased back under the thick, warm water, her eyes closed. Once, there had been another segment to these nights— she'd walk her dogs, then take her bath, then hope to sleep. Always ready to go outside, the dogs would chew on their leather leashes in anticipation. The two of them were no protection; they'd lift their snouts, wag their tails at rapists, muggers, and killers. Her boys, Kristine called them. Uno was thin and black, rangy, some cross between a Labrador and a hyena; low-slung hips, hair all bristle, his hard tail slapped the legs of tables and chairs, left bruises along her shins. Rastus was part boxer and part pug, with short legs and his smashed-in face, eyes bulging manic, breath wheezing—an ugly, affectionate, flatulent dog. She couldn't imagine he would travel far.

It had been almost a month, now. She had let them loose to run at the dog park, had looked away for a moment, and they had never come back. That simple.

~~

The two men entered the restaurant, taking mincing steps, as if their shoes were too tight. Their cheap, black suits were definitely too small, binding here and there, exposing dark socks and white cuffs where golden cuff links flashed. The two men followed Charles, the maître d', who led them to their table without speaking. They were white men, thin, one older than the other, both with their hair cut close against their scalps. They appeared to be foreign—German, perhaps Austrian—or as if they had been packed away in some other time and had then stepped out of a closet. If one leaned close to them, it seemed likely that they would smell of moth-balls, hair oil. And tonight, like every Friday night, these men did not even have to point at Kristine; it was under-stood that she would be their waitress.

"Gentlemen," she said. "Good evening."

They looked up at her with anticipation, as a kind of greeting, and then turned their attention back to their menus, pointing as they went, making certain that she could see.

Kristine waited as they decided; she studied the men. They did not seem to use sign language, or any complicated hand signals, but they were able to make themselves understood. She had never seen them smile, never even seen their teeth. The older man had flecks of gray in his hair, deeper wrinkles around his sunken eyes. The golden cuff links at his wrists were scratched, tarnished. Both men had slender, hooked noses, thin-lipped mouths. Were they father and son? Lovers? As usual, they chose the most expensive entrées—the filet mignon, the apple bacon–wrapped venison.

"Excellent choices," she said.

At first, the men's weekly visits to the restaurant had aroused anxiety in Kristine, even dread; over time, these feelings had settled into a mixture of irritation and curiosity. Now she stood next to the kitchen door and watched as they simply sat there, gazing calmly across at each other. They did not look around themselves, at the other diners or at the linen napkins folded like origami; they ignored the flaming desserts and the special escargot plates, the curtains that took several men to hang. Kristine had tried speaking French to them—her accent decent after two years of college, six years ago, the classes providing a perfect restaurant vocabulary—but it did not change their response.

She had asked them if they'd taken a vow of silence, once, and they'd gazed serenely at her, as if she were far from the truth or perhaps close to it. There was something sad about the men, something slightly threatening. She could understand, she wanted to tell them.

She herself often grew tired of talking—just going out and making up the words to say to strangers could be exhausting.

She watched Vincent, the sommelier, perform his part of the charade, uncorking and pouring the wine without waiting for one of the men to taste it. They wouldn't taste it; the thick red wine would remain unwavering until the men were gone and the bottle was taken to the kitchen, for the chef's enjoyment. The silent men only ordered the finest vintages.

When their food arrived, the two men wouldn't even lift their silverware. They would sit over the meal for half an hour, sometimes longer, the time it would take for someone to actually eat the meal they had ordered, and then—after selecting something from the five-tiered dessert cart—they'd rise, leaving all the food and their payment, in cash, behind them on the table. They'd tip Kristine fifty, maybe more, which went a long way toward strengthening her patience.

After the two men left, before the busboys swept in, she picked up the plates and carried them back through the kitchen, to where the dishwashers, Seiko and Hervé, worked in their white T-shirts, aprons around their waists.

"Friday night," Seiko said, pulling a tray of glasses from the machine. Steam rolled up the wall, across the ceiling. "Damn! I never eat so well. My good, silent friends."

"Absolutely," Hervé said. He set the plate on the counter, began to saw at the steak.

Columns of stacked white china tilted slightly next to rows of hand-polished wine glasses. Fans blew hot air in and sucked it out, the door open to the dirty cobblestones of the alley. A battered AM radio played soft, almost inaudible salsa; the chef was always after the dishwashers to turn it down, fearing the sound would seep out and dilute the five classical CDs that rotated, playing from hidden speakers in the dining room.

"Those two," Kristine said. "Sometimes it's just frustrating."

"They're getting off on it," Seiko said, his face wide and cheerful. "Some way or other."

"It doesn't seem like it," she said.

He stabbed at the venison, cut a piece loose; he chewed, his right and then his left cheek bulging, a muscle flexing in his temple. Seiko ate no starch; he did not touch the garlic potatoes. Kristine ate them, quickly, since she had other tables, all the timing in her mind— how long each appetizer lasted, when the entrées would be ready.

"Any plans?" Seiko said. "After work tonight?"

"I don't know," she said.

"It's been a while since we did anything outside of work."

"I know," she said. "It's just everything, lately, you know?"

She watched Seiko eat. He was slightly taller than she was, and twice as wide, a bodybuilder. His muscles stretched the fabric of his shirt and his dark hair was cut short, bristly, his bright scalp showing through when he angled his head. His name was a nickname from elementary school, a joke about someone's wristwatch. He was Korean, not Japanese, but that was not a distinction nine-year-olds made. He didn't mind the name, even introduced himself with it; his actual name, he claimed, could only be correctly pronounced by his parents.

"Yes," he said. "Everything, lately. Any word on the dogs?"

Kristine almost mentioned the phone call of the night before, yet hesitated, uncertain how much to disclose. After all, the conversation had not exactly been about the dogs.

"I've been thinking," Seiko said, "of all those dogs who show up years later, after being lost, all skinny and happy and worn-out."

"That's a movie," she said. "Or a story on the radio. That's not my life."

The night picked up, food cut and cooked, eaten and digested, Kristine too occupied to think of the dogs, or of her caller. This morning she'd gotten up after eleven, still hearing the voice in her head as she stood before the mirror, looking at herself. There was no arguing that she was thirty-four, despite the firmness of her chin, her steady brown eyes staring back. She braided her hair, clipped it up. Smiling, she turned to the left, then the right; some people found her crooked, sharp-edged teeth sexy. She might describe herself as cheerful, or resourceful. She would never say she looked lonely.

The hours spun past. She did not pause to talk with Seiko, at the end of the night, did not really consider going with him, as she sometimes had—one time they'd even done it in the walk-in, all that cold air blowing down, the compressor's copper coils trembling above. Seiko had been behind her, her skirt over her head. She'd opened her eyes and seen bulbs of leeks like white fists, long silver mackerel with sharp teeth, spines on their backs.

It wasn't so much the look of Seiko's muscles as it was the fact of them, the strength to pick her up, to bend her all around. He could be gentle, but he knew when not to be. Usually this all happened in the front of his jacked-up pickup, her legs kicking everything, her head against the metal ceiling with a rhythmic, dimpled sound. It surprised her, how many positions they could find in that tight space, how well they did, parked some-where down along the river or in a corner of the WalMart parking lot, three in the morning. One time she'd even fainted; when she came back around, they were driving—Seiko running all the red lights, heading for a hospital. Her head was in his lap, her underwear still on the dashboard. She laughed, sitting up, and he'd almost hit a parked car.

Perhaps he expected her to want something more,

to start meeting in the daytime; perhaps he was waiting for her. If that were the case, he would wait a long time. He had never even seen the inside of her apartment; she wasn't even certain where he lived. He was a dishwasher, after all, with no real ambition—she knew that, but it was difficult, finding the right situation to meet someone, in a place where she could be recognized as the kind of person she actually was.

~~

"You must miss them," the caller said. "Have you checked the pounds?"

"Of course I have."

Two nights had passed since the first call. Kristine was already out of the bath, lying awake in bed, her body loose from the hot water. She had begun to believe she'd sleep.

"Why are you calling me?" she said. "Where are you?"

"My body, you mean? That doesn't matter. We're having a conversation."

"I'm kind of wondering why you're not asleep. It's almost three. I'm in bed."

"Am I keeping you up? I apologize. I was under the impression that you're something of a night owl."

"It's just kind of an intrusion," Kristine said.

"Well, you have to admit that it's a little odd,

hanging your picture and phone number all over town. And sometimes it helps to intrude on someone else's life to really see the edges of your own. That's a notion I've been turning over."

Kristine wasn't sure how to respond, so she remained silent. If this voice were a man's, would these words be threatening, sinister? Perhaps. Would she like to feel this person's arms around her? She considered hanging up the phone, but the voice kept talking.

"Anyway, I'm calling to help, to sympathize. Don't you remember all that I said about loneliness?"

"I do."

"Maybe that's what we're trying to get to, here."

"Are you a woman?" Kristine said.

"What do I sound like, a talking bird?"

"So you are a woman."

"It really is such a strange situation. Do you miss them?"

"You already asked that," Kristine said. "You already said I did. Let's not talk about the dogs. Let's not talk about whether I'm lonely. Why don't we hear some more about you?"

"I like to walk around during the day," the woman said—it was a woman, Kristine decided, without a doubt.

"I think it's underrated," the woman said, "the daylight; it's every bit as mysterious when the sun's out, all sorts of surprises happening. I close my eyes a little and

look through my eyelashes. That helps me see some of
the mysteries, it really cuts down on all the distractions,
closes them out. You understand."

"I'm not so sure I do," Kristine said.

"You will, unless you stay lazy. And you know I've
seen you out there, walking around. I recognize you
from the poster. I'd recognize your dogs, but I certainly
haven't seen them."

"If you believe all that," Kristine said, "about the day
and the daylight and mysteries and everything, why do
you keep calling me in the middle of the night?"

"Because the distinction still means something to
you. Besides that, I'm not trying to be mysterious. I'm
interested in you, your situation."

"Are you just trying to make me feel worse? It's terrible, especially calling so late like this."

"'Terrible' has its positive connotations," the woman
said.

"What?"

"Like the way they call dinosaurs 'terrible lizards.'
Did you ever read T. S. Eliot? 'Terrible' was his favorite
compliment."

"I did not mean it as a compliment," Kristine said.

"I just see your face on the poster and I want to talk
with you," the woman said, "but then I do talk with you
and I don't know if it does any good—so many things
people don't talk about, but even then the words don't
catch. Even myself, sometimes; I hear the words come

out of me and I wish I'd stayed silent, that I never talked at all."

"That you never talked at all?"

"As if I spent my days in silence. Correct."

"That's very interesting," Kristine said.

~~

The silent men kept a very strict schedule. Since they'd first appeared, three years before, it had never varied. They dined on Friday nights, and they came in on Wednesday afternoons to make their reservation. They never called on the phone; they never spoke a word. Their presence added something to the restaurant, a certain mystery that the entire staff shared. Some looked on this odd relationship with a sort of pride, while others preferred to maintain a distance. Based on the men's consistency—and their overtipping—Charles, the maître d', had tried to make it clear, several times, that they could have a standing reservation, that it could be understood that a table would be held every Friday night. But the men did not want this, or they did not understand. They continued to make their reservations in person, pointing at the same date and time in the book. They never left a name. In that space, Charles simply wrote, *The Silent Men.*

"They're not hurting anyone," Seiko said, that Wednesday afternoon. "Why not let them be?"

"I don't want you to do anything," Kristine said. "Just follow them for an hour or so, find out a little more. They won't even know you're there."

It was almost four o'clock; the restaurant was preparing for the evening's dining. Seiko had been peeling potatoes; white starch marked the muscles of his forearms.

"You may have noticed that I'm at work," he said.

"An hour or two," Kristine said. "Hervé can cover things until then, no problem."

Within half an hour, the two men appeared. They seemed to nod in Kristine's direction, then leaned over Charles's wooden podium, where a small light shone on the bound reservation book as if it were piano music. They pointed at the expected time and date, then turned to go.

The two of them passed in the large window, outside, walking in their way—it seemed they should be moving faster, with their arms jerking, their legs going like that, but their progress was decidedly slow. After a moment, Seiko passed; his walk had a muscular roll to it, his shoulders back. No one would suspect that he could have any relation to the two men, that he was following them. They seemed to be from another world.

Tables began to arrive. Dinners were served. Kristine checked the kitchen when she could, the dishwashing room where Hervé was barely keeping up. Seiko did not return in an hour, nor in two. He did not return to the restaurant at all. He had the next day off, and then she had a day off, and the results of his following remained as unknown as his own whereabouts. He had disappeared so quickly; she had looked away, and he had not returned.

~~

For three nights, the phone did not ring, and this disappointed Kristine. She lay in the bath with only her knees and nose above the surface; she opened her eyes and stared through the burn of the water, at the cracks in the ceiling's plaster. The lines looked like rivers, seen from miles above. She bent one leg over the tub's edge and used the shower massage on herself, thinking all kinds of things. She lay there with the phone not ringing until the water went cool around her, and then she surfaced and walked still dripping to bed, the drain gasping behind her.

The phone rang on the fourth night after Seiko's disappearance.

"It doesn't seem fair," Kristine said, answering it, "that you have my number and I don't have yours."

"You do have my number, Kristine. You just don't ever choose to call it."

It was her mother, far away in Colorado. Her mother, always ready to point out that waitressing could begin as a job and become a career. Kristine leaned forward in the tub; the cigarette in her hand sizzled as she jabbed its tip downward and water climbed to darken its paper.

"I'm sorry," she said. "I thought it was someone else."

"Who?" her mother said. "Isn't it extremely late, there?"

"Exactly, Mom. I should get off the phone. I'll call you tomorrow."

"So you are expecting a call."

"No, I'm not. I'm expecting to be asleep, very soon."

"I was just calling, thinking we can chat."

"So we can do that during the day."

"Well, I hope you're in a better mood tomorrow, then."

Kristine hung up, and slipped more deeply into the warm water. When the phone rang a minute later, she picked it up, but did not speak. Holding her breath, she listened.

"I keep thinking about those dogs of yours," the caller said. "I mean, what could those two be doing? How far could they have gone? Do you think it's possible they're in another state by now?"

"Anything's possible," Kristine said.

"You've been on the phone. Who have you been talking to, in the middle of the night?"

"Jealous?" she said.

"Pardon me?"

"Do you know Seiko?"

"You were talking to whom?"

"How about the silent men?" Kristine said, and enjoyed the pause, the silence—was it uneasiness, or honest confusion?—that followed her questions. She reached for the wine glass, balanced on the edge of the tub. The wine was thick, red, cooler in her mouth than the bathwater around her.

"Let's get back to basics," the woman said. "I called you because I saw your lonely face hanging on a telephone pole, looking out at me. Simple as that. Some people things happen to, some make things happen."

"That's like a cliché," Kristine said. "You could put it on a poster with a rainbow or some courageous animal."

"You certainly could," the woman said. "Some make them, some buy them. That's what I'm saying."

"Have you ever had a dog?" Kristine said. "Any pet at all?"

"I see people every day, out with their dogs, carrying the plastic bags and all that, talking on their cellular phones, impatient, just waiting for the dog to do its business. It's not exactly an ennobling relationship, is it? We're talking about animals who once were hunters, after all—it's just that people project emotions onto dogs, and their brains are so small."

As Kristine listened, she fantasized about someday meeting this woman, out on the street, of this voice in her ear and the arms closing around her from behind.

"It's not like your dogs planned it, or it was anything malicious. Not necessarily. They just wandered off, most likely, and couldn't find their way back."

~~

The silent men came in as usual on Friday evening. Nothing strayed in their behavior, or suggested that they knew anything about Seiko, that they were aware of having been followed. Kristine felt she had betrayed them, somehow, by trying to find out about their lives beyond the restaurant—yet the men themselves would have to admit, if they were willing to talk, that the way they acted might give rise to curiosity.

She cheerfully served them; she accepted their tip; she gave their dinners to Hervé and Tom, the new dish-washer. The night was busy, all the timing in her head, all the choreography with trays and hot dishes, the spin-ning between tables and down narrow corridors.

Later, after work, she had walked less than a block when a man's voice called out from a dark alleyway.

"Kristine, wait."

She heard the footsteps, approaching on the cobble-stones, but she did not slow. Her job meant she gave out her name fifty times a night. Anyone could know it.

"Wait. Hold on. It's me."

Only then did she recognize the voice as Seiko's. He stepped out, under the streetlamp, wearing dark slacks and black cowboy boots, a clingy black T-shirt that showed off his muscles. He smiled at her.

"Where have you been?" she said. "When are you coming back?"

"I'm not coming back." Seiko shrugged; he seemed relaxed, yet full of energy. Confident.

"Did they fire you?"

"No," he said. "I quit."

A cab passed, its driver slowing in case they were interested.

"It's not the job, so much," Seiko said, "but the way I've been going about things, you know?"

"So what have you been doing?" she said.

"Chasing some options down—there's so much more out there than I ever thought."

"Like what?"

"It was you who started it," he said, "who sent me after those guys."

"And you never came back."

"Well, I've come back now."

"But you haven't been following them this whole time."

"Oh, no," Seiko said, laughing, his hands up, palms facing her. "No, no. I was only with them that one night."

"You were with them?"

"Hold on," he said. "If you stop interrupting, I'll try to tell it right. Let's find somewhere to sit down or something."

At an all-night diner, she ordered a piece of cherry pie, and Seiko had a ginger ale. They sat at a table in a dim corner.

"Waitresses are always nicer to waitresses," he said, after they'd ordered.

"Maybe so," Kristine said. She looked across at him, waiting for the story. It was obvious that he sensed her anticipation. He seemed more formal, somehow, more composed than she remembered. She wondered if he was on something, but she had heard him denounce steroids and all other poisons so many times—she had never even seen him drink a beer—that she knew this could not be the case. Now he glanced around the diner, then closed his eyes for a moment, as if allowing the story to return to him. Finally, laying his hands flat on the table, he opened his eyes and began to tell it.

"It was easy to follow them. I got into it, actually—I mean, everyone at the restaurant wondered about those two, and I was going to find out their secrets. They didn't walk fast, but they got on this bus I didn't expect and I barely caught it. They sat together, legs crossed, barely moving, staring straight ahead. I sat two seats behind them and I thought they'd say something to each other, maybe, since they were away from the restaurant, but they didn't.

"They got off the bus down by Rittenhouse Square, in a rich neighborhood, started walking down this street of redbrick rowhouses. Locust? Anyway, I was behind them, and they didn't look back, not even to the side. And then one of them reached out and lifted a brick from the wall—it was a fake brick, a tiny door made to look like a brick, and inside there was a key pad, the numbers lit up. The younger guy punched in a combination and this dark wood garage door jerked open, next to them, rising without barely a sound. I saw a Cadillac in there, and a Mercedes, shining. The men walked between those cars, then the door came down and I was left outside."

"You couldn't have followed?" Kristine said. She had already eaten half her pie, then forgotten it, listening.

"I almost went around back, to see if there was a way in off an alley, but then I also wanted to watch the front door of the house they went into. The front door was made of that same kind of wood, at the top of these curving stone steps. Up above the door were these black metal letters spelling V-E-N-E-Z V-O-I-R."

"Venez voir," she said. "'Come and see.'"

"I know that," Seiko said. "You think I've just worked in a French restaurant all these years?"

"Go on."

"The windows were too high to see through," he said, "and curtains were hanging there, anyway. I walked back and forth, a few houses up, a few houses down; above, on roof decks, green plants were hanging over. Across the street, in a high window, I saw a child's face, watching me, but that was it.

"And then the front door swung open. One of those guys, then the other came out. They waved to me, then started pointing toward the open doorway. 'You want me to come inside?' I said, but I already knew I was going, I was climbing the steps. They just leaned so I could get past, then closed the door, and it was like the street outside was miles and miles away. Man. It was like a catalogue for rich people in there, or a magazine. Velvet and leather everything. I didn't know what to do; I barely dared to step on the carpets. I was really nervous.

"'You guys probably think I was following you,' I said, but they didn't even seem like they heard me."

"What were they doing?"

"They were pointing at me, pointing at a table and chairs, like they were really relaxed and they expected me or something. And they had these rubber sandals on—and they still wore their white shirts, and ties—and the sandals made this slapping sound when they walked. That was all. There was a cart with crystal pitchers of liquor, and the young guy pointed at that, and I shook my head. It was weird—already I wasn't speaking, just like them. I felt kind of sleepy, sitting there at this table on this fancy chair, and the two of them each pulled a chair aside and one sat on a three-legged stool, one on a milk crate. All the furniture was fancy, though; the tabletop was so shiny I could see my face in it, stretching away from me, flat, staring at the ceiling, and those guys were reflected there, too, so our heads almost touched, in the center of the table. And then the younger guy got out the Monopoly board and started passing out the money to me and the older guy—"

"Monopoly money?" Kristine said.

"Yes," Seiko said. "And we just started playing. I mean, damn. The whole situation didn't seem normal, but it didn't seem dangerous, either. I thought if I acted like it was normal for me they might smile or let me in on their whole deal. It wasn't like asking questions was going to get me anywhere."

"Right," she said. "So you played Monopoly."

"The younger guy was the bank. He did all the math by tapping his fingers on the tabletop—some kind of method they used to advertise on TV?"

"Chisenbop," she said, not wanting to interrupt, to slow Seiko's story. She leaned across the table, closer. Something about the way he was talking—both how he told it, and how he'd acted—attracted her.

"They're good players," he said, "but they never really seemed to be having fun about it. They were serious, paying attention, just not competitive. It's hard to explain. After about an hour, I had the railroads—that was about it. A couple utilities. The only sounds were the dice, and those tapping fingers, and our game pieces, and the whistling in the older guy's nose, him breathing."

"Do you think someone else could have been in the house?"

"No," he said. "I mean, there could have been, but if there was I didn't see them—I never really left that front room."

"Right," she said.

"So after a while they offered me a drink again and I had a cup of green tea. First I tasted the hot water, and I checked the foil wrapper of the tea bag, to be safe. Those two both had a glass of water on a cork coaster in front of them, but neither one took a drink. Instead, after a couple more moves, they started pointing at me, then pretending to unbutton their shirts, then at the rent I owed, back and forth like that."

"Like what?" Kristine said. "Strip Monopoly?"

"I don't know. I just wanted to go along with them, to call their bluff, you know? So I pulled my shirt over my head and hung it on the back of my chair."

"And then what did they do?"

"Nothing. They just looked at me, and then we kept playing."

Seiko paused, smiling in disbelief, remembering. He drummed his fingernails against his teeth. Kristine imagined him there with his shirt off, all those muscles he worked for. Under the table, his calf rested alongside hers; she could not recall when they'd begun to touch. She did not pull away.

"Did you like it?" she said. "And then what did you take off?"

"That's the thing," he said. "They didn't ask any more

than that. It felt all right, I guess. I was just trying to act like it was all normal, but then I just kept losing properties, and before long I was bankrupt. The older guy just picked up my piece, that little wheelbarrow, and set it back into the box. They didn't gloat or anything like that.

"I stood up, like I was going to leave, and they both looked at me with no expression at all and I could tell I had to stay, so I sat back down until the game was finished. The younger guy had all the red, green, and blue monopolies, so it was only a matter of time. I put my shirt back on, and they didn't seem to mind. I didn't mind watching, actually. I liked it, I guess. The whole situation was so ridiculous, it was kind of exciting and unreal to be in the middle of it. I had to keep reminding myself that I was actually there.

"And then I wasn't there. I mean, it was fast. The older guy went bankrupt—and there wasn't any celebration or complaining or anything, and then they carefully put the pieces back and fit the top on the box. We all stood up and walked to the front door, none of us saying a word. I stepped outside. It must have been close to midnight. I looked back, from the bottom of the steps, but the door was closed and those two guys were gone, inside."

"What if they had made you do something?" Kristine said. "What if they'd had a gun?"

"Those two?" He laughed. "They'd never have a gun."

Kristine leaned back, tapping her plate with her fork. She found the story hard to believe, though it was even more difficult to fathom why or how Seiko would make it up.

"They don't have your dogs," he said. "If that's what you were thinking."

"What?"

"Two men, two dogs," he said. "I know it makes a kind of sense, but I think you have to let that go."

"I didn't think that," she said. "Not exactly. Listen, though, I'm glad you came and told me. It's good to see you."

"Well," he said, "it was kind of a strange evening, there."

"Have you seen them again? Have you gone back?"

"No," Seiko said. "I don't know why I would."

"It's late," she said, setting down the money for the bill, a generous tip. "What next?"

"Oh, man," Seiko said, checking his watch. "I got all caught up, talking. I'm late, I'm really late." He scribbled something on the paper placemat, tore off the corner, and handed it to her. Standing and leaning in, he kissed her cheek, then turned and walked away.

He moved quickly, his boots clocking along the checkered linoleum. Kristine, feeling surprisingly disappointed, watched him go. She opened her hand and unfolded the paper, revealing a telephone number.

~~

In the days following her talk with Seiko, Kristine called the number, wanting to speak with him, to see him again; there was never any answer. It rang and rang. If he wanted to reach her, she knew, he could find her at the restaurant.

Her attention slightly shifted, her routines slipped. Some nights after work she did not even go directly home. Instead, she walked; she did not stay on the busy streets, nor under the lights; she wandered alleyways and dark corners, using the city like a maze, turning left, turning right, every decision as random as the last and yet she did not slow or waver, did not even seem to choose.

Sometimes she did not return home until near dawn. It was one of those mornings that she opened her door and the phone began to ring.

"You've been out," the woman said. "Where have you been?"

"Very well," Kristine said. "And how about you?"

"Did you ever see a lamprey?" the woman said, unflustered.

"Those things on sharks?"

"They're like big leeches with sucker mouths ringed with teeth. That's the kind of parasite a dog is—it's been their whole evolution, learning how to manipulate us."

"I imagine you have a fascinating life," Kristine said. "All this mystery, and probably luxury and sex, all sorts of forbidden things. That's how I think of you. It amazes me that you ever find time to call."

"You're growing stronger," the woman said. "You'll see mysteries in the daylight, if you keep this up."

~~

Tonight Kristine came across one of her own LOST DOGS posters—stapled to a telephone pole, stiffened and corrugated by rain—and she tore it down, shredded it. Hanging her name and photo all over the city had been a mistake. She didn't need any more callers, wasn't even certain she needed the one caller she did have. Yet she knew that the prospect of more callers was not the only reason; she also tore down the poster as an answer to the question that the woman's late-night voice had asked again and again—Did she miss her dogs?

If she missed them more, now, perhaps they would never have run away. Kristine knew that, and she realized that she did not want her dogs to be found. As she walked, she imagined them at the end of long leashes, Rastus and Uno standing heavy on the bottom of the ocean, their eight legs down, fish swimming between them. Her boys. They look up, their sad eyes through the water, and she cuts the leashes, the anchor lines. She moves with the current, tearing on a riptide, walking the city.

The words catch in the corner of her eye; she almost walks past them; she could not have passed them. VENEZ VOIR, the black letters pounded into the white stone above the doorway. The street is empty, all the windows flat black rectangles against the night. Without hesitating, Kristine climbs the stone steps. The doorknob turns in her hand without a sound. She waits for a word, an alarm, a face in the opened gap. There's nothing. She steps inside, into the hot air, the thick scents of leather and furniture polish.

The wall against her hand is soft, a hanging Persian rug. A pale streetlamp shines through the window; she stands for a moment, her eyes adjusting. There's no sound except the ticking of the grandfather clock—its round glass face glints in the darkness—and a low wind that is not, she realizes, a wind at all. It's breathing.

The two men sleep on the floor, on wooden pallets. Their bodies rise and fall; they breathe in synchrony, hands folded flat under their cheeks, legs drawn up so the four points of their elbows and knees jut out, the pale tips of their penises flopping there. Without their clothes, they don't look so similar. The younger man is almost entirely hairless, his skin pink even in the dim light. A straight line marks his side, where he'd rested on the edge of the pallet. Folds of flesh hang along his waist, as if he'd once, not so long ago, carried much more weight, as if his skin does not have the elasticity to hold his new shape.

There is a gap of a few inches between the pallets. The older man is even thinner than the other. Skeletal, and his bones covered with whorls of hair. Kristine crouches behind a sofa, less than three feet from the men. The sofa is leather and stainless steel, and there are two matching armchairs on the other side of the men.

The grandfather clock sounds the half hour; the men stir and settle. They look so peaceful. Like children. Even the chance of waking them does not seem frightening. Had they ever appeared threatening, or merely odd? Was there a difference? She leans closer, barely holding back from reaching out and touching them. And then—slowly, silently—she stands. Stepping out of her shoes, she heads past the men, deeper into the house; turning around and leaving does not even occur to her. She climbs heavily carpeted stairs, under a chandelier that drips with shadowy glass tears.

Upstairs, it is even warmer, the air close. She enters a study, past shelves of leather-bound books, floor lamps with slender, bending necks, and passes through another doorway, into a bedroom, which is empty, and covered in silk—she can tell simply by touch, the slippery smoothness against her fingers. The bed is a canopied four-poster; she walks around it, her reflection a dark ghost in the mirror over the dresser, and then she passes back into the hallway.

"Uno," she whispers. "Rastus." It's a joke, a little joke for herself, and on the dogs, wherever they are—far away, underwater or running across a wide field.

At the sound of her voice she suddenly worries that perhaps she is not alone here, considers the possibility that the house might hold more than the two sleeping, silent men. Quietly, she continues. In the second bedroom, she turns on a small light. She has to risk it. The art on the walls, the paintings look real; nudes, mostly, heavy men and women, flesh stretched out. They seem familiar, as if she'd studied the artist in college, but she can not quite remember. On a low table, photographs reflect the light, and at first glance she believes they are of Seiko—skin, and muscles, men's bodies oiled and flexing—but they are not Seiko. It is a magazine, lying open; some of the men kneel on mattresses, bent at their waists and looking over their shoulders, while others grimace, gripping their long, curved cocks like scimitars. Kristine closes the magazine. She stacks it atop the copies of *House Beautiful*.

Designer suits hang in the walk-in closet, fifteen or twenty of them, the tags still attached. White shirts, ties, shining, unworn shoes. No one has ever worn any of this. No one has ever slept in these rooms. The bed here is low, king-sized, its frame a wooden sleigh; she runs her hand along its smooth, polished curves. She could so easily climb into one of these beds, strip down and slip between the silk sheets, wake up tomorrow and ask the men for breakfast.

As she leaves the room, another face startles her, another person that is only herself, her reflection in another mirror. Strands of hair have escaped her bun and hang loose, like a spider's legs around her head. Her skin shines with sweat, her eyes manic and hungry, all wound up.

She descends a different, back stairway, into the kitchen. There are smooth ceramic tiles beneath her feet; heavy pans hang from the ceiling; long knives shine, sharp against the darkness, in a rack along the wall. Every countertop and appliance is stainless steel, still holding some of the previous day's dull light. Inside the refrigerator there are wheels of brie, and pâté, every rich thing—all untouched, just as she'd expected.

Kristine can see, through an arched doorway, the heavy table where the Monopoly game must have been played, the chair where Seiko had sat. His phone number is on her dresser, back at her apartment, under a charm bracelet. Beyond the table, she can see into the front room, the shapes of the men, still sleeping. It occurs to her that perhaps it is not Seiko's phone number at all, there in her bedroom. He had never said it was his. The number could belong to the silent men, though she sees no phone here; they'd be unable to answer one if there were. With a shiver, then, she realizes that the number belongs to the night caller, the woman—Kristine has been calling at the wrong hours, during the day, to get through, to make the connection.

She turns and opens a white door next to the refrigerator. Cold air rushes up a dim, wooden staircase; the wind smells like dirt. She descends, stepping with one foot, then joining it with the other, pausing on each step.

Her hands, out in front of her, tear cobwebs. At the bottom of the stairs, she stands in the darkness, the open doorway a pale rectangle above her. The floor beneath her feet is damp, gritty. A string swings along the skin of her face; she pulls it, and a bare lightbulb snaps on.

She is startled by two headless, human shapes, and steps back, her hands up, stumbling on the stairs. It's only the suits, hanging empty, awaiting the men.

Kristine pulls more light cords. Bulbs in metal cages illuminate the basement's far corners, the mousetraps along the walls. She is careful where she steps. There are shelves, stacked with cans and bottles of cleaning solutions. A toilet with no seat or lid stands in the corner, not walled in at all, a sink nearby. A three-legged stool sits beside a plastic milk crate. Here, people have lived. The men live here. They do not sleep here, though; they need to be surrounded by temptation even while they sleep.

She holds herself still, holds her breath. She can't tell if she'd heard something or if she'd made the sound herself. She realizes that when she had just seen the men, sleeping on the other side of the table, they seemed to have switched places. Had they? The sound above is the easing shut of the door atop the stairs, the click of a lock. No one will hear her if she calls, she knows this. No sound can escape this house.

She looks around herself, her black shadow bent at the neck, her body on the floor and her head on the wall. A dented saucepan hangs from a nail, there, a bent ladle next to it. A hot plate, a galvanized tub. Still, no sign of food, not even a loaf of bread, a can of soup. Through a doorway, she can see into the garage, the dark gleam of cars' hoods.

The garage door does not open; there is a numbered key pad, glowing, its digits a riddle she can't solve. Yet here, hanging from a pegboard, is a skeleton key, almost hidden.

Quietly, Kristine climbs the stairs, eases the key into the keyhole. It does not fit. But when she tries the knob it turns, and she feels that her thinking has unlocked it. When the door swings open, no one is there.

Kristine walks through the kitchen, down a hallway, past where the silent men still sleep, or pretend to sleep. Opening the door, she steps into her shoes and looks out onto the street. The wider she stretches her eyes, the more the shadows ease and dissolve, the more quickly light rises from the sky and street, the more the air shivers and opens. She feels wonderful, terrible. Once more, she looks over the pale bodies of the silent men, breathing together, and then she steps outside and gently closes the door.

~~

It is three o'clock in the morning when Kristine returns to her apartment. She finds the scrap of paper atop her dresser, then the phone, and dials.

"Hello?" a man's voice says.

"Who is this?"

"Kristine? It's Seiko."

"Seiko?"

"I hoped you'd call."

"Some things happened."

"What?" he says. "The dogs?"

"I went there. The house."

"Where?"

"The silent men," she says.

"What did they do to you?"

"Nothing. They were sleeping."

"What are you talking about?" he says. "It's late. I've missed you."

"I want to see you," Kristine says. "Can you come here?"

"Yes," he says. "Yes, I can."

"Hurry," she says, and then she tells him how.

Halo Effect

Randall stands in his small kitchen, next to the sink. He watches his quiet street through the window. In three hours, Celia is coming to take a bath with him. They'll face each other across his old tub, her feet under his armpits, her long toes tickling him.

In the late afternoons, on odd-numbered days, they bathe as the sun comes through the bathroom window and lights the wall. His bony knees break the surface, and Celia's gray hair is piled up on her head, the loose strands wet and darker, floating around her shoulders. The white bar of soap slips between them, sometimes thick, other days worn to a sliver. It is relaxing—they listen to Randall's portable phonograph, set on the floor, the vinyl albums out of their jackets and within reach. Show tunes, mostly, happy voices singing of farms and highways and love possibilities. The black records spin, the diamond tooth of the needle spirals toward the center, and Celia holds her makeshift rock tumbler—an empty peanut butter jar full of fine gravel and coins, some dish soap and water—she rolls and shakes it to the rhythm, polishing up whatever she's found.

When the bath grows cool, they stand and towel each other off, drying the water from their wrinkles. They laugh and boast of how their bodies used to be, of their once-great appetites and capabilities. He used to have so much hair on his legs. Where did it go? Celia often doesn't wear underpants; her trousers are silky, tight at the ankles and loose everywhere else. She calls herself an old hippie.

Randall is eighty-two. Long ago he retired from working insurance; he says he traded reading actuarial tables for being a statistic within them. Celia's sixty-seven. She helps him get dressed, after their baths, tucks him in, buttons him down. He has arthritis, but her fingers are quick, decisive. She has no problems with her joints, her eyesight is sharp, and she smells like vanilla. Celia is a hunter, has been for some time. She's the one who drew Randall in, even if that pull already existed. She is taller than he is, inches. She can follow a deep signal, is always seeking an unexpected cache.

Waiting at the window this afternoon, Randall hears the rattle of a bicycle, sees a raggedy man with a trophy tied to the rack above the back wheel. The trophy is two feet tall, a golden figure on top, a champion. Later,

Randall will tell Celia about this, what a wonderful gesture and declaration, a perfect way to feel, to coast along.

Next, two young mothers pushing strollers; one smokes while the other, an Oriental woman, happily complains into a telephone. She hasn't slept, her nipples hurt, the sky is too bright, the world too unpredictable. Randall spends a lot of time at his window. He looks down, he closes his eyes and listens, tries to guess at what's coming. The slap of joggers' feet, the drunken music of the ice-cream man, he anticipates the rattle of bicycles, children riding with no hands, the jangle of a shopping cart full of cans and bottles.

Now it's a sound he hasn't heard before, like a huge scratching rake sweeping closer. It's a girl dragging a tree branch down the middle of the street, an angry expression on her face, her hair dyed orange and black. She doesn't care about physics; she's a vegetarian; she's tired of her parents being flexible and understanding. She's tired of her job at the amusement park. She's tired of all these trees surrounding her.

Randall watches her turn the corner, her shoulders angry. He pats the top of his head with the tips of his fingers and it's like the sound of clapping hands. He imagines a crowd of bald men, in a concert hall, applauding a performance in this fashion. The rings hurt, however—he has a gold wedding band on every finger. Ten, counting his thumbs. Some, Celia gave to him, some he found for himself. He has a more difficult time taking the rings off than putting them on. And he's hardly dressed to go anywhere—he wears his brown Sansabelt trousers, a white V-neck T-shirt. Turning, he steps into his bedroom. He puts on a white dress shirt, fights the buttons; his tie, already knotted for him, hangs from the doorknob. His shoes are good ones, white leather and Velcro. Orthotic.

Out the side door there's a narrow concrete walkway. Randall's metal detector rests here, his Bounty Hunter Tracker IV; he leaves it out in the rain like this, drags it around on the concrete because he wants it to look old, weathered, more like Bruce's. He picks up the unit, turns it over, touches the search coil, checks to be certain that the batteries aren't connected, getting drained. On the days after he hunts, his wrists and shoulders are sore. Today is not one of the days; he sets the Bounty Hunter down again and leaves it behind him.

Cobwebs stretch like smoke in the green bushes surrounding his house. He stares down the street, the direction he's headed. He does not shuffle. He imagines his neighbors watching him pass, recognizing him, wondering about his thoughts and plans. The girl in the window of the drive-through coffee shack—short blond curls, she looks like a Sally, a Bernice—waves as he passes. Randall has seen Bruce there, some mornings, with his dog and shopping cart, buying the expensive coffee. They pretend not to recognize each other.

Out on the schoolyard, the grass is pitted with dig-holes, like it's been hunted and probed and turned over. Have they ever hunted here, so close to his house? He cannot recall it. The last time, four days ago, was at a cemetery on the edge of the city. Early in the morning, before any mourners or funerals, and Rhoda and Leslie were joking about picking up signals through coffins, the jewelry of the dead. The units can only reach eight to twelve inches, though—Glenn loves to talk about that, claim deeper penetration. There's those three, and Bruce, and then Randall and Celia, plus lately the three Mexican guys who might be brothers, *hermanos*, friendly though they don't speak English. People drift in and out; long absences aren't mentioned. Hunters are drawn together, gather through curiosity and quiet accretion. Randall's seen other groups, in distant parts of the city, people he doesn't know, who probably don't even know each other. There's nothing to do but accept it, to nod and make small talk, to gather afterward, perhaps, to show and trade what has been found.

There's not a lot of talking; it's all business. People can hunt for months and disappear and Randall never learns their names. No one asks or offers. The names he uses are ones he's made up, to help him remember, to use in conversation with Celia. Only Glenn is actually Glenn's name—it's hard not to miss it, as he struts around with his hipmount and his kneepads, his apron full of pockets and his probes, his digging tools hanging off him. He talks so much, naming himself: *Sometimes people say to me, 'Glenn, you're obsessed, you son-of-a-gun, talking about your LCD and your discrimination, out coin-shooting after every concert or ball game and probably finding only beaver tails. Glenn! You and your* Lost Treasure *subscription! I tell them you got to dig trash, you know, even if you suspect it, because maybe you're wrong, you got to trust the machine only so far, and anyway you got to clean up the area if you're going to ever return and hunt it. I'm working my threshold tone, homing on my target. Don't crowd me, now!*

That's how it was, in the cemetery, and Bruce out on the perimeter, with his shirt off and all his muscles and long hair and beard, swinging his detector slowly back and forth. His dog is huge, like a wolf, and it had gotten hold of a dangling, broken tree branch and was yanking at it with its teeth, its front legs off the ground. Bruce could be twenty-five, he could be forty; he has about as much luck as Glenn—not much. Rhoda and Leslie are the successful ones; that day at the cemetery they came away with a silver brooch and a cigarette case with a broken hinge. They wear painter pants and drive a pickup truck. They love to hunt cemeteries, shouting and laughing. Celia says they're lesbians, and she and Randall try to emulate them, one working a counterclockwise spiral, the other clockwise, never so close as to cause signal interference but many times they'll even gently collide, so intent they are on the hunt, staring down, eyes raking the ground. They seek the same targets; they're drawn together. He calls her his girlfriend and she calls him her man.

Randall looks up as the bus approaches, lurching into the stop. The doors slap open; the front of the bus kneels down with a whoosh, so it's easier for him to step inside.

"Hey Randall," the driver says. "Surprise, surprise."

His rings sound on the metal headrests of the seats as he walks down the aisle. He sits in the back so he can observe all the people inside as well as those outside, the scenery passing. There are poems posted up near the ceiling, but he does not read the words. He prefers the windows, all the people moving with their hopes and expectations, searching.

Sports bar, bookstore, antique shop. The bus stops at the light, waits. Outside the veterinarian's office, a dented white truck is parked, yellow paint scraped along its side. Blue used to be his favorite color; now it's yellow, and he's always looking, always happy to see yellow. It rises up in him, filling his chest.

Three people stand next to the dented white truck—the vet in a lab coat and a young couple, talking with their hands in the air. As the bus pulls around, Randall can see that the truck's tailgate is open, and he can see that a dog is lying there, a big dog with only its four straight white legs visible. He leans forward, close to the window, but the white truck is gone, lost around a corner.

Randall slides his orthotic shoes along the floor of the bus. Four people are riding with him, none sitting together, all alone. He straightens one aching leg to get his bus pass back in his front pocket and touches the pocket knife he found at the cemetery. Bone and sterling silver, its blade is snapped off so he can hold the broken end against his side, pretend he's been stabbed. He searched and searched for the lost piece of the knife, the tip, that metal triangle gone deeper or in a pocket, on a bookshelf, a keepsake, or even lost in someone's body.

When he finds something, he considers it a reparation. Not that he'd ever try to locate the owner, attempt a physical return. It's more tenuous and disconnected than that. Some things are meant to be lost, after all, by some people. And finding takes patience, all the circling and wandering, the sifting, the sideways attention. He likes to imagine the people, the times, the losses and futile searching, the gradual giving up. He tries to travel back and understand what happened; usually it takes both of them—him and Celia—to piece together a story.

Ball games, couples arguing in cars, a boy with a broken umbrella. Two weeks back he saw a fire, while riding the bus, and it had not surprised him that within days they'd converged to hunt there. His shoes and cuffs were lost to ash, gray, as he kicked aside all the charred pink fiberglass, as he dug out the forgotten piggy bank full of pennies. That day, Bruce found a skeleton key. He'd tied his dog to the shopping cart, so he wouldn't get dirty. Randall likes to pet the dog, to pound him on the rib cage and tell him he's good; Cyclops, he calls him in his mind, though the dog has two eyes and Bruce has never mentioned his real name. Cyclops pulled the cart back and forth on the sidewalk in front of the burned-down house, and Celia joked about sled dogs. Bruce didn't laugh, he only scratched at his bare chest. He'd look a little like Jesus, if Jesus pushed a shopping cart full of empty cans and bottles and was so muscular and went everywhere with a shaggy malamute at the end of a thick, frayed rope.

A boy with a shaved head climbs on the bus, saunters down the aisle, and sits directly in front of Randall. Wires stretch out of his ears, which are buzzing and make Randall think of the music they'll listen to later, in the bath, and also how sometimes late at night, lying awake, he'll hear a sprinkler's ratcheting circle, the water ringing once on a metal pole with each revolution, and then atop this rhythm a car alarm or the random clinking, the melody of some late-night person collecting bottles put out on the curb to recycle.

That day at the burned-down house, Glenn circled with his headphones stretched to his Bounty Hunter, talking the whole time. He had brought a sheet of Plexiglas, to hold down tall grass and make hunting easier—a technique from *Lost Treasure*—so he was disappointed there was no grass around. *Even a glimpse away at some children watching you, a car passing,* he was saying, *and you'll miss that tone, miss your target. What's that? Zinc, silver, or clad? Beaver tail? Man, those pull tabs give the same signal as gold rings, so how are you going to set your discrimination?* Celia told him that talking was another way to miss a signal, but he didn't hear her. He has read all the books, knows the verbiage or makes it up. *Halo effect,* he says, *you know, certain metals will oxidize and leach out through the soil, so there's a metallic halo around the object, underground.*

Having a name for something doesn't change it or make it easier to understand—whenever Glenn lectures, Randall's mind goes in a different direction, spinning definitions. The halo effect is a hot lasso that can hold a person to you, it is a term involving weather and stars, it is a pull and a push, gold and silver and stainless steel, it's made of bone. Halo effect is invisible. It causes men and women to love you. It's an electrical impulse in cities, combing neighborhoods, binding them together.

Celia is taller than Randall is, her fingers buttoning and unbuttoning. She hunts, she is haloed. Her tricks: she checks where the storm drains empty, along the river, where everything lost in the streets comes out; she follows the routes of moles who have torn up the ground; she can puzzle together where a house once stood, all the outbuildings, and can guess where the mailbox was, where so many things were dropped. She'll trade away anything, with no regard for its worth or rarity, kind of like Bruce. Randall sometimes wonders if Bruce even has batteries in his weathered, beaten-up detectors; he'll find targets—wooden beads, a plastic box, the jawbone of a deer—that aren't even metal, then smile and shrug, abashed and proud, looking around happily at everyone.

Targets need to be found, as much or even more than the hunters need to find them. Treasures call out, unseen and hidden, underground, the same way people are buried in their bodies and can be unearthed by others. Buses roll in straight lines, even while they circle and wander. Some searches are vertical, others horizontal. Randall first saw Celia from the bus; she was crisscrossing a schoolyard, holding something he mistook for a mop. He simply pulled the cord, disembarked, walked back to get a closer look.

Randall opens his eyes. He likes to do this, to awaken in disequilibrium, to close them for half an hour at a time and to then guess and see which side of the river he's on, which neighborhood, and who is now riding, replacing those who were. A man in a suit sits next to him, though the bus is almost empty. The man smells of cologne; his leg presses against Randall's for a moment, and then he stands and disembarks and slides smoothly away.

All the way down the aisle, through the wide windshield, Randall can see a police car's flashing lights, and a tow truck. A yellow car is on the sidewalk, crashed into a tree. He stands, unsteady, and pulls the cord.

On the sidewalk, outside again, he walks back toward the flashing lights, the accident. Traffic slows as it passes. Horns honk impatiently. People stand in the windows of the apartment building, watching, telling each other what happened. Their mouths move; he can't hear them.

"Careful, sir," a policeman says. "Move along. Careful, there."

One policeman is writing in a notebook; another measures everything with a tape, takes photographs. Shattered glass crunches under Randall's feet as he walks close to the yellow car, looking in as he passes. A broken cassette player rests in the back seat, black tape strewn and tangled everywhere, the upholstery all torn with foam showing through. Someone is talking about the jaws of life. A ripped map rests on the front seat, orange Cheetos everywhere. Empty soda cans spill out from under the front of the car, which is lifted up as if it rests atop something that looks like a metal cage, shiny bars crisscrossing each other. All the tree's bark, down low, has been skinned off, revealing the white, splintery trunk. The tow truck driver pulls on his hook, a steel cable unwinding from a huge spool with a rasping sound.

Randall keeps moving, just as they asked. The day is turning hot; the air smells like rain. After a soaking rain, the signals are clearer, the machine can go deeper. He wanders through a neighborhood. Dogs bark through chain-link fences. Cats watch from under parked cars. The heads of three children, three girls rise above the top of a tall fence, their faces smiling and weightless; they are attempting to fly, eager to see him, their long dark hair wild around their heads. The sun is hot, every-where, unseen. As he turns the corner, Randall sees the round black trampoline, the girls' bare feet.

He is short of breath, his feet sweaty. He's walked farther than he expected, and should ask what time it is, if he sees someone wearing a watch. Now he sees the old amusement park, rides that can jumble your bones and your organs—and the crematorium on the hill, where he may live, someday, sand in a vase sifting upon him-self, day after day. From this rise he can see the black river, sliding under the bridges, and the green grass of the city park along the water. He'll sit at one of the picnic tables close to the river and rest.

A kayak, a sailboat, two fishermen on the shore. Before he reaches the river, Randall turns right on a side path. He doesn't think about it. The dirt beneath his feet is packed hard. Wild blackberries, not yet ripe, thick vines covered in sharp, snaring thorns. He holds each vine between thumb and forefinger, going deeper. He'll sit alone, where no one can see him, and watch the cold water and think back through the day and the people, and then he'll return to the warm water of his bath with

Celia. He'll tell her everything he's collected today, all he's seen; she'll do the same, and together they'll make sense of it all.

The bushes thicken, undergrowth and overgrowth, whiplike branches he pushes away from his face. Closer to the river, there is a small clearing of tangled, beaten-down grass. A woman sits there, her long hair loose, her bare back facing Randall. He slows; he stops; he pulls back into the bushes, moves around to the side.

Two crows fly over, about to settle in the clearing and then change their minds, clapping away. Randall pauses, holds a branch aside to see. It is not a woman—it's Bruce, sitting alone with his two detectors laid out next to him. He wears jeans; his feet are bare. Cyclops is nowhere to be seen—perhaps he is tied to the shopping cart, somewhere outside of the thicket. The sun comes down, bright on Bruce's skin. His eyes are open, but he is not looking at the river, not looking at anything at all. His face shines, beneath his eyes, tears sliding into his beard.

And there's something on the other side of him, a red flash in the bushes. Randall shifts again, to see better, careful to avoid detection. The flash of red is a shirt; it's Celia's shirt. It is Celia, sitting perfectly still, smiling sadly, a strand of her gray hair held out by a thorny vine. Has she seen Randall? No, she is watching Bruce, and she is also crying.

Slowly, slowly Randall kneels and turns. Quietly he

crawls from the thicket, toward home, where he will draw the hot bath and wait. The phonograph's diamond needle will poise above a record already spinning, ready to be pricked into sound, into words.

Disappeared Girls

Miranda had never been on such a long train ride. Not by herself, at least. Carrying a bouquet of pink and orange chrysanthemums, she stepped from the platform to the train and started down the aisle. Just ahead of her walked a man with a backpack like she had only seen little girls wear—it was made of clear plastic, so all the contents were visible.

The man was tall, which made it easy to see what he was carrying. A flashlight, and something wrapped in a brown paper bag, and a book with a brass lock across the pages, like a diary. Higher in the pack, there was a coil of rope, a pocket knife, and a small adjustable wrench; if he only had a candlestick, a lead pipe and a revolver, Miranda thought, he'd have all the weapons from Clue. She had played Clue the night before, with her parents. She had been Colonel Mustard, and had solved the murder.

The floor of the train was sticky, strewn with old newspapers. Miranda chose a seat, and set her flowers gently down, next to her. She wore a wool skirt, a white blouse, her peacoat—a series of arguments lost to her mother. All Miranda was allowed to keep were her black Timberland boots; they matched her hair, dyed by her friend, Cindy, and cut as short as a boy's.

Out the window, two dirty pigeons shivered, hopping along the platform. The train began to roll. Miranda's mother, who had dropped her off at 30th Street Station, was already driving away, headed to work. Neither of her parents could make this trip, which was why they'd sent Miranda. They trusted her.

North Philadelphia slid past, crumbling buildings and windows with no glass; even the graffiti looked old. Miranda noticed, then, that the man with the transparent pack sat only two seats ahead of her. There was no one between them.

"Hey," she said, her voice just above a whisper. When he did not turn, she picked up her flowers and moved forward; she leaned until her mouth was close to his ear.

"One time," she said. "I saw a grown man wearing a backpack that looked like a teddy bear, with a zipper up its belly."

The man looked over his shoulder. His hair was pale blond, thinning on top, his blue eyes set close together.

The skin of his narrow face was flushed, and very smooth, as if whiskers had never grown there.

"I found this pack," he said. "I didn't choose it."

When he spoke, she saw the braces on his teeth; he seemed a little old for braces, but it was difficult to guess his age.

"Everyone can see everything you're carrying," she said.

The man shrugged, as if he had nothing to hide. Miranda leaned closer, to see over the back of his seat, where his pack was resting.

"Is that book in there your diary?" she said.

He looked at her flowers and then, slowly, at every feature of her face. He paused, as if to understand them all in relation to each other.

"Do I know you?" he finally said. When she didn't answer, he turned to face forward again.

Miranda stared at the back of his neck, where dark, twisting hairs grew. Past him, in the front of the car, two black boys about her age—fifteen—sat, handing a pair of headphones back and forth, rapping with a song. The land outside looked gray and cold and dreary, dirty snow on the ground. Wissinoming, Tacony, Holmesburg Junction. The conductor called out the names. Miranda would switch trains at Trenton, then meet her grandmother at Princeton Junction, on the platform. A man from the retirement home was driving the old woman to the train station. She wore diapers, and needed a walker to get around. Miranda would bring her back to Philadelphia; tomorrow was Thanksgiving.

Now she watched a man with long sideburns, who was brushing a little girl's hair. The girl was missing a tooth. Strands of her hair rose up, full of static, and the man licked his finger and smoothed them down. He and the girl got off the train at Bristol.

"Listen," said the man sitting in front of Miranda. He turned slightly; his voice was low. "It's not a diary. It's more like a journal. I write my dreams in it."

"Fine," Miranda said.

"That's why I'm on this trip," he said. "Why I'm on this train. Because of a dream I had last night."

"About this train?"

"Well, I'm not really certain." He licked his chapped lips, which looked sore, cut by his braces. His hands came up and gripped the top of his seat, and he twisted his body farther, bringing his face closer to hers. "All I remember from this dream," he said, "is an address. It's a street up in Hamilton—I know that, because I grew up there. I didn't have to work today, so I thought I'd ride up there, see if I remember any more."

"You don't have anything better to do?" Miranda said.

"Not really," he said. "I mean, I never know what this kind of situation might lead to. You'd be surprised."

"I'd like to see that," Miranda said, almost laughing.

"No," the man said. "I didn't mean to give you that

notion. This will have to be more of a solo type of thing."

"Whatever," Miranda said.

"Trenton!" the conductor shouted. "Final stop! The New Jersey Transit north to Penn Station is on this track, directly in front of us. Walk forward, please. You have five minutes to make the connection."

Everyone rushed to get off the train. The air outside was cold and smelled greasy; the edge of the platform was covered in yellow nubs, rubberized. In the crowd, the tall people and backflung scarves and shopping bags, Miranda lost sight of the man with the transparent pack. This both frustrated and relieved her.

She walked farther than most of the crowd, until the doors of the new train were about to close. The cars at the front were mostly empty; she chose one, then sat in a seat that faced backward, just as the train began to move. In less than an hour, she'd be with her grandmother, responsible for her; Princeton Junction was the second stop after Trenton. Her grandmother was probably getting ready, fixing her makeup in her room at the nursing home. She was old, but lively. Peppy, everyone said, and that wasn't always a compliment. Whatever passed through the old woman's mind came out her mouth, as if nothing could be held inside. Miranda knew it would be a long ride back to Philadelphia, listening.

The door at the end of the car slid open, and the man with the transparent backpack stepped through. He wore a red cardigan sweater, scuffed penny loafers with waffle soles. His pants rode high, revealing socks that were the same red as his sweater. Seeing Miranda, he waved, his approach not slowing. She picked up her flowers just in time. He sat next to her, blocking the aisle.

"Here you are," he said.

"What do you want?" Miranda watched him out of the corner of her eye. He seemed too nervous, too timid to be afraid of.

"Actually," he said. "I've changed my mind. I think you should come with me. I don't know why. It's a feeling."

Miranda thought of the stories she'd heard about disappeared girls. Girls with duct tape over their mouths, girls who left nothing but their shoes behind. She shifted and stared at the man, trying to figure if that was what he wanted, to make her disappear.

"How old are you?" she said.

"Thirty-one," he said. "My name's Edward."

"I'm not going to tell you my name," she said. "And I want you to show me where you wrote the address, in your diary, so I know you're not just making up the story to trick me."

Leaning forward and shrugging his bony shoulders, Edward pulled his left arm free of the strap, swung the pack around, and unzipped the top. A tiny key, threaded onto a rubber band, circled his left wrist; he unlocked the book, thumbed through the pages, then held it out, open, for her to read.

763 Sandalwood Avenue, the last line said. Yesterday's date was written above the address; over the date, a thick line had been drawn, as if to cut off this dream from the one before it. Squinting, Miranda tried to read what was written above this line, the record of a previous dream. Edward's fingers covered all but a few words: *She screamed and screamed and screamed.*

"You could have written that address in after you told me about it," Miranda said. "Before you found me on this train."

"I could have," he said. "True. Either you trust me or you don't."

"Hamilton," a voice said, through the static of a speaker.

"All right, then," Miranda said, standing at the same time Edward did.

They did not pause, on the platform at Hamilton. Miranda hurried to keep up with Edward as they exited the station and crossed the icy parking lot, between the empty cars.

"You didn't think I would," she said.

"I had a feeling," he said.

"Another feeling," she said, trying to tease him, and then she had a thought. "Was I in your dream? Was that it?"

"No," he said. "Not that I know of."

They entered a neighborhood of tall houses, some fixed up and some run down. There was slush in the gutters, snow in the yards, ice in the bare branches of the trees overhead. Miranda's orange and pink flowers looked out of place. She walked behind Edward, looking at the contents of his pack.

"That thing wrapped in the paper bag," she said. "Is that a revolver?"

"What?"

"Is it a gun, wrapped in there?"

"It's a sandwich," he said. "My lunch."

The middle of the street was the clearest place; not everyone had shoveled their sidewalks.

"Do you have dreams about sex?" she said.

"Yes, I do," he said. "Sometimes."

"Can I read them?"

Edward just kicked a shard of ice ahead of him, with his right foot, then his left.

"You're trying to take me somewhere," she said.

"Yes, I am. Obviously."

"Are you trying to have sex with me?"

"I don't think so." He kicked the ice into a snowdrift; it was lost.

"But you're not sure?" she said.

"Do those boots have steel toes?" he said.

"They're waterproof," Miranda said. "Aren't you cold?"

"I guess so."

They kept walking. In the silence, there was only the sound of their footsteps, and Miranda felt the space all around her, the fact that no one knew where she was. She'd always been told that she could do anything, and had understood that to be about achievements, and graduations, and success; now she felt some of the other side of what that meant—she could do anything, and this, today, was only one example.

She hurried to catch up with Edward, eager not to miss anything. She switched the bouquet to her left hand, and pulled her cold right hand into the cuff of her coat. They walked on Sloan Street, across Princeton, and onto Sandalwood. Crossing Amherst, she memorized the names, so she could find her way back to the station if something happened. She wanted something to happen. They passed a park where some kids were shouting, running around a collapsed snowman. The snowballs they threw at each other came apart into powder before they went anywhere. Miranda could still hear trains at the station, and highways, not so distant.

Edward stepped sideways. Without warning, he hid behind a tree, peering around it at a red brick house.

"What?" Miranda said.

"Yes," he said. "This is the one."

"From the dream? Why are you acting like that?"

Edward stepped out from behind the tree, not taking his eyes from the house. "It's the upstairs bedroom," he said. "That's where I was. That's where it happened."

"And what happened?" Miranda said. "What was there?"

"I don't know that, yet," he said.

"Come on," Miranda said. She crossed the sidewalk, not looking back. By the time she rang the doorbell, he was standing next to her.

Minutes passed before a woman opened the door. She was a black woman, old, and didn't seem happy to be bothered. A flight of stairs rose behind her, into darkness.

"He'd like to come inside your house," Miranda said. "Just that bedroom, upstairs." She pointed above her head.

"Pardon me?" The woman looked quickly from Miranda's face to Edward's, then back again.

"I had a dream about your house," Edward said. "I grew up in this neighborhood."

"My house?" The woman's hair was streaked with gray, pulled into a bun. Darker spots marked the skin of her face, freckles under her eyes. "You're too young," she said, "to have grown up in my house. I would've been here."

"No," Miranda said. "He only dreamed about it."

"I understand that it's a very peculiar request," Edward said. "Perhaps it's too much to ask."

"I don't see exactly what it is you want," the woman said. "And I sure can't see what I get from it."

"You can have these flowers," Miranda said.

"I just want to go into the room," Edward said, "to see if that helps me remember the dream. Five minutes, is all."

"The holidays," the woman said, "is when all the scams and con games happen. They warn us old folks about it, you know. But this one, you two, I can't figure what it is. That room is completely empty."

"All the same," Edward said.

"Five minutes," Miranda said. "That's all he needs."

"And my son lives next door," the woman said. "All I'd have to do is give a shout. I'll hear by the floorboards, too, if you walk anywhere else, try to steal anything."

"So you'll let me?" Edward said.

"For the flowers." Suddenly, the woman opened the door wide enough to reach out and take them, then stepped aside, to let Edward pass. "Not you," she said, her hand on Miranda's arm. "I'd rather you stay here."

The woman's grip was strong; when she let loose, the door closed, between them. Miranda watched Edward disappear up the stairs.

"Is that your brother, then?" The woman spoke through the thick, clear plastic of the storm door.

"I don't have a brother," Miranda said.

The woman just nodded, as if this cemented a suspicion she'd been harboring about Miranda and Edward. She stood across the doorway with the bright flowers in one hand, her other resting on the lock of the door.

Miranda's toes were cold. She wondered how long five minutes could last. Closing her eyes, she thought of Edward in the room upstairs; the window was ten feet above her head. She imagined him crouching down, crawling on a wooden floor. The room was bare, and dim; the wallpaper, torn in places, was all covered wagons. Edward had to use his flashlight to see. He was bent down as if he had caught a scent and was moving by smell.

"Why aren't you in school?"

Miranda opened her eyes. "Thanksgiving," she said.

"I don't like this." The woman's words fogged the window.

"But you like the flowers all right," Miranda said. She was enjoying the feeling of the woman being suspicious of her, the uneasiness that couldn't be hidden. She leaned sideways, and could see down a hallway, candlesticks on a table; she wondered what else the house held. She was not familiar with many black people, and knew they were different in the most unexpected ways. In the drugstore she had seen hair relaxers, and products for the bumps black men got from shaving.

"He better be finishing up," the woman said.

"Tell me," Miranda said. "Did anyone ever die in that room?"

"Pardon me? No. No one I ever heard of."

"Are you having a big Thanksgiving dinner?"

"That's none of your business," the woman said. Behind her, then, Edward appeared, descending the stairs. His feet, his legs, his body and arms, his hands rubbing together, his smiling face.

"I told you it was empty," the woman said, turning

at the sound.

"Pretty much," Edward said. "I appreciate it. Not many people would understand."

"I didn't understand," the woman said. "I don't. And I wouldn't do it again."

"Thank you," Miranda said.

The heavy door swung closed, and then there was the click of the lock, the sound of the deadbolt sliding across. Miranda and Edward went down the stairs, the walk. At the edge of the street, they both turned to look up at the window of the second-floor bedroom.

"Was it really empty?" she said.

"I remembered more," he said, "once I was up there. I lied before, even if I didn't mean to—you were in the dream."

"What was I doing?"

"I think it was the flowers, today," he said. "That's how I recognized you."

"I had them in the dream?"

A car passed, spraying them both with slush; they did not move out of the way.

"You didn't really do anything," Edward said. "Except that, when I was in the room, you appeared in the window, looking in, just kind of floating there, watching me, with those flowers in your hand."

"Floating?" she said. "What was I watching you do?"

"Exactly what I was doing, just now. There weren't any lights in the room, so I had to use my flashlight. The room was bare, no furniture at all, and dusty, like no one had been in there for a long time."

"But you did find something," Miranda said.

"Once I was inside," he said, "I remembered more, and I kind of knew what I was looking for. Down along the baseboard, I saw what seemed like a crack or smudge; when I looked closer, though, I saw it was words. I bent down to read them, and that's when I felt you watching me through the window."

"What did it say?"

"I wrote it down," he said, opening his backpack, unlocking his journal. "Let me tell you exactly. Here, I'll copy it for you—you might want your own copy."

He took out a pen; Miranda waited for him to finish writing. Her neck ached from looking up, listening to him. She took the scrap of paper that he held out to her.

Miranda Covington, it said, *you are a wicked young woman. Do not be ashamed—this is the right path for you, and it's only partially your choice. Embrace it.*

Her fingers were numb, difficult to work. She folded the paper and put it in her pocket.

"That's that," Edward said, barely breaking the silence.

"That's not that," she said. "That's hardly any kind of dream. How did it end?"

"Well," he said, "I came down the stairs and walked outside and stood here, next to you, just like this."

"And then what did I do?"

"You rose up," he said. "You flew low, through the trees, over those houses, and I couldn't see you anymore."

"That's not going to happen," she said.

"No?" Edward smiled. His braces looked sharp and cruel.

"I can't fly," she said.

"You can," Edward said. "I'd rather believe that you can."

With that, he turned and began walking away from her, in the opposite direction from the train station. She stood there for a long time, waiting, watching him grow smaller and smaller. His head straight, his body rigid, he never once turned to look back at her.

Pergrine Falcon

At a certain time of the year, the sun sets behind my house and casts the roof's silhouette, a pointed shadow, onto the street out front. This sharp triangle juts across the asphalt, lengthening as the sun descends. Like the bow of a ship, the shadow slowly forges toward the empty schoolyard across the street; just as it touches the curb, the sun slips away, beneath the horizon, and dusk falls. All lines disappear.

On the night I'm recalling, the shadow was not yet halfway across the empty street. I sat at my chair in the window, encyclopedia in my lap, trying to read about electricity—about neutrons and electrons, how current flows through a wire like water through a pipe. I couldn't grasp it. Many things conspired to distract me. My cat, for one, cried from the windowbox, where he sat crushing flowers. I ignored him. I was anticipating the beginning of *60 Minutes*, my favorite television program, and a telephone call from my parents, who live across town. They also watch *60 Minutes*, and our routine is that they call me every Sunday night, after the show, to discuss the interview by Mike Wallace.

I glanced up that evening, checking the shadow's progress, and saw that now its point was almost touching a car parked across the street. A big yellow '70s sedan. A man with a round, bald head sat inside, the skin of his face startlingly white against the dusk as he flashed his attention away from my house.

I switched on the television, impatient with the introductions, that ticking clock. At last, Mike Wallace came on, his sharply wrinkled face tinted orange. I always watch with the sound turned off, to better study his attack—that's how I think of it, and the pleasure I derive is the same as that enjoyed by people who watch shows of wildlife, of predator and prey. Why would anyone agree to such an interview?

Mike Wallace pointed with a crooked finger. His expression said he wished he could believe his pathetic victim. I didn't even try to read his lips. He blinked and blinked and blinked, as if lies brought him physical pain. I sat close to the set, reveling, twisting the controls back and forth, taking Mike from full pumpkinhead to an almost gray pallor, leaching his face of color. His technique is a riddling, but also a jujitsu of sorts, using peoples' own strength and weight against them. He lets a person believe they're free, that they're winning. When they try to escape, he stays with them. When they try to surprise him, take him in an unexpected direction, he surprises them by following, traveling easily in their slipstream, catching them out. I like to watch the people Mike questions, to see them squirm. I like to imagine that I am Mike Wallace, and that weaselly people collapse under the sharp, relentless nature of my questioning.

The phone rang. There were twenty minutes left in the show, but Mike was finished, and sometimes my parents are precipitous, jumpy. I lifted the headset. There was a pause, an intake of breath, and then a tangle of tones, someone randomly hitting their phone's buttons. Then a voice—not my mother's voice, not my father's voice—

"Stop fucking my sister!"

"Pardon me?" I said. "You must have the wrong number."

"Don't try that shit with me. I know who you are, where you are. Stop fucking her."

It was a man's voice, but high-pitched. Perhaps a boy's.

"Hold on," I said.

"Hold on, nothing," he said. "Just stop fucking her. That's all."

He slammed down the phone, and in a moment there was a dial tone. My heart was really going; I felt accused, even guilty. I wheeled back through my memory. I had not fucked anyone—not for a long time, anyway. I was hard-pressed to think of anyone who would suspect me of having done so. I wondered if I'd ever even thought of it in those terms—fucking someone.

I switched off the television; the credits were rolling. Outside, the shadow of my house was now touching the yellow car across the street, and the man inside it was staring in my direction.

I laced my shoes; I buttoned my shirt; I set my book aside, stood, and stepped to the front door. I opened the door, crossed my cracked sidewalk, and stood in the middle of the street with my hands on my hips.

"What?" he said. "Do I even know you?" His voice rose, slightly shrill. The light was fading, but I could see a Band-Aid, stuck along his jaw, another on the back of his head. His head was large and round, the skin of his face like a raccoon's mask; it was clear that he'd just shaved off his hair and beard—his cheeks and head were pale, while his nose and the skin around his eyes were tanned, weathered.

"I'm curious just what is your business here," I said.

"Business?" he said. "I'm thinking."

"Thinking," I said.

"I'm just working some things out. It's a free country, man. Far as parking it is, anyway."

"Is that car equipped with a car phone?" I said.

"What's with the questions?"

"Do you possess a cellular phone?"

"No, and no," he said. "Those things cost money."

"Well," I said. "I know you're out here." I turned and walked back to my house, the hard soles of my shoes slapping the asphalt, my cat slipping back inside, almost tripping me as I opened the door.

It's a large house, certainly larger than I needed, alone. I had rented it for five years; I was thirty-two.

That evening, I had just sat down and reopened my encyclopedia when the phone rang. Once again, I expected my parents, and once again it was not my parents. This time, it was a woman's voice.

"I called to apologize," she said, "for that prank call you received. My younger brother is very immature. I overheard him from the other room, so I thought I should hit the redial button and explain, apologize."

"Do I know you?" I said.

"It was just a random call," she said. "It won't happen again."

"Hold on," I said, but she was already gone. I set down the receiver, slightly disappointed. It occurred to me that this second call was also a prank, or that the first call might have been the true one. Perhaps I did know this sister, from some other time, and there was some truth, or could be, to the brother's accusation. These were interesting possibilities. I wished I still had the sister on the line, that I could ask her some questions.

I glanced out the window. The yellow car glowed

faintly against the dusk, the man still in it, the mask of his face flashing at me.

This time, as I approached, he didn't speak. Instead, he turned the key in the ignition; the engine kicked once, but did not catch.

"Hold on," I said, before he tried again. "I want to talk with you."

"I have to be somewhere," he said.

"You can't just take off," I said.

"Why not?"

"Well, you've been out here for the better part of an hour, and then there's the matter of the phone calls and everything else. It's been a peculiar evening."

"First I can't stay here, and then I can't go?" he said. "What is your deal?"

I walked around the front of his car, opened the passenger door, and sat down. A thick phone book, both white and yellow pages, crowded my feet.

"Where do you have to go?" I said.

"That I don't even know—all I have is an address."

"Kind of mysterious," I said.

"Not really. It's happened before."

"I'd like to accompany you," I said.

"Just go back inside," he said. "Go back to what you were doing." He tapped the face of his watch with the index finger of his other hand.

"Let's go," I said. "If time's so tight."

The interior smelled like old vinyl, cooked by years

of sun. I pulled down my shoulder belt and buckled it; he watched me, then did the same. Despite my expectation that he would peel out, put the pedal down and take off with some aggression, he merely shifted and eased away from the curb. We swooped around a corner, leaving the dark windows of my house behind.

The thinness of the man's body was accentuated by the size of his head; his slightness surprised me. He was younger than I was, somewhere in his twenties, his jeans torn, holes in the elbows of his flannel shirt. There was dirt beneath his fingernails, as if he'd been digging with his hands. We drove north on 99-E, past the furniture stores and the clown supply warehouse, past the Mexican restaurants. He told me his name was Parker.

"Parker," I said. "That's an interesting name for you. I was wondering what you were doing, parked like that; you must also have been curious what I was doing, inside the house."

"Not really," he said. "I was thinking."

"Well," I said. "I was watching *60 Minutes*."

"The television show? Jesus."

"What?" I said. "You don't like *60 Minutes*?"

"I don't know."

"Did you ever watch it?"

"Not really," he said, "but I hate that old guy, that guy at the end. The ornery one."

"Andy Rooney?" I said. "He's a curmudgeon—no one likes him. That's kind of the point."

"What kind of point is that?" Parker said. "I mean, that's the problem with everything, man."

"What is?" I said.

"People pick things apart. If there's something good, they change it around."

"Provide an example," I said.

A few raindrops fell, then more. Parker hit the wipers and the blades dragged across, smearing the windshield. Sitting close to him, I could see where he'd missed some places, shaving. Tufts of whiskers on his throat, dark hairs behind his ear.

"Signs," he said. "Signs. People have to change them around. If there's God Bless America out in front of a church or cleaner's, someone's going to steal that *B*; or you see all those Portland signs with letters blacked out to say Potland or Poland or something."

"I used to know a Chinese restaurant," I said, "a place called 'Grand Canal Take-Out,' and people kept painting over that *C*. These folks were dedicated—they had to climb up on a roof to do it."

"Exactly!" Parker gestured with his right hand, almost slapping me, as he steered with his left.

"Like pranks," I said. "I mean, why do people do pranks?"

"Pranksters," Parker said, spitting out the word. "Fuckers."

His voice cracked, shifting even higher, the last word bent and extended so it sounded like "fuck-her" and reminded me of the phone call.

"I don't appreciate hard language," I said.

"Neither do I," Parker said. "Not at all. Sorry."

The rain slashed against the car. We turned right on Hawthorne, then jogged up a couple blocks, to Belmont, and kept heading east.

"We're probably going to see a band," he said. "A musical performance. That's my best guess, anyway."

"I'm easy," I said. "Whatever you want to do, that's where I'll go."

"All right," Parker said, after a moment. "Here's one for you. Say this woman I knew, from where I'm from— a while ago she was going away to a competition, and one of her neighbors painted a sign on the wall of their barn that said Good Luck Debbie—"

"Did it work?" I said.

"Someone came by," he said, "overnight, and changed that *L* to an *F*, you know? And she just came apart, her reputation and everything, it all went downhill."

"What kind of competition was it?" I said.

Parker did not answer; he looked out my window, past me, scanning addresses.

"Forgive me for pursuing this line of questioning," I said, "but was that with a comma, like a congratulation— Good Fuck, Debbie—or was it more of a nickname?"

"Stop pointing at me," he said. "And don't blink like that, either. Is something wrong with your eyes?"

"Is this Debbie your sister, by any chance? I could

see how that fact would be upsetting."

"Man, no," Parker said. "A person can really get going about a sister, but that's completely different. This was a love thing."

"How is it different?" I said.

"Leave that alone," he said. "We're around here, somewhere."

He parked in front of an old theater, the name AVALON spelled vertically, in lights. A sign under it read WUNDERLAND 5¢; another THE ELECTRIC CASTLE. We did not enter this building, however. Parker ran across the street, through the rain, and I followed.

We walked back and forth up the block. Sometimes he turned so fast, switching back, that we almost collided. I stayed close. At last he led me down a driveway, behind a rundown Victorian house, to a cinderblock garage from which pale blue light flickered.

A few young people stood near the door, but did not greet or try to slow us as we stepped through the hanging vinyl shower curtains. Inside, it smelled smoky—cigarettes and cloves and marijuana; campfire, even—all close and mixed together. Christmas lights were strung overhead, and under this dim illumination people sat on bales of straw and on broken-down couches along the back wall. Voices rose and trailed away, crossing each other. An area had been cleared as a stage, where an unattended drum kit stood, a guitar lay on the dirt floor, and a banjo leaned against a chair.

Three video monitors faced the audience—one was playing a cooking show; one, blue static; the third, a tape loop of a cheetah running in slow motion.

I paused at a rickety card table, where tallboys of Pabst Blue Ribbon stood lined next to Styrofoam cups and a dented pot of steaming cider. The cans of beer were warm, slightly sticky. Parker cracked one open, took a sip. In that dim light, the skin of his face almost appeared to be one color. I ladled out some cider for myself, sniffed it, then set it aside. The show was about to begin. The people on the straw bales shifted closer together, crowded; some of them were young children, brought by their parents.

A woman wearing a gingham dress—a girl, really, with cropped, red hair—picked up an accordion. Next to her, a heavy, dark-haired woman in corduroy overalls strapped on an electric bass. The drummer had acne on his face, a pompadour, a pencil-thin mustache. A skinny guy with a ponytail sat in a chair holding the banjo; he wore pointy cowboy boots, his belt cinched by a seatbelt buckle from a car. His shirt had snaps for buttons, long sharp collars, and one sleeve completely torn away at the shoulder. Cloth bracelets and rubber bands circled his thin, bare arm.

"All right," the girl with accordion said. "Some of these haven't been practiced much. This first one is called 'Polyester Lover.'"

The drummer played a trombone to open the song,

then set it down and started in on the high hat. The televisions flickered and kept shining. A melody snaked from the noise and a few people held lighters aloft in half-serious tribute. The band didn't seem to notice, or even to be aware of where they were. The red-haired girl's small white fingers pressed the accordion's keys; the squeeze box yawned open and pinched down as she sang with the other woman, their harmonies so innocent and right that they seemed to have traveled from some lost place. They sang about vinyl people in suede trees and their mouths were perfect circles, slowly bending into smiles. The beat lagged, then sped, then jerked to circle back. I caught myself swaying; I felt a tenderness rising in me, and I was not ashamed.

At the close of the song, I took my hands from my pockets and clapped. A woman crushed an empty can in her hand, then threw it at a window; I winced, anticipating a crash, but there was no windowpane and the can merely slipped through the air, out into the darkness and rain.

"This one," the singer said, "is called 'Who Wouldn't Kill for Girls in Tights?'"

The banjo player switched to an electric guitar; the drummer played the snare with one hand, a muted trumpet with the other. The music seemed in tune with the cheetah on the screen, his every bound covering twenty feet and still not tiring, never arriving. As I watched, as I listened, as I softly sang along with the chorus, a slow suspicion started inside me. It seemed that the drummer's mustache was not merely pencil-thin, it was penciled-in. The guitarist, now that the background vocals kicked in, was also clearly a woman. I looked around me, realizing that I had mistaken many women for men. Yet I was not the only man, I reassured myself; there were others. Parker, for instance, with those tufts of whiskers, though he no longer stood next to me and I could not see where he'd gone.

This realization, this insight came so gradually that I would not call it a shock. It did not change the way I was feeling; in fact, I chuckled at myself, at my misapprehension. And the music didn't allow me to stray. Now the bass player had an upside-down metal washtub propped up on a brick, attached to a broomstick and string pulled tight for plucking. The drummer held a washboard.

"This one," the accordion player said. "It's called 'Catamount' or 'Catamite'—we can't decide."

The banjo returned, racing the cheetah, and the disparate instruments first cluttered and clattered in the air, only slowly coming together, the drummer howling through the middle. The sounds, the words rose up from below and at the same time descended; they wheeled outward and pulled us in, surging down a forbidden trail, past cliffs full of caves, trees growing sideways, vines reaching out. As the music spun and buckled, as the singing voices intertwined, my lungs felt squeezed in and then let out. I moved closer to the person standing in front of me—a woman, I believe, with long blond hair—and I began to gently, slowly rub my lower body against her hip. My eyes were closed, and through the lids I saw colors. Blue, red, green, orange and yellow. The stick on the washboard notched up and down the vertebrae of my spine. If the woman noticed our contact, she did not say; she did not pull away. The music resonated with the rain, uncoiling around the room and then pulling itself tight, and the friction was delicious, startling—

The song did not so much stop as it collapsed, came apart. The band lay down their instruments, taking a break, and when I stepped away from the woman she did not turn toward me. No one said a thing. I kept moving, backward, the vinyl curtains sliding around me.

I was outside again, in the rain, everything darker now as I hurried out the gravel driveway to the street, the lighted sign of the Avalon, under which Parker's yellow car was no longer parked. I checked behind me. No one followed, no one shouted. The cold night air was refreshing in my lungs. I did not feel the rain falling on my bare head; I barely felt the pavement beneath my feet. I punched the air, then raised both arms, a sudden wave of exultation surprising me. I felt amazing, wonderful.

Across the street from the old theater was a wine bar, and I stepped inside, out of the rain. I sat down at a table and ordered myself a glass of champagne.

Water ran down the windowpanes, bending the lights outside. Cars passed, faintly slithering, splashing. The music playing from the speakers, overhead, sounded artificial, synthesized, but this didn't rankle me. I don't know what I was thinking about, only that I wasn't in a particularly reflective mood; I was not far enough outside to reflect. I wasn't musing about Parker, or my time listening to the band, what I'd done and felt in the cinderblock building—not, at least, consciously. I simply felt wonderful, suspended in wonder.

About the time I ordered a second glass of champagne, a woman approached my table. She wore a yellow rain slicker, a matching hat.

"Is this seat being used?" she said.

I thought she was going to take the chair away, drag it to join friends at one of the crowded tables, but she sat down across from me.

"Celebrating?" she said.

"No," I said. "Not exactly. Maybe."

"Sounds complicated." She ordered a beer, then took off her hat. Her hair was bleached, peroxided white and yellow, cut asymmetrically. Her smile revealed buck teeth, and her fingernails were dark red, the polish chipped.

"I've been playing Skee-Ball," she said. "Might have sprained my arm."

"Pardon me?" I said.

"Over at the Avalon," she said. "On the game room

side. I was also working that machine with the metal claw behind glass, where you grab things. 'Action Claw,' it's called."

Our glasses marked the aluminum tabletop with faint, interlocking circles.

"And what did you grab?" I said.

"Well," she said. "Really you only win tickets, and then you can buy things, prizes, with the tickets."

"And what did you buy?"

"Nothing for me," she said. "Just something small for my brother."

"How old is he?"

"He likes things he should be too old for," she said. "We live together—I'm raising him, more or less."

"Must be a lot of work," I said.

"He's a troublemaker, but he's worth it."

"Is he a prankster?" I said.

"What do you do?" she said.

"I ask questions," I said.

She laughed. "Here," she said, spilling a handful of licorice and Tootsie Rolls on the table. "I bought these with my leftover tickets."

"Is your name Debbie?" I said.

"Sure," she said. "What's yours?"

"So you know Parker," I said. "He said he'd be back."

"No," she said. "I don't believe I know Parker."

"But you did recognize his car?"

"I have no idea what you're talking about."

"Let's back up, then," I said. "I understand. You say you had leftover tickets, correct?"

"Yes," she said. "That's how I bought the candy."

"Left over from what?"

She held up an envelope with a fierce red and blue bird painted on it. The bird had angry eyes, a sharp, curved beak, golden talons. Beneath it were the words PERGRINE FALCON.

"That's not even spelled right," I said. "It's missing an 'E.'"

"I know," she said. "I think it's made in France or something. Listen to these directions: 'The higher it fly depending on the more you exert yourself to throw (and the stronger you will be).'"

"Do you think that's true?" I said.

"In general?" She smiled. "You never know."

She handed the envelope across the table. I could feel the flat balsa wood pieces inside, the stiff outline of the falcon. I was about to ask her name again, but she spoke first.

"What did you think of the band?" she said.

"What?"

"The band you just saw," she said, "who you were listening to?" Unwrapping a piece of candy, she kept her eyes on me.

"I thought you'd been playing Skee-Ball," I said.

"That was earlier."

"I liked them," I said. "I have to admit, though, they

confused me, a little."

"How's that?"

"I thought they were men," I said. "The guitar player and the drummer, I mean. I did like the music."

"Are those two connected?" she said.

"What two?" I said.

"Your admiration for the music and the musicians' gender," she said. "That's not important—I'm joking with you."

"Were you there?" I said.

"I saw you," she said. "I saw what you were doing. You looked so happy—transported. There's a word for rubbing yourself against strangers, I just can't remember it."

"I didn't," I said.

"I was right there."

"Well," I said, "I've never done that before, nothing like it. I don't know." I struggled to swallow the licorice I was chewing; I washed it down with champagne. "If you want to know why I did it," I said, "I'm not so sure I can help you there—"

"Oh I know why you did it," she said.

I turned the envelope over and over in my hands, uncertain what to say. I felt caught, pinched.

"I liked it," she said. "I followed you, didn't I?"

The word *peregrine* means foreign, alien, roving, migratory. This I learned, later, sitting in my house with the *P* encyclopedia open in my lap. The peregrine falcon is the fastest bird in the air, flying over sixty miles per hour, even faster when diving to strike its prey from above. It is a swift and graceful hunter. This is not true of the pergrine falcon, whose brittle wings can be rattled and jolted by rain, whose body may splinter when landing on pavement. I know this because I have a piece of that bird, a shard of wing, in my desk drawer as I write this. Debbie's phone number is written on it, indented where the pen pressed into the soft wood of the wing. If you called that number right now, you would be told that it's no longer in service, disconnected, that she no longer lives there. That's because now she lives with me, in my house. We fit the falcon together, that night; we stood, left our drinks unfinished behind us, and headed out into the rainy streets.

The pergrine would not fly straight. It veered into buildings, it swooped into traffic, it dove spiraling into parked cars. She threw it. I threw it. We ran down side streets, the two of us uncertain, exactly, what we were running from, what we were running toward. Splashing wet, we ran laughing with pieces of that broken falcon in our hands.

Disentangling

I. Walter Austin

The edges of the Schuylkill are frozen, the ice faintly reflecting the lights spaced along the bridge above. Out in the middle of the river, the water runs thick and black and slow. Michael sees a few people walking on the bridge, only their heads visible, sliding there; he's down on the bank, searching, skirting frozen puddles. Sixteen years old, he wears a nylon jacket with round cigarette burns in the shell, dirty cotton batting seeping out. He carries an empty canvas mailbag over his shoulder. His pants are a special kind that can be turned into shorts; the legs zip off. Now the zippers, circling his thighs, are icy cold against his skin. Wind slips between the metal teeth.

He has been searching for hours without much luck.

It's late, after midnight, and cold, and he wishes he could sleep.

"White boy!"

Someone throws a can from above, but it misses him, clattering twenty feet away. At the sound, the birds rise from their night places; they clap their wide, black wings and settle again. Michael heads under the bridge, kicking at the piles of trash, checking the coils of old wire, the abandoned clothing. He knows what Walter Austin wants. It can't be too fresh—for that, Michael could just kill any dog, and he wouldn't ever do that—but it can't be just bones, either. He steps under a street-light, takes the assignment from his pocket; the ten-dollar bill and the strip of paper inside the envelope, both folded twice.

> ASSIGNMENT: ROADKILL OR DEAD DOG.
> LARGE SIZE BEST. AND FRESH. DROP OFF
> TOMORROW. 8 AM. 24TH AND LUDLOW.
> YOU ARE THE MEANS + THE CAUSE.
> SILENCE ALWAYS

He has worked for Walter Austin since April, and now it's almost Christmas. He has never met him, directly; he can't even be certain he's ever seen him. The assignments keep coming, and asking questions might change that. Michael does whatever is asked of him. Once, he met a woman in a red hat and told her,

"Wednesday." Another time, he watched a street corner for three days, taking notes about anyone who lingered, worrying about his spelling.

The envelopes are delivered by all kinds of people, always different. And the slips of paper the assignments come on always say that he is the means, the cause, but they never hint at the end or the effect. Michael never stays behind, nor tries to follow. His restraint is not from fear of Walter Austin, of losing the money or receiving some kind of punishment; it is closer to a sort of honor, an agreement that he respects, that provides a place where he can understand himself.

~~

Plastic bags, broken glass, and scraps of clothing litter the on-ramp. Here he's even more exposed to the wind, which slices right through, barely slowed by his thin body. There's something farther along, down on the shoulder, but it's only a dirty blue blanket, empty when he unfolds it.

Then he's worn out his bad luck, and everything begins to turn. The dog is thirty feet from the highway, where the shoulder slopes away and a chainlink fence, at the bottom, sifts all the trash.

It's a long, rangy kind of animal. Black, with a curved tail and floppy ears, a dried tongue that twists out, only three teeth at the front of its snout. Perhaps it was hit so hard it was knocked all this way, or it dragged itself this far before collapsing, or perhaps someone left it here. None of that matters; all that matters is that he's found it. Few things have looked so beautiful to him. He leans closer, his nose almost touching the fur, and still he smells nothing but the frost, the cold air. It's too cold for the dog to stink, too cold for bugs.

A rag in his hand, Michael takes hold. The dog's legs move a little, but its knees don't bend. It wears a half-rotted leather collar, no tags. One eyeball is gone and the other is like an old grape, loose in the socket. The skin is unbroken, but Michael can tell just by the feel that things aren't right inside. Broken bones, organs swollen and torn up. Unclasping the buckle from the cord, he pulls the mail bag's mouth open wide and, with his feet, slides the dog inside.

Walking, he carries the bag, then sets it down and rests, then drags it half a block, then picks it up again. Sirens cry out, not far distant. He stays in the shadows. Just because he's not doing anything illegal doesn't mean he'd be able to explain it, or wishes to try. Now he turns on 23rd Street, out of the wind, and follows the river at a distance. Closer, along the bank, he knows Denny and the other boys are working the bushes, waiting for the men who will pay them. Michael won't go back to hustling; he has his new place, his assignments.

He crosses the train tracks, goes under the bridge at Market Street, then Chestnut. Beneath the bridge at

Walnut, he pauses. Dragging the canvas bag into the tall grass, he opens it a little and pulls it back around the dog's head, in case anyone gets curious.

A rope hangs close along one of the thick round bridge supports; above it, far out of reach, is a metal ladder, screwed there when they were putting all the wires and everything inside, when they built the bridge. Michael checks that no one's watching, that no police cars are rolling past with their headlights dimmed.

His breath whistles through his teeth as he climbs. The ladder is so cold it hurts his fingers, though they're already numb. At the top of the ladder, he slides the piece of plywood away and sticks his head through, into the hollow space between the bottom of the bridge and the street above.

At least twenty people are sleeping around him, all wedged into their places, their breathing collecting with the hum of the pipes. Michael slides the plywood back. He can stand up straight, barely, between the girders. Farther along, two boys sit around a camping lantern that smells like it's burning gasoline; it casts light over a purse and two wallets, round coins, a car radio with wires snaking from it. The boys' wrists are bleeding a little, the kind of cuts Michael has had himself, from reaching through broken windows. That explains the sirens, before.

"What are you looking at?" one of the boys says.

In his corner, Michael has a double thickness of

dirty foam rubber, two sleeping bags with broken zippers. He listens to the water slapping gently below, the cars and buses and trucks—he can tell the difference—close overhead. He tries to sleep, his back against a warm steam pipe, and his feet pressed to it, farther down. His teeth hurt.

~~

In the morning, the dog is exactly where Michael left it. Looking up, he checks the time, the lighted numbers circling the top of the PECO building: 7:36. He spits up a gob of black phlegm, then shakes his head against the muzziness of breathing exhaust all night. Closing the bag, he lifts it in his arms and begins to walk.

The morning is cold and gray, with no chance of sun. A bus rolls past, blurred faces staring out the windows. He sets the bag down, catches his breath, then starts again. The corner is not far, only a couple blocks; he is thankful for that.

No one is around. He eases the bag down off his shoulder, onto the pavement, right at the edge of the street. Stepping back, he leans against the brick wall. He wonders if anyone would guess that it's a dog inside the bag; the stiff legs stick straight out in four points, making it look like the side of a box.

A white van passes. The second time, it stops. A man climbs out, leaving the engine to idle as he opens the two back doors. The man wears a blue knit ski mask, with round holes for his eyes and mouth, and an orange down vest that looks like it's for hunting. He is barely taller than Michael, but much heavier.

"Walter Austin sent me," he says, taking hold of the dog. His gloves are also orange; the fingers are thick, rubbery.

Michael moves closer. He watches as the man gently sets the bag inside the van, which is completely empty, and clean, with a white metal gate separating the seats from the back. The man does not open the bag, doesn't ask about its contents.

"Didn't think you were supposed to be here," he says.

"I probably wasn't," Michael says.

"Not that it matters." The man slams the double doors. "Not that I know a damn thing about it."

Michael watches the tailpipe cough, once, as the van drives away.

~~

Hours later, he's found half a piece of pizza, three chicken wings with plenty of skin left on them. Michael doesn't like to spend money on food. Wrapping it all in a piece of foil from a hotdog wrapper, he sets it on a steam grate, to warm; an old man's sleeping there, too— shoes under his head, icicles on his sleeve and pantleg where they've settled off the edge. Clouds of steam slip under his arms, between his legs. Sleeping that way keeps you warm, Michael knows, but it can make your skin go all soggy and strange, it can leave pockets of water beneath the surface.

Another man stands behind Michael, at the payphone—checking the coin return for change, from the sound of it—and then walks away, repeating a number aloud, his voice fading. Michael sits in the sun, gnawing on the chicken bones, his expression serious. He's bored, but wants people to believe he's doing something, or waiting, or thinking a problem through. Men and women in suits hurry past, not even looking his way. The Chinese delivery guy clatters down the sidewalk, his bicycle's rear tire flat. Time passes; the line of shadow shifts. Pigeons pick cigarette butts out of the cracks in the pavement.

The payphone rings. Four times, then it stops. A minute later, it rings again. Five times. It seems the man on the steam grate is stirring, as if he might answer the phone, but he is only turning over, cooking his other side.

The next time the phone starts, Michael stands and steps closer. He shivers, but he feels good, the food settling inside him. He picks up the receiver before the fifth ring.

"Hello?" he says.

"Yes." It's a woman's voice. "We have to get together."

"We what?"

"You're interested in love, right? People coming together?"

"I think you don't know who this is," Michael says.

"The boy wearing those pants with the zippers all over them? Is that you? That's who I want."

Her voice sounds black. Michael holds the phone to his ear, thinking. The man on the steam grate sits up, laces his shoes, and slaps the icicles from his clothes; they shatter around him, and he walks away, eating the crust of pizza Michael didn't finish.

"Are you there?" the woman says.

"Yes."

"We have to meet."

"You said that," Michael says. "You know where I am, I guess."

She pauses between words, waiting to answer, as if she's covering the receiver while she asks someone else what to say.

"But I'm busy," she says. "I'm thinking in a few hours. I'm thinking like 5:15."

"Is this a special assignment?" he says.

"You can call it whatever you want."

"I found the dog," he says. "I dropped it off this morning."

"A young man like yourself," she says.

"What?"

"You're lucky," she says. "Ninth and Diamond. In front of Kentucky Fried Chicken."

"That's a ways from here," he says, then waits out the pause. He stares down a businessman who's waiting for the phone.

"You've been chosen," the woman says. "It can be no other place."

Then she whistles, and it hurts his ear, and when he listens again there's no one there.

~~

Michael wastes the hours. It's too cold to sit on the benches in Rittenhouse Square, or to rest anywhere, outside. He zips up his jacket, tight, until the zipper bites his throat. He walks, thinking of the woman's voice on the phone, everything she said. He wonders if the phone call was a new way to get assignments; he is uncertain, but can't risk the chance that it was a message from Walter Austin. The details are always changing, and he is proud to be able to follow.

As he walks, he sucks on a fake sugar packet until the paper gives way; when the sweetness is gone he spits the pink pulp against a parked car. It sticks. Days like this, mostly, he just tries to stay warm; sometimes he talks to someone, a little bit, a person waiting for a bus or working somewhere where they can't turn away. Today, though, he doesn't really feel like talking, even if anyone wanted to talk with him. He just keeps moving— through City Hall, onto Market Street, walking deeper into the afternoon. Patches of ice catch the light, salt resting on bare stretches of pavement. There is no one he's looking for, no one he wants to find. He does not have a mother or a father. No sisters, no brothers. Since he never had them, he does not miss them. All he knows is his feet are cold, that he's dependable, that his broken shoelaces are fixed with knots that won't go through the eyelets. His shoes are loose, but these are not bad times, when the sun is shining and he's not hungry, when he has an assignment for Walter Austin and he does it well.

~~

Around four o'clock, he opens a door and steps into the warmth of the mall. The escalator carries him down, among the fake plants and wooden benches, mannequins watching through windows. Michael eats another packet of fake sugar. He doesn't like the feeling of other people's eyes on him, especially the other people his age, traveling in groups. They hold him off with their eyes, keep him at a distance—really, he'd like to be closer to the girls, to say something and have them listen. It's not figuring what to say, for him, it's the approach that has to be gotten past. No one will let him get close enough. And if he hangs around too long, watching, some of the boys will come ask him if he has a problem. He remembers the woman's voice on the phone, what she said about love, about people coming together. He wonders how it would be if one of the girls came and sat next to him, and talked to him, telling all about her room and her house, inviting him there. He imagines her thigh brushing against his own on the narrow bench. He wonders if she would listen to him, if he would lie to her.

~~

It's after 5:30, and the sun is gone. Michael stands below the fan that vents from the kitchen of the Kentucky Fried Chicken; warm, greasy air blows around him, making him hungry. Inside the restaurant, it's bright, the plastic chairs and tables shining. Most of the tables are empty, but a few people are working their way through buckets of chicken, eating little cups of coleslaw and mashed potatoes. Looking in, Michael gently kicks the wall, trying to keep his toes from going numb. He doesn't like it this far north, or east; he feels more comfortable when he's closer to the Schuylkill than the Delaware.

Across the street, there's a boarded-up drugstore, next to a tall building that's covered, down low, with that Mexican graffiti he can't read; the sign next to the door says HOTEL LANCASTER. He waits, watching for the woman he talked to on the phone. He imagines what she'll look like—probably wearing some kind of boots, and a matching coat, slippery, with her hair in tight braids and her eyes on him. All her words will be saucy, teasing. He tries to imagine what those boots will sound like, their sharp heels leaving no echo at all.

Finally, a man approaches, coming along the sidewalk. Huge, looming, in a black overcoat that almost reaches the ground; his shoulders are rounded, as if by the weight of the two leather suitcases he carries, one in each hand. When he sets them down, there's the sound of metal, settling. He looks at Michael, then across the street, then at Michael again. His skin is pale, yellow in the light from the restaurant. His black hair is long, lank, hanging almost to his shoulders, swept back from his forehead. A mustache rests on his thin upper lip.

"I was very much afraid you would not make it." His eyes are set close together, his nose thickens at its tip, and his small mouth stretches as he speaks. He is somewhere between middle-aged and old. "I hope you weren't waiting long," he says. "The bus was very slow, this evening. They are not always dependable."

The man's voice is low, almost a whisper, the ends of words slightly lisped off. He holds out his hand, short fingers thick as broomsticks. Michael takes a step back rather than shake the hand. He doesn't want the man to have hold of him.

"Is something the matter?" The man withdraws his hand. "I realize things are not entirely clear. For the moment, that must be the case."

"I think you're mixed up," Michael says.

"The phone call," the man says. "That is what has brought the two of us together. There has been no mix-up."

"I might have to go pretty soon," Michael says. "I'll probably have to get going."

"You will not," the man says. "This will be worth your time, I can assure you of that. You will have to trust me. I'm afraid I can't say it any other way."

Now there is a ten-dollar bill in his hand, extended.

"I'm not doing anything for ten," Michael says.

"You are not going to do anything," the man says. "No one will even touch you, and you will not touch anyone."

"What about the woman on the phone?" Michael says.

"She told you the truth." The man's hands are empty again, the money put away somewhere. "Only it's more complicated than that. You'll have to come along with me, if you wish to find out. Are you hungry, before we start?"

"Start what?" Michael says. "No, I'm not hungry."

"There is no reason to have anxiety. No cause. Did I tell you my name? I'm sorry. My name is Bender."

"Bender?" Michael says.

"Yes. Now, you see that hotel across the street? I'd like it very much if the two of us could go in there together. I'd like that very much. There's something inside that I'd like for you to see."

The man, Bender, takes a step forward, and Michael turns away, steps into the street. He feels trapped, yet curious. Bender walks slightly behind him, hulking, ready to reach out if he turns aside or tries to run. There's the whispering scrape of galoshes, sliding on the pavement, and the metallic sound inside the suitcases, as if they are filled with silverware, filled with knives.

The floor of the small lobby is dirty tile, pale lights flickering overhead. Behind a high desk, an old woman nods at them. She wears a Phillies cap, a hearing aid. Michael keeps walking, Bender silently herding him. A radio, mumbling through static, rests on a shelf above the old woman's head. On a pad of paper, she marks one X, then another.

Bender reaches a huge hand past Michael, taking hold of a door with a round, wire-reinforced window; he swings it open and pushes aside a metal gate, which folds in on itself. The floor of the elevator is a slight step up. Michael enters first. There are mirrors in the corners, where the walls meet the ceiling, and Bender's head almost touches them; the reflection shows the round bald spot on the back of his head. Michael sees himself—small, his white face shining and scared, his body tailing away to nothing, down by the floor. He presses himself against the far wall of the elevator, but he's still within reach. He watches as Bender hits the 14 button with a thick finger.

They begin to rise, very slowly. Michael realizes his

face only reaches the middle of Bender's chest. He is breaking one of his main rules—no enclosed spaces— but he has his reasons. His suspicions are gathering. Perhaps this man can impersonate voices, can sound like a woman or anything else. Then there was the ten-dollar bill—very familiar.

In the window, floors pass; he catches glimpses of empty hallways, each like the last. The elevator loses momentum, then lurches upward again, as if remembering itself. Michael keeps his gaze turned down, so he won't meet Bender's eyes. On the suitcases, next to the shiny steel hasps, tiny numbers are set on metal wheels. Combinations. He resists the temptation to reach out and spin them.

"What's in there?" he says, pointing.

"Instruments," Bender says. "You need not concern yourself with them."

"Do you know Walter Austin?" Michael says.

"No. I am not familiar with that name."

The answer comes a little quickly, perhaps; Michael is not sure what to believe. It's even possible that this man *is* Walter Austin, but recognizing that aloud would not be wise.

At the fourteenth floor, Bender curses under his breath, then punches the 4 button. The elevator begins a jerky descent.

"I apologize," he says. "That was not the correct floor." His body seizes into a kind of shiver, then relaxes again. He turns his head one way, then the other, cracking the vertebrae in his neck; his hair hardly swings at the movement, all its strands together in a solid mass.

Michael cannot tell if Bender is nervous, excited, or if this is how he always acts. The front of his overcoat, Michael notices now, is covered in short, black hairs. The cologne in the air is like medicine, like mouthwash, and it mixes with the smell of sweet, stale smoke. Michael almost asks if he knows anything about the dead dog, but decides to wait, for now. Even if this is related, if it is part of the whole plan, it is probably best to be quiet. It is never his place to understand.

"What is your name?" Bender suddenly asks.

"Michael," he says, not sure if the man already knows, or if he is only checking, to be certain.

"You won't see me again, after this evening," Bender says. Then, as they reach the fourth floor, he hesitates. He takes off his galoshes and holds them in one hand. His hair hangs in front of his eyes, a black curtain; he sticks out his lower lip and tries to blow it out of the way.

"Quiet," he says.

"I haven't said anything."

"What I mean is no talking from this point forward. No sound at all. If we are discovered, it would be a terrible misfortune."

He pulls the gate aside, then holds the door open. Michael steps into the hall. The carpet is matted, with hard dark shapes where things once spilled. One door is open, revealing only a toilet; the air smells like a subway tunnel. Above, paint has peeled, hanging from the ceiling in stiff white tongues.

Bender takes a single key from his pocket and scrapes its tip along the plaster of the wall, the sound a dry kind of whistle. There are straight lines above and below the key, identical to the groove it's making; there are also lines on the other side of the hall.

The key opens the door to room 419. The hinges give way unevenly, like the knuckles of fingers, inter-locked. Bender stands aside, so Michael can enter.

Beneath his feet, the floor is gritty. He takes another step, expecting to stumble or to kick something. Bender closes the door behind them, then stands still, as if allowing the room to settle. Michael keeps waiting for the lights to be switched on, but they are not. Gradually, his eyes adjust.

The room is square, twenty feet across. A sawhorse stands in one corner, and a metal chair with bent legs rests on its side. One of the two windows is covered with cardboard; a streetlight shines dimly through the dirty glass of the other.

Michael steps to the window. Mouse droppings line the narrow sill. Down below, he can see the cold yellow lights, the sidewalk where he'd stood. If he was back there, half an hour ago, he would not wait; he would not be here now.

It is not cold in the room, though not exactly warm.

Somewhere, unseen, a radiator is clanking away. Turning, he watches as Bender takes off his overcoat, opens a door, and hangs it carefully in a closet. Now he wears a long white coat, like a doctor's, which makes him easier to see, in the dim light. His body seems to hang suspended; it almost glows.

Michael would like to ask if Bender is a doctor, and why they're here and what they're waiting for, how long it will be before the suitcases are opened. He wants to remind Bender how the old woman at the desk downstairs made the two Xs, how she has counted the number of people who entered the hotel and how she must expect the same number to eventually come back out.

Next, Bender crosses the room, steps around behind, and takes hold of Michael's collar; the jacket's zipper gives way as he gently pulls, and then the sleeves slide off Michael's arms, and then Bender is hanging the jacket in the closet, next to his overcoat. Michael watches this. He does not ask any questions. He was told not to speak at all, and he believes that questions would be met with action, not answers.

Bender now holds up his hands, the pale palms as wide as Michael's face, as if something is about to begin. He stands next to a square on the wall that is slightly darker, a piece of cardboard hanging by one nail. He spins the cardboard on the nail, so it slides upward, and then, there, in the space that had been covered, something shines.

It is a hole in the wall. An inch across, or less, the size of an eye. A wedge of light is cast from it, almost like the pale beam of a movie projector. The beam grows wider, then dissipates before it can reach across the room.

Bender motions for Michael to come closer, and he does so. A heavy hand on his shoulder, he bends slightly, facing the hole in the wall; he closes his left eye and squints with his right.

Two people are standing still, facing each other, in the next room, through the wall. They are only fifteen feet away from him. A man and a woman, wearing loose white clothing, and they stand so still that at first it's hard for him to tell if they're real. The room is the same shape as the one Michael is in, only cleaner, with no furniture except a brass bed, set out in the middle. There are lights shining from a hidden place, in different directions; the man and woman each have two shadows, in Vs behind them, joined at the feet. The man's sideburns are thin and sharp, pointing at the corners of his mouth. He is a little shorter than the woman, and he is black. She is white, and her dark hair is up, piled atop her head, away from her pale face. Her dark eyes blink once, then again. That's the only movement.

And then, slowly, the man raises his arm. He reaches out and takes the pins from her hair, so it loosens in sections, unfolding around her. He bends down and sets the pins in a straight line on the wooden floor, then stands and gently touches the woman's cheek.

She smiles at his touch, but there's something sad in her smile, a tremble in her lips. She steps past him, and he turns to watch as she stands at the window, looking out. Again, all movement ceases. A streetlight shines, the same light at the window in the room where Michael stands, watching.

He can tell, by the expressions on their faces, that the man and woman have known each other for a long time, that they care for each other. His forehead is pressed against the rough, gritty plaster of the wall, sharp against his nose. He fights off a sneeze; he can hear Bender's ragged breathing, he can feel the warm breath on the skin of his face. Pulling back, opening both eyes, Michael sees that Bender is only six inches away, staring at him. For some reason, he feels less afraid, less wary; he is not sure why. He gestures for Bender to look through the hole, into the other room, but Bender just shakes his enormous head and points back, nodding as if no time should be lost.

The man and woman resume their movement. She turns, smiles, and steps away from the window. Neither of them has said a word, as if this whole floor of the hotel is silent. Next, she undoes laces, and buckles, and her white skirt slips away—but there's another skirt beneath that one, and then another. They rustle, loosened, collapsing down. The man does not help her; he only watches as the skirts settle around her ankles, as she slips away from them. There's only one thin layer left, the shadows of her legs visible through it.

Next, she unlaces the bow at her neck as she keeps walking, the V of her shadow tilting and sliding across the floor, dragged behind her. She sits on the edge of the bed, her nightgown hanging slightly open. Dark shadows collect along the curved line of her clavicle, and in the hollow of her smooth throat. Slowly, she stretches backward, then rolls over, on her side, facing away.

Michael hears a low whistling, and wonders if it is her, or the wind, somehow. He cannot tell. As he watches, he tries to keep it from happening, but still his dick gets hard, pushing against the zipper of his pants. He keeps expecting Bender's hands on him, but they do not come; there is only the ragged breathing, to the left, the crack and whinge of the floorboards when Bender shifts his weight.

Through the wall, in the other room, the man now moves. His hands come alive, rising in front of him; he undoes the drawstring of his pants, and they drop around his feet. He steps out of them, his legs so black they look burned into the white sheets behind them. The shirt he wears reaches halfway to his knees, and he sits on the edge of the bed, rubbing his hand up and down the woman's bare arm, as if smoothing or polishing it. His other hand rests on her hip, then her thigh.

The man is saying something, his lips moving, but his voice is only a murmur, the words impossible to make out. She doesn't turn over; she still faces away from him. He rests his hand along the nape of her neck, now, then takes hold of her robe, there. She bends her elbows, slips her hands through the armholes of her gown so it can slip farther down, revealing the pale skin of her back, arching slightly, and the dark shadow of her spine, the sharp curves of her shoulder blades. The man's fingers trace shapes across her skin, as if he is spelling words for her, as if she might guess. She reaches behind, where she cannot see, and strokes his leg, just once, very gently.

Slowly, slowly, he pulls up the hem of her gown, until all the fabric is bunched there, around her middle. The edges of her legs are hard to see, against the white sheets. Her hips are wide, but her thighs are thin, so there is a space between them though her knees touch, resting one on the other. His hand slips from her hip, out of sight, and then the tips of his dark fingers show, in that space between her thighs.

The woman laughs, then coughs. Soft, then harder, folding in on herself. Once she falls silent, both she and the man are motionless again. There is the sound of the wind, the glare of the lights, time passing around them, and then the man stands and slowly walks around the head of the bed. He kneels there for a long time, his face wide and full of care, all open as if nothing can be hidden or held back. His mouth moves again, his whispers lost.

Michael had not noticed the man's hand straying toward the foot of the bed, but then the sheet is being pulled up, without stopping, all the way over the woman's head and settling, hiding her entirely. Now that the man and woman have fallen motionless again, Michael is not certain what has happened, only that everything is finished, that it can go no further. He feels it—sharp, like a surprise, as if nothing in the other room will ever move again; and if it does, it they manage to rise, they will no longer be the same people. It is an ending, and he feels it spreading to him, as well. As if he, too, must change.

A pulse ticks in his eye, and at his wrists, and at the back of his knees. He feels hot inside, heat rising off his skin. He stares at the man, kneeling next to the bed, and the shape of the woman beneath the sheet; he does not want to forget them.

When Michael finally steps away, Bender is standing calmly beside him, holding out his jacket, open, so he can slip his arms back inside.

II. Auguste Dupin

Outside the Lancaster Hotel, Dr. Ralston Bender pauses to pull on his galoshes. He kneels on the cold pavement, and the boy stands nearby, watching, as if waiting for something more. The two have not spoken since before they went into the hotel room; inside the room, it was silent; they finished their business, then descended, without words, in the elevator. The silence between them is unbreakable.

Now, finally, the boy turns and walks away. Dr. Bender does not call out after him, he just watches him go. That all went quite well, he believes. Just as he'd planned. Now, for the rest of it, he can only hope; he can only believe. He hasn't felt this hopeful since he was a boy, over fifty years before.

Dr. Bender senses that he is needed, somewhere; his eyes search for a payphone. He'll never wear a pager or a cell phone, since he wants to always concentrate on the time and place where he is, to frustrate all distractions. He does not even have a telephone in his apartment.

Picking up his murder bags, one in each hand, he begins to walk. The darkness closes around him. People are hurting tonight, that is certain. The neighborhood slips past. He can walk anywhere without fear, and this is not only due to his size; the way he spends his days renders him impervious. No outcome is unforeseen— neither dreadful nor surprising.

Three boys with hoods over their heads stand around the payphone. Brightly colored pagers show on the waists of their low-slung jeans.

"Yo," they say. "White giant. Use another phone."

"No," Dr. Ralston says. "This one is convenient. I will

not be long."

"Fuck you," they say, but do not come any closer.

The receiver is cold against his ear. His frozen mustache bristles. He dials the number of the answering service.

"Dr. Ralston Bender," he says.

The woman on the other end says the call came in just minutes before. She wants to know how he does that.

"Is it urgent?" he says.

There is a case that needs his attention. At 16th and Locust. If he can alert them as to his whereabouts, they will send a car to pick him up. They await him before proceeding.

"I will not need a car," he says. "I will arrive there in between half an hour and forty-five minutes. Please relay this message, as I am not currently in a position to do so. And, please, make it extremely clear that the scene is not to be breached until I am present."

He hangs up the phone, then looks back and forth, searching for a bus stop. Most of the streetlamps are dark. Shoes festoon electrical lines, hanging from laces like sinews.

Glancing once at the boys, who still wait, he picks up his bags and begins to walk. The bags seem to have become heavier, as he's grown older; at night, his shoulders ache, their joints gone rough and arthritic, but he has no choice. He needs every single thing he carries. The scissors and forceps, tweezers, scalpel handles and blades. The syringes, needles, cotton swabs. The gloves, sponges, sketchpads and notepads. The thermometer, the chalk and tape, the body bags and ID tags, the evidence scale and the cameras, both regular and Polaroid—he's learned not to rely on the police photographers. And no matter how many tools he carries, how essential they are, Dr. Bender never forgets that the most important thing he takes to a crime scene is his common sense.

As a medical examiner, he is somewhere between a detective and a doctor. There's an *M.D.* after his name, and he is admired in the cold rooms of the morgue, but he's earned his respect on the street. He has to remain attuned to feel the clues; he's learned their ways, how they arise from people and the spaces between people. This is why he is always ready, why he carries everything with him. He rarely goes to his office, for he needs to be out among it all, surrounded, to feel the gentle push and pull, the tendencies and possibilities all around him.

Eighteen thousand to twenty thousand people die, each year in Philadelphia, and he sees a fair fraction. The cause of death is natural, accidental, homicide or suicide. Only he has the power to say what happened, to lock it down. He's seen the skin of a hand come off like a glove, the scar from a braided whip, and the dark nostrils where a double-barreled shotgun's been placed. He can figure the shooting distance from the spray of the pellets, spread through a body, or the presence of gunpowder, if the weapon shot a solid bullet. In a skull, he knows the difference between entry and exit wounds. Bullets go haywire, ricocheting inside people; knife wounds are so much cleaner, simpler. He's seen mummification, and how rigor mortis comes and goes, and the pinkness of carbon monoxide poisoning. He's tested the food left behind, uneaten; he's sniffed for the bitter almond smell of cyanide.

~~

It is not long before the bus eases toward him, the square lights of its windows coming into focus. Dr. Bender climbs on board, drops his token in the slot. He likes buses, the way they sway and moan, how they hold strangers together for a time, how all the scenery wheels through the windows. He likes them best at rush hour— all the people standing and leaning in the aisles, their bodies pressed against one another. Now, the bus begins to move. He prevents himself from speculating about tonight's case; he prefers to arrive at the scene with his mind clear and unsullied, with every explanation still possible.

He's in a good mood still, from helping that boy. Michael, back at the hotel. Dr. Bender had tricked him a little, paying a woman to talk on the phone this morning, but now he sees that wasn't even necessary—the plan was so pure that the boy sensed it, that he wanted to come, that it was clear in his eyes. A sense of duty, even, more than curiosity. And there is no doubt that Dr. Bender chose correctly; he had never seen the boy before, yet he sensed the need, a coiled aimlessness, an energy waiting for purpose. The sight of him lit on Dr. Bender like a surprise, the answer to a question he had been struggling to formulate. *How might I spread hope?*

The brakes catch when the bus slows; the driver's hand waves the wheel around as they swoop through corners. Outside, people lean into the cold wind, clutching the lapels of their coats. All the trees' branches are bare, fragile. Dr. Bender prefers the night; any point requiring reflection can be examined to better purpose in the darkness.

Now the bus is passing through his neighborhood, his apartment only short blocks away. He imagines it now, the place he's lived for over thirty years, with the pale red light seeping through the windows and his cat, Pluto—who does not fear the smell of him, who likes everything about him—asleep or patiently waiting, holding the room still.

One single lamp hangs from a slender gold chain, its bulb hidden behind a ground-glass shade. An octagonal table rests in the middle of the room. On the walls hang two large paintings—a landscape holding barren hills, one lone tree; a portrait of a dark-haired woman he does not know. He bought them both at an estate sale.

There are no mirrors, no shining surfaces; the heavy

curtains are capable of blocking all light. The red velvet sofa is covered in black cat hair. Often, Dr. Bender falls asleep here, and he awakens in the early afternoon, with Pluto on his chest.

The large window behind the red velvet sofa frames the yard next door, which holds a black, wrought-iron raven, its outspread wings over six feet across. As wide as Dr. Bender's own arms, held out to his sides. It perches there, atop a post, because the house there was once rented by Edgar Allan Poe. Poe lived in those rooms over a hundred years before, with his young wife and his mother-in-law; he wrote his best tales here, marked down the words. Now the house is a National Historic Site, and Rangers lead tours, most days. What would Poe make of them, in their stiff polyester uniforms and wide-brimmed hats, the ties that close with metal snaps around their necks?

Tours do not interest Dr. Bender. Some nights he looks through this window, though, and imagines that a dark figure stands in the windows of the house, looking back at him, sharing his thoughts. This does not frighten Dr. Bender—far from it. Some nights he even descends from his fire escape, the rusted ladder scrolling loose from inside itself, and walks across Poe's lawn. He looks through the low window, into the basement, the low ceiling and the crumbling mortar of the false fireplace, a perfect place to hide a body. He feels close to Poe, these nights, a chill burning inside, where effects find their causes and do not fork away.

Before he moved here, he'd never read Poe. And once he began, he could not stop; now he's read it all. The tales, the poetry, the criticism, the letters. He reads the collected works, all thirteen volumes, circling through them as if they have no beginning or end, which they do not. His fingers still tense and shock, holding the pages.

It's true that Dr. Bender has grown the mustache, and let his hair stretch toward his shoulders; it's true, perhaps, that he and Poe share a sensibility, their nerves wound tight, that there is a similarity in their eyes. But it's preposterous to imagine he's trying to perfect a further similarity—at six-four and over two-fifty, Dr. Bender is twice Poe's size.

In any case, it was never Poe whom Dr. Bender emulated. Not exactly. It was Auguste Dupin. It still is. Dupin, Poe's detective, who went out only at night, when the mysteries were illuminated for him. Dupin, who solved the Rue Morgue murders, who outthought both criminals and policemen. Dupin, the occasional poet who developed every side of his brain, who was fond of enigmas, of revealing the complex as far from profound.

Poe never really described Dupin, physically, though Dr. Bender suspects the detective looked very much like himself. A larger, stronger Poe, with equal acumen yet more ability to survive in the world. Like Dupin, Dr.

Bender smokes a meerschaum pipe, filled with cheap tobacco. Even with the smoke thick in his clothes, and his cologne—musk, it says on the bottle—people still sense there is something about him, a reason to step back. He cannot help this. He has changed in tiny increments, so gradually, to become what he is, until his loneliness is like a scent, a kind of electrical membrane cast around that holds everyone away.

~~

At Walnut Street, Dr. Bender transfers from the 57 to the 21. This bus is almost empty. Copies of the *Inquirer* and the *Weekly* cover the seats. Only a week ago, they'd both run articles about him, about his upcoming retirement. They recalled some of his most famous cases—the blowfly eggs taken from the nose of a corpse, the pupae tested to provide toxicology information on the victim; the dismembered body whose parts were matched by the marks of the same vise on the ankles, wrists, and skull; how he matched the jagged circles around the nipples of a victim by taking casts of the suspects' teeth, then tested them on Jane Does in the morgue, corpses still fresh enough to bruise.

He refused interviews; he does not desire publicity. The papers had talked to some of the technicians, though, and to Detective Farnsworth, and had even gotten a quote from the police chief, a man Dr. Bender has never met.

Once, though it sickens him to think of it now, he had considered collecting the cases himself, detailing them in a book. Adipocere formation vs. mummification, his theories on fingertip-type bruising, a chapter on rationality and the criminal mind. He had bought a bound notebook of expensive paper, a fountain pen with a gold nib. On the first page, he wrote the title he'd been saving—DISENTANGLING—and, below it, his epigraph, a description of Auguste Dupin by Poe:

> *As the strong man exults in his physical*
> *ability, delighting in such exercises as*
> *call his muscles into action, so glories*
> *the analyst in that moral activity which*
> *disentangles.*

The remaining pages in Dr. Bender's expensive notebook are blank; they will remain blank. The idea was self-serving and beyond that. Distasteful. People's curiosity is not about the disentangling at all—it is for the details that shock and thrill them, a thirst for all the sexual deviance cases that some consider his specialty. And, Dr. Bender admits to himself, he has not always been innocent of pandering to such people. On more than one occasion—at dinner parties or receptions he could not avoid—he'd let someone start questioning him. He'd warm up by explaining that hair and fingernails did not, in fact, grow after death, and before long he would hear himself regaling a growing crowd with tales of mutilation and postmortem ejaculation, with every prurient detail. The sound of his voice, in these times, came to disgust him. It made him question whether his work was, in fact, a "moral activity"; it made him wonder what he might do to make it so.

Dr. Bender has realized that he's never known a happiness he could not pick apart. He has practiced too long at looking backward—all his work has been in the past, about things that have, always, already happened. This is why he is retiring early, while there is still time to change.

No one knows how effects are managed like he does, few have traced them so far back. Poe found purity, but he'd never been able to move forward—Dr. Bender believes he can go beyond this. All the polarities inside him have been reversed; instead of explaining past tragedy and sadness, he will project future happiness. He will plant the causes deeper than anyone could know or recognize. Tonight in the hotel was only a beginning, one beginning. There will be others.

~~

The bus departs, and Dr. Bender walks the block and a half to Locust Street. All his senses bloom in anticipation. The traffic is easing; there are few pedestrians on the dark sidewalks. As he approaches his destination, he sees that there are no reporters yet, no press waiting. That is fortunate.

One police car is double-parked out front, and the door of the row house is propped open. He steps inside the narrow, haphazardly lit hallway. Cracks run through the brown paint, stretching along a stairway where the three men sit waiting. Detective Farnsworth sits at the bottom, the two policemen spaced equally above him. All three stand and begin talking at once; Farnsworth looks back and the officers go silent. He takes a step forward, with his slouching body, the loose skin around his sad eyes, his pale gray halo of hair.

"Good evening, Detective," Dr. Bender says. He holds out his official ID for inspection. "I know who you are, Bender," he says. "Christ. It's been how many years, now? How many cases? And you're a short-timer now, too. Relax a little."

"I understand there's a situation here," Dr. Bender says. "How do the facts stand?"

"Well, the smell is what alerted the landlord."

Dr. Bender has already taken note of the odor of decomposition; he has unconsciously switched to breathing through his mouth.

"And it's clearly coming from behind that door."

It is the only door in the hallway. Below the brass #1, someone has drawn a black shape—rather hastily, it seems—with a piece of charcoal.

"A crow," Farnsworth says,
"or some kind of blackbird."

"I beg to differ," Dr. Bender says.
"That bird is decidedly a raven."

The two policeman are still on
the stairs, prepared to begin.

"And what," Dr. Bender says, "has
your initial investigation revealed?"

"The landlord is upstairs, awaiting
questioning," Farnsworth says.

"And behind this door?"

"We haven't opened it, yet. We were waiting for you."

Dr. Bender takes off his overcoat and hangs it on the
newel post of the bannister. He pockets his cuff links, then
briskly, with a snapping sound, rolls his shirt sleeves to his
elbows. He takes off his galoshes, then dials the combination of one of his murder bags, so its hinges open like jaws.
Inside, it is extremely organized. He takes out his sketchbook, a dark graphite pencil, and stands. Looking once at
the expectant men, he opens to a blank page.

As he begins to sketch, he is assembling what he has
to work with, here. Farnsworth is dependable, in his
way, yet extremely squeamish—he avoids a corpse every
single time. And the policemen are so young; the white
one has acne on his cheeks, razor burn at his throat. The
black officer, Wilson, has worked with Dr. Bender
before, on a recent case. Wilson had cut himself,
somehow, and had refused help, had said he'd wait for a

doctor who handled living people. That's how it is—they keep their distance, fear his touch. They never shake his hand, always lean away when he tries to clap them on the back. Still, they are not bad men, not stupid men. It's after eight now, and they're already thinking of going home to their wives, their families.

Just as Dr. Bender finishes his sketch, Detective Farnsworth clears his throat.

"Can we begin?" he says.

The policemen, who had returned to their seats on the stairs, rise again.

"Are you ready?" Dr. Bender asks.

"We've been ready for the last hour."

"I realize that. I appreciate that fact. Have you heard any movements behind this door?" From his bag, he takes out four paper face masks, four pairs of latex gloves.

"Nothing at all," Farnsworth says. "And it might be best—I mean, in light of preserving fragile evidence, you know—you might not want a lot of people in there, milling around."

"Of course," Dr. Bender says. "I'll go in alone, with these two gentlemen prepared to respond, should I require their assistance. Until that time, I will require, as usual, absolute silence."

He cannot have the air busied with talk, words loose in his head. Taking the key from Farnsworth, Dr. Bender unlocks the door, holds his breath, and pushes it open. A wall of hot, foul air collapses over him; the other men gasp. He hits the light switch and steps inside.

One bare bulb swings from the high ceiling, two hundred watts or more. The ceiling is perhaps fourteen feet high, the room perhaps twenty-five across, and square. It is empty, not one stick of furniture. One window faces the street; there are two doors, closed, on his right. On the wall straight across from him, written in the same charcoal, is the word

T E L L — T A L E

The letters are over a foot tall, perhaps midway between the ceiling and the shining hardwood floor. The odor of decomposition is stronger here, thick and strangling.

Yes, they were right to wait for him. Turning, Dr. Bender sees the policemen waiting in the doorway, pale blue masks over their silent mouths. They find nothing dramatic about this; they want to have it behind them, to be on to the next thing, or at least out driving the streets.

Now he notices the galley kitchen, which had been behind him, half-hidden behind a sliding door. His footsteps are heavy, too loud; he pauses after each one, his ears straining. The chrome of the faucet shines. The cupboards are clean and hold nothing—no plates, no glasses, no utensils. There is no sign of habitation whatsoever.

Turning again, he crosses to the closed doors. The first is an empty closet, holding only three wire hangers. The second door opens into the bathroom. He pulls the hanging string and a fluorescent light flickers over the medicine cabinet. The mirror reflects his tie, his shoulders. The tile is covered with a layer of dust; there are no footprints, no messages written in it. There is no curtain on the shower, and there's no body here. When he turns on the spigot, rusty water coughs out. He closes it down, pulls the string, steps back onto the hardwood floor. On his right, the round thermostat juts from the wall. The red arrow points just past 98°. He dials it down, into the fifties.

Standing motionless in the center of the room, he feels his muscles tightening around his bones. He must restrain himself from hastening toward conclusions.

"What do you make of it?" he says suddenly, whispering.

"Nothing through those doors?" Wilson says.

"The apartment appears to be empty," Dr. Bender says. "Perhaps the mystery here is *too* plain, do you think? A little *too* self-evident?" He gestures to the word on the wall, but they do not seem to notice his movement, nor the implication.

"We could bring in the dogs," says the white officer.

Dr. Bender cuts that idea short by narrowing his eyes. The canine corps always wants to bring in the dogs; the mounted police always believe horses are the answer; the officers in the wetsuits, the frogmen, suspect all answers are underwater. Such complication is more than unnecessary—it invites distraction. Dr. Bender steps into the hall, reaches into his open bag, and hands a roll of yellow CRIME SCENE tape to Wilson. The other officer, it says on the badge, is named Jim O'Connor. He looks ready to suggest the dogs again.

"Perhaps," Dr. Bender says, standing, stepping back into the room, "you, Detective Farnsworth, could prepare the landlord for questioning. I will be with you shortly." He unlocks, then opens the window. "We must pause before proceeding, to ascertain our direction."

"To let the air clear," Wilson says.

"Exactly."

Dr. Bender is beginning to feel acclimated. Sitting on the window's sill, he writes in his sketchbook: *Entry at 8:36 PM. Strong odor of decomposition evident. Room temp extremely high. Initial inspection reveals no body. Fragile evidence not apparent. Physical layout as below.*

As he begins to draw his diagram, he hears Farnsworth's footsteps, wearily climbing the stairs. There is traffic outside—horns, car radios—yet Dr. Bender is not distracted, not even by Wilson's low voice, telling O'Connor a story.

"Dude had a wire going into a copper pipe," he's saying, "and that plugged straight into his asshole. Yes way. Would I make that up? Plus, another wire attached to an alligator clip, you know, and that clamped onto his lower lip, and he's got an electrode taped to each nipple, spliced into some speaker wire—"

Dr. Bender hardly hears it. He looks up, then back into his sketchbook. He must not let himself begin guessing, bringing his subjectivity into play. He must move in increments, attentive to every sensation, every clue. Does he feel threatened, is he in danger? He does not believe so.

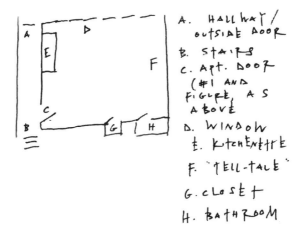

"So," Wilson is saying, "this dude had taken pictures from skin mags, you know, and glued the faces of his family and friends onto the bodies. Then, and I shit you not, the doctor here decides to hook the whole thing up to the amplifier again, just to see how strong a shock it was putting out! I mean, the dude's dead, but I thought the body was going to get up and dance!"

Dr. Bender closes his sketchbook with a slap. Both officers look up, startled, masks still on their faces. The yellow CRIME SCENE tape bisects their chests. Stepping closer, he bends to get under the tape, then stands next to them.

"This room can be contained," he says. "Perhaps one of you might circle the block and see if anything arouses your suspicions."

~~

The landlord's apartment smells like an ashtray. Newspapers stand in unsteady columns as tall as most men. There are enough tables and chairs, stacked precariously atop one another, to furnish the room downstairs, as well. Dr. Bender steps carefully, afraid of setting off an avalanche.

The man himself, Joseph Kimmel, sits in a kind of clearing, deep in a threadbare armchair. He is a retired white male of sixty-seven years, who has resided in this house for thirty-nine of them. His white hair tangles around his head; his eyes blink rapidly. He looks at Dr. Bender and Detective Farnsworth as if he is happy to have company, proud to play the host.

"He lives here alone," Farnsworth says.

"I do," he says, with a note of triumph. "I own it. What I don't understand is why you don't just take the body out—hell, you've been here for hours, and the smell's just getting worse."

"This is not an everyday situation, sir." Dr. Bender shakes Kimmel's hand; he has not taken off his latex gloves, for he expects to need them. "We will," he says, "return this situation to its previous condition. This will be accelerated with your cooperation."

"Here's the lease," Farnsworth says.

Dr. Bender takes the folded document, but he does not open it.

"It's legal," Kimmel says. "He paid for a year, cash, so there's three months left on it."

"The room downstairs shows few signs of habitation," Dr. Bender says. "Were you under the impression that your tenant lived alone?"

"He was a black guy, nice clothes, I don't know. I didn't ask too many questions. I guess I saw different people go in there—men, women, different kinds of clothes, whatever."

Kimmel holds up his hands; talking seems to tire him. Through a doorway, colored light flickers along a wall, where a television has been left on. There are voices, laughter, increasing in volume for the commercials.

"Did you ever see," Dr. Bender says, "more than one person enter that downstairs apartment at one time?"

"No. I did not," Kimmel says, after some hesitation.

"In your opinion, could the people you describe possibly have been the same person, wearing a variety of disguises?"

"Bender," Farnsworth says. "Really."

"They came in, they went out," Kimmel says. "Sometimes I heard the phone ringing, through the floor, and then it stopped."

"Is there next of kin on that lease?" Farnsworth says.

"Contact information?"

Dr. Bender unfolds the paper and begins to read it. He stands still for a long time before speaking.

"Do your recall your tenant's name, Mr. Kimmel?"

"I only met him that one time, when I showed him the place, gave him the key."

"The name on the lease is 'Auguste Dupin.'" Dr. Bender pauses. "Does nothing about that name strike you as strange? 'Auguste Dupin.'"

"I never saw his driver's license, if that's what you mean." Kimmel blinks, clearly confused. "What answer do you want? I just can't tell what you're getting at."

~~

Both policemen stand at the bottom of the stairs, waiting. Dr. Bender can feel their impatience; he sees their watches' faces flash. No one likes to slow down, to hold back so things can clarify, so it's possible to recognize the correct moment to begin.

"Listen," Officer O'Connor says, "are we doing anything, here? Because already I feel like I'm going to have to burn this uniform I'm wearing, the stink's in so deep, and so far it seems like we're not seeing any action at all."

"Next," Dr. Bender says, "we are going to exhume the body. I assume that will be sufficient action?" Kneeling, he opens his second murder bag; he hands a hammer to Wilson, a short pry bar to O'Connor.

"I have a feeling," Farnsworth says, "that I may no longer be needed here. I don't want to get in the way—I'll head down to the station, start the paperwork, so when you come in you can just fill in the blanks."

"Very well," Dr. Bender says, turning away, dismissing him. "Now, gentlemen, if you will be so kind."

He leads them into the middle of the room.

"The body," he says, "is directly beneath our feet."

"In the cellar?" O'Connor says.

"No." Dr. Bender points to the wall, the word TELL—TALE. "Beneath the floorboards, of course—you know the story."

"Now what?" O'Connor says. "No, I don't."

"The boards look perfectly fit together," Wilson says.

"Exactly. Someone has spent a lot of effort to do this right." Dr. Bender takes the tools from the officers. He widens one groove between the floorboards; wood splinters along the seam. Chipping out enough so he can get a bite with the pry bar, he uses the hammer's head as a fulcrum, then leans in with his weight. Nails whinge, giving way. The smell rises, thick through the narrow gap; he's guessed correctly.

The officers reach out their hands without taking hold of anything, like boys watching their father work; they won't face the task straight on, either, as if something might erupt from the floor, a hand scratching for their eyes.

Dr. Bender works methodically, but he is far from

calm. Every detail of this case points to him, every clue is in his language. He levers up the floorboard and sees the foot, then the leg. He slides the prybar farther, lifts, and the board cracks. As it gives way, something shines, reflecting. A photograph, then another, then a third.

"Stay back!" he says, but the officers are already in the hall, their gloved hands over their noses and mouths, their eyes squinting back at him.

He palms the photographs, shielding them, then slides them into the pages of his sketchbook, which rests on the floor. He lifts the next floorboard.

"What is it?" Wilson says, his voice low. "One body or more?"

"This is an unusual situation," Dr. Bender says. "What we have here does not seem to be human. It appears to be the remains of a dog, in a moderate state of putrefaction."

"A dog?"

"Exactly."

"Why?"

"Yes," Dr. Bender says. As the officers slowly approach, he holds out his magnifying glass. His hand, usually steady, is shaking; he must not let his agitation show. At least there are no more photographs, none he can see.

Standing, he bends floorboards until they give—a strongman trick, almost, the officers watching—and the dog's whole length is uncovered. Next, he returns his sketchbook to his bag, and returns with the cameras.

Even if he is only going through the motions, he must do so correctly. He checks his watch; it is now 9:44. The dog is gaunt, rangy, its coat black. He photographs it with the Polaroid, from each side, then with the 35 millimeter; between the flashes of light, there is only the sound of breathing.

"That's some kind of pit bull mix," Wilson finally says. "That's one big dog."

"Satanism," O'Connor says. "Some kind of ritual or something."

"That's a very romantic notion," Dr. Bender says. He carefully puts the cameras away, then opens a plastic body bag and lays it on the floor, next to and above the dog.

He feels the officers watching as he touches the body with his latex-gloved hand. A greenish mold is growing along the dog's jaw. An insect slithers out its ear, disappears under its fur. The dog is still, yet the weight shifts inside. The body sags as he lifts the head, then the tail end. He slides it into the body bag, then zips it shut.

In the space where the dog had been hidden, there is nothing but dirty boards, a puddle of thick fluid in the shape of the body, the rough edges where the pink insulation was torn out. Dr. Bender looks into this hole, then up at the officers.

"I'd like you to deliver this body to the morgue," he says.

"But it's a dog," Wilson says.

"I'd like you to treat it as if it were a human body."

"This is not our job," O'Connor says. "Crime technicians, maybe. Animal welfare, probably. It's just a damn dog."

"At the very least, it's evidence," Dr. Bender says.

"Evidence of what? It's not like you're going to pull a fingerprint off that thing."

"There are many facts," Dr. Bender says, "that we do not know about this animal. The circumstances under which we found it might lead us to proceed with some caution." He holds up his hand to stave off interruptions. He wants to be alone, to have a closer look at the photographs; he is as eager for the officers to leave as they are, yet he does not want them to sense this. He wants them thinking in other directions.

"If not fingerprints," he says, "we may find strands of human hair, tangled in the animal's fur. I have even read of cases where human remains are hidden, found within a body such as this one. The morgue would be the correct place to investigate such a possibility."

"Don't argue with him," Wilson says, taking hold of the body bag, the handle on one end. "Let's end this."

They lift the body, duck under the CRIME SCENE tape, and turn around in the hall.

"Happy holidays to you, too, doctor," O'Connor says, disappearing.

Dr. Bender can hear their voices outside, blurred—*ridiculous* is the only word he understands—and then the trunk slamming, and the doors, and then the rattle of the squad car's engine as they pull away.

He is relieved to be alone again; now there are no distractions. Stepping into the hall, he retrieves his murder bags and his overcoat, brings them inside the room, and closes the door. He sits on the floor with his back against the wall, fresh air blowing through the window, onto his face. This night is only beginning.

He takes out his sketchbook, opens it to the page where he'd slipped the photographs.

The first image is of a city street, in the summer—people wear shorts and sandals, dark glasses; they make way for the large figure in the middle of the sidewalk. It is Dr. Bender himself, in his dark suit, a heavy bag swinging from each hand. His head is higher than anyone's, alone at that height, and the expression on his wide, white face suggests that he is not there at all, not among these people, that he is working out a distant confusion.

Dr. Bender is not surprised, not exactly. He chuckles to himself, rummages through his coat's pockets for his pipe. He packs in the tobacco, then lights it. The photographs still smell of the dog, the air caught in the space between them. He shuffles the top one under, and realizes the next image is actually a postcard. It is the one they sell in Poe's house, in the gift shop there—the engraving from a daguerreotype, Edgar with his tight high collar, tie knotted like a noose, his wide brow, his uneven mustache, his eyes dark, gleaming with sensibility and soul. Dr. Bender turns the card over; only one word is written there, stretching from edge to edge. NEVERMORE.

He does not feel threatened; challenged, perhaps, yet whoever set up these clues is mistaken, has arrived too late. Who could it be? Dr. Bender is scarcely curious— yes, it is all very clever, he won't dispute that, yet the time has passed when he might have risen to this, when he might have let it concern him. It's a taunt that can't touch him now, for his concerns are beyond himself.

The final photograph is grainy, out of focus, yet he immediately recognizes the dark silhouettes. His own hulking figure leans to look into a window—the window at Poe's house. Above him, against the pale night sky, is the jagged wrought-iron shape of the raven. Higher above, the moon, waxing full.

Smoke weaves around the bare bulb, settles in the high corners of the room. Dr. Bender stacks, then places the photographs in the sketchbook, and the book into its place in the bag. He unrolls his sleeves, his pipe clamped in his teeth, and replaces his cuff links. He prepares to leave, to let this settle inside him; he sits one last moment, on the verge of embarking.

And then the phone begins to ring. Distantly, as if in another room. He taps the pipe's bowl against his palm, and throws the tobacco out the window before it burns him. The phone rings five times, six, and then it stops. There is a voice; a muffled, woman's voice. Dr. Bender stands, maintaining all silence except the voice, locating its source.

He steps over the hole in the floorboards, across the room. When he opens the door to the closet, the voice is louder—its tone insistent, as if trapped—and yet the words are still indistinct, and the closet is empty.

The voice stops. Dr. Bender holds the small prybar in his hand; he does not remember picking it up, and he doesn't need it. With his fingertips, he gently pushes upward on the edge of the ceiling. It gives. He slides the loose sheetrock over and, reaching above his head, grasps the telephone.

It's a phone and answering machine in one, with a tiny speaker next to the headset. Phone and electrical cords snake from it, down inside the wall. Dr. Bender opens the phone's plastic case, and takes out the tiny microcassette. He puts it in his pocket, then places the phone back into its hiding place. Carefully, he replaces the false panel, so the ceiling once again appears whole, unsuspicious.

He closes the closet door, then locks the window, draws the plastic blinds. Carefully, he repacks his murder bags, then snaps the hasps, spins the numbers of the combination locks. He puts on his coat, smoothes his mustache, opens the door, and ducks under the yellow CRIME SCENE tape.

In the hallway, Dr. Ralston Bender kneels and pulls on his galoshes. He peels off his latex gloves. Closing the apartment's door, he affixes a paper seal that stretches from the door to its jamb, that cannot be broken. Along the bottom of the seal, he signs his name.

III. Sylvester

It is cold in the hotel room, the bed out in the middle and exposed to every draft. Lily rests on her side, facing away from Sylvester. His hand is warm, his palm soft. He strokes her bare hip, down along her leg, and then his hand rests, for a moment, between her thighs. Lily's breath whistles faintly through her nostrils, blurs into the sound of the wind. She feels so much desire, energy inside her—romance built up only to be buckled down.

She laughs, gently, then coughs, forcing the breath from her lungs, her body curling so her cold breasts press against her ribs. The springs of the mattress complain and adjust when Sylvester stands. He walks around the bed and kneels, facing her. His warm hands are clasped, touching only each other. His skin smells sweet, faintly of vanilla. His fingernails, Lily knows, are perfectly manicured, smooth and shiny, their edges filed.

The scene is softened through her lashes, her eyes half-closed. She opens them more widely, and he is looking at her, into her, his eyes unwavering and true, not slipping away.

"And true love caresses, leave them apart. They're light on the tresses, but hard on the heart."

He says these words softly, under his breath, as she knew he would. Over his shoulder, she can see out the window, where a deflated balloon hangs sadly from a tree branch, its string tangled. Once, while she and Sylvester were here, a phone lineman in a yellow hardhat appeared in the window, standing on a one-man crane. He waved once, as if apologizing, then swung from view. He had no idea what he'd seen.

Now Sylvester pulls the sheet over Lily's head. Everything is white. She feels him there, through the sheet, though she can no longer see him. She is not allowed to move, but she wants to. She wants to reach out and take hold of him, to hold him close.

And then the silence is cut by the sound of something scratching along the plaster of the hallway, outside the room. Sylvester stands and gently rubs his hands together, as if clearing them of dust, a whisper between them as her dried skin is shaken loose. He steps away.

Lily could throw the sheet aside, but she likes the light way it rests on her, tenting from her shoulder and hip. She likes the anticipation, the chance that Sylvester will pull it from her body. She listens to him as he puts things in the closet, as he closes the closet door. She waits for him to return, to say something; instead, she hears the whine of the hinges, of the door leading into the hall, and then the sound of that door closing.

She imagines Sylvester walking to the elevator, descending three floors in twice the time stairs would take; she imagines him walking a little sideways, like he always does, as if he's constantly coming through a doorway. He's on the street, sauntering now, perhaps looking back, once, up to the window.

With one hand, Lily tosses the sheet aside. The room is dim, the lamps turned off; the only illumination comes from the streetlight outside. She sets her bare feet on the floor; all the plaster and dirt have been swept against one wall. Standing, she goes to the window. Dirty raindrops, dried on the pane, are only visible up close, and through them she sees the yellow circles under the streetlights, and the light spilling from the window of the Kentucky Fried. She can see her car, parked below, a green Pinto wagon with wooden siding made of plastic. Even thieves disdain it.

There is no sign of Sylvester. Perhaps he began running, once he left the hotel; perhaps he felt no desire to linger. Lily is not crying. She has no reason. Nothing has happened, really, yet she feels a collapsing inside.

She scratches her head, then lifts the long straight wig free and holds it out in front of her. Her own hair is short and dark, cut close to the nape of her neck. Usually, Sylvester stays behind, helps her pin up the wig's long strands. There are no mirrors in the room. There is no furniture except the bed. Turning, she pulls the sheets tight, makes the bed, though she knows the bedding will be washed before they next return. Every time, the sheets seem whiter, bleached so hard it burns her lungs.

Lily hangs the wig from its hook in the closet, then retrieves the petticoats from the floor, carefully folds them, and puts them away. She unhooks her garter belt, which pinches her for no purpose—she has no stockings for it to hold. She pulls the thin nightgown over her head, and stands in nothing but her panties; quickly, she fastens her bra, buttons her blouse. She shivers as she pulls on her stonewashed jeans, her suede boots that zip up the side. Her ski jacket is bright red, her cap striped with colors like a stack of LifeSavers.

Lily looks the room over, one last time. Standing in the hallway, she locks the door to room 418 and heads for home.

~~

The way things are with Sylvester is worse than nothing at all. It's been a frustrating kind of tease, the thinnest sliver of possibility. Today, it all felt different. Lily wants to straighten it, to try something, to talk until everything's been said. She must find him.

When this all began, five months before, it was light outside—they meet after she gets out of work. Now the days are shorter, and the streets are darker; this makes everything seem less hopeful.

She works nine to five, transcribing legal documents,

typing with headphones in her ears—tapes of recorded meetings, of lawyers talking to themselves in empty offices. There are seven other women like her at the law firm, in a cluster of eight cubicles. When she turns off her machine and removes her headphones, she hears the buzzing murmur of all the others' headphones, all the tiny words. Below this static is the women's low breathing, as slow as if they were asleep. Their fingers tap, spidering across keyboards, and their eyes stare into the monitors where the processed words surface.

After four years at this job, Lily began to make adjustments to her transcriptions. Not grammatical changes, but slight shifts of facts; insignificant details, mostly, never names or dates. She inserts adjectives, adverbs. So far, no one has noticed.

Often, she'll work with a magazine or newspaper open in her lap. She'll read, in pauses, or when the tapes are rewinding. She reads the *Philadelphia Weekly* from the front to the back, where she finds her favorite section: the Personals. Her interest began with the **I Saw You** ads, in which strangers try to translate a coincidence or chance encounter into something more, and then she graduated to the **Men Seeking Women** and the **Women Seeking Men**—and then all the possibilities and variations. She considered whether any of them could concern her.

Lily is thirty-two years old. Her figure is nothing special, but it's not bad, and it's holding up; her face is plain, yet not unpleasant. And now there is Sylvester. She wants it to end, and she wants it to continue. She wants it to come to something beyond where it is, beyond anticipation. How is the romance of fulfillment different? She does not know. Perhaps it's shallower, knowing how things stand—perhaps it's no romance at all?

Finally, it was the **Anything Goes!** ads that had drawn her in, that brought her to room 418. She'd always read them furtively, not wanting to be caught. It was there—among the "Naughty Committed Couple," the "Hung, Hirsute Lady Lover," and the "Talented Tongue"—that all this began.

GOT MILK?

Generous WM seeks pregnant or nursing mother. Any size, shape, race. No other involvement sought. Who will let me suckle?
Call Box 5693

WOMAN NEEDED

Discretion necessary. Age, race, looks negotiable. Dramatic encounters. Longing and Love. Regular. Details upon verification of suitability. Call Box 5701

LOOKING FOR MY SOULMATE

SWM–early 40's seeks kind-hearted caring helpmate who can tie the best knots this side of the US Navy. Other interests: golf, country music, astronomy.
Call Box 5773

WANTED: SEXY, WET PUSSY

19 YO WM, blonde hair/blue eyed track star ISO female 18–28 to hear scream as I eat her for hours and reach ecstasy only dreamed of.
Call Box 5754

The ads abashed Lily, and they excited her. She imagined answering them, following through; sometimes she even called to hear more information. She never left her name. It was number 5701 that spoke to her—she was a woman, and one was needed. She knew longing, and she could use drama. Would she be found suitable?

She had not planned to leave her actual name, her real number. The words escaped, a slip of her unguarded desire. The man called her back in less than an hour. His voice was calm, dignified. He did not give her more information, he only told her to come alone, to meet him in a Kentucky Fried Chicken. Why did she agree? She wonders if there is a difference between curiosity and desperation.

~~

Lily had waited at a shining, plastic table, the fluorescent light reflecting all around her. She knew he was the one as soon as he came in—he so obviously didn't belong there. Where did he belong? She stood as he approached, and it surprised her, how tall he was, the bulk of him, his shadow falling across her and changing everything. For a moment, in that silence, she imagined him lying on top of her—she would be entirely covered, he would break her in two.

You may call me Dr. Bender, he said.

He was dressed as if for a costume party set in a different era—in a dark suit, despite the heat, buckled shoes, his lank hair swept from his shining forehead. His speech seemed old, also, his words formal and carefully chosen, sifted through his mustache.

I'm delighted that you made it, he said, reaching to take her hand from her side. He smelled like alcohol, she thought, then decided it was some kind of medicine.

She tried to tell him that there had been a mistake, that she didn't know him, that she'd had second thoughts.

Nonsense, he told her. He told her she had come in a spirit of goodwill, and that he appreciated it. *I assure you*, he said, laughing under his breath, *that it is not I who is to be the object of your affection*. He promised she would not be disappointed.

The words Dr. Bender said were ridiculous, yet something—sincerity?—about the way he spoke made Lily follow when he guided her across the street and through the hotel's lobby, into the elevator and down the hallway, to room 418.

When he opened the door, she stepped into the dilapidated room, the white bed glowing; against one wall rested two bright lamps, a cassette player on the floor between them.

I must leave you here, Dr. Bender told her. *I will return in under fifteen minutes.*

He closed the door behind him, and Lily was left alone. After a moment, she stepped to the single window. Below, she saw Dr. Bender slowly crossing the street, entering the Kentucky Fried. She re-crossed the room, reached for the doorknob. It was unlocked. Stepping into the hallway, she looked both ways; she could run, but then she would never know. He'd left the door open, perhaps, to show her that it was her decision. That she was not going to run was the scariest and most exciting fact of all.

She stepped back into the room and closed the door, then walked around the perimeter. She pushed the Play button on the tape recorder; in a moment, there was a low, rough whistling, its pitch shifting. Hitting Eject, she read the tape's label—*WIND*. She continued circling, spiraling inward until she reached the bed; she checked underneath it, then sat down to wait.

When the doorknob turned, she stood. Dr. Bender entered the room first, but he was not alone. The other man was smaller, more Lily's size. His skin was black, his body slim. She liked the way he looked, and how he looked at her. If he was nervous, it was only slightly. He wore a brown leather jacket, the same color as his pointed shoes. His beard was shaved precisely, as if the edges were painted on; his mustache was just a sliver, four whiskers thick, balanced on his upper lip.

Lily felt something, as she stood ten feet away. A faint twinge in her rib cage, an edge of pain. Not exactly recognition, though Sylvester always felt familiar to her, at the same time as he made her uneasy. Later, he told her that he, too, had answered an ad; Dr. Bender wanted to be sure they didn't already know each other.

That first day, standing by the bed, she was ready for anything; she forced herself not to turn away. Earlier, she'd chosen a black dress that had grown tighter than she liked; she hoped it would be right for this, whatever this was. She'd pulled back her hair, and taken off all her jewelry. She wore black eyeliner, dark red lipstick. Shoes with low, sharp heels. She felt Sylvester's eyes on her, and sensed that he liked what he saw. He smiled, and his teeth looked sharp and white.

~~

In the beginning, they met twice, even three times a week, in room 418. Now, when she needs it most, the frequency has dropped to once every two weeks, or even less. Lily waits for the calls, checks her answering machine ten times a day, drives out of her way to pass the hotel.

That first night ended after the introductions; it was only for Dr. Bender to be certain that Lily and Sylvester would do, that they could be trusted.

There will be compensation, he told them, *but I could not tell you that, before now—this is not prostitution, but people's thoughts tend toward the literal. Most of your compensation, however, will not be in money. Listen carefully to me: these times in this hotel are the only connection the three of us will have. Outside of this room, we do not exist for each other. Any breach of this, any attempt at contact, will mean the end. Are we in agreement?*

The second time they met, he brought a duffel bag filled with their costumes. Both she and Sylvester had to change out of their clothes before they began. No nylon, no bright colors, no sneakers were allowed to be seen. They were all hidden away in the closet.

The first few times were only rehearsals, really. Dr. Bender had to show them how it was all supposed to go. He was very serious about it; he never joked. He held their costumes against his body, playing both their parts. He even wore her wig, and they didn't laugh. They watched as he shifted the way he moved—not becoming them, but revealing a way they might be. He taught them exactly how to touch each other, the stiffness of their gestures, their expressions like something was being lost, slipping away.

Every movement had to be repeated the same way. Every word, the lines built from some kind of old poetry. Dr. Bender worked and worked with Sylvester, repeating the words, helping him memorize them. Before long, Sylvester changed his beard to pointed sideburns; he was complimented for his authenticity.

You must do it with honesty, he told them, and his belief made it seem possible, as he stood aside and listened, as he watched with his pipe clenched in his teeth and a perfect whirlwind of smoke obscuring his face. *And don't ever ask me why. Your innocence is essential.*

Eventually, he spent less time in room 418 with them; he interrupted less frequently. There was nothing except the taped sound of the wind, the bright lights, Sylvester reciting the poetry, touching her only so far. Each time Lily became more aroused, as if she returned to find her excitement where she'd left it.

Unity of effect, Dr. Bender said, and soon he did not come into the room at all. There was only the phone call alerting them to be there, and then the scratch of his key in the hallway—the signal that he'd arrived and then the signal that he'd departed. Envelopes of money were there ahead of time, in the closet. They were not to talk outside of the words he gave them; Sylvester was to leave at the end of the scene, and once he was gone she could rise from the bed.

Both she and Sylvester realized that Dr. Bender was in the next room, his eye watching through the hole in the wall. They knew better than to look at it, directly, yet it was always there, in their peripheral vision, switching back and forth. Sometimes she almost forgot they were being watched, but still she felt the weight of that eye, still she felt her movements subtly guided. Even when hours were lost in seconds and she felt a weightlessness, even when she saw Sylvester's erection, pushing out his nightshirt, the tip pulsing with his heartbeat. She never reached out and grasped it.

Be honest, Dr. Bender told them, yet until now the words and actions have felt stilted, slightly false. Today was the first time that they seemed to make sense, to feel as if they applied to her, to Sylvester: *And true love*

*caresses, leave them apart. They're light on the tresses, but
hard on the heart.*

~~

As she accelerates down her street, Lily realizes she
can't remember any of her drive from the hotel. She
parks at the curb, locks the Club across the steering
wheel, then opens the passenger door and slides across.

The walk is icy, unshoveled; hurrying, finding the
front door key, she almost falls.

"Hello?"

There's no answer. She shares the row house with
two college girls, both ten years younger than she is.
They study at Temple—Julie's in the education school,
Kristin can't decide—and Lily has nothing in common
with them. In the living room, there are posters of bands
she's never heard, and a musty, broken-down couch, and
a television with a tinfoil halo. She kicks her way toward
the kitchen, where she picks up the phone.

This is the only number she has for Sylvester. As it
rings, as she figures what to say, she glances at the bills
stuck to the refrigerator by magnets. The cupboards are
filled with mismatched plates and cups, everything
chipped, left behind by prior tenants who are now far
away, living better lives. Lily rinses out a glass and fills it
with water, sets it next to a two-foot-tall bong she's
never seen before—it's made of clear purple plastic,
blackened around the bowl. She can't believe she lives in

this world, and in the hotel, and at work, typing the lawyers' words. In each place, she feels like a different person; they are not subtle adjustments.

Sylvester's not there. He never is. Lily pauses. She almost hangs up without leaving a message, then can't stop herself.

"You took off on me! I need to talk to you, we need to get together. Outside of the hotel. Call me. We can't wait for that jackass elephant man to set it up. The times are too far apart. Call me."

She hangs up the phone, and is not certain what to do next, only that it has to be something. Her car keys are still in her hand.

~~

Lily had been ready for Sylvester since the first rehearsal—that is the truth. She'd wanted to throw the sheet aside, to open her legs and catch him there. They didn't have to talk, to plan it. They spoke with their eyes, the tremors in their outstretched hands. It took almost three months before they acted, before they touched in ways they hadn't been taught.

That first time, they waited for the signal of Dr. Bender's departure, and then Lily slid out from under the sheet, and made the bed, and they started the scene from the beginning—carefully, like a spell, for no one except themselves. And after Sylvester covered her with the sheet, he uncovered her; he was no longer wearing his nightshirt. At the sight, she wrestled free from her gown, and then, at last, she felt his skin on her. She cried out, and he covered her mouth. He was quiet, but his hands were strong, his pale palms gently slapping her, his long dark fingers, finally, and his fingernails at the back of her neck, her thighs, the round cheeks of her ass. His eyes were wide, rolling and still on her. What she wanted was to feel his tip just forcing its way into her and then loose again and coming back inside; he wanted to be deep as he could be. They worked their compromise, again and again.

It is always like that—only in room 418, and only after the scene has been played through, as a continuation. The possibility of Dr. Bender's return only heightens the thrill. Is it that he would punish them? Take the game away? Or is the possibility of disappointing him what tinges the act with delicious fear?

They rested, that first night, after their shadows had buckled and rolled along the far wall; they laughed into each other's skin as the tape ran out and the wind clicked off. Lily almost told him he didn't look like a Sylvester, that it was a cat's name, but in that same moment she realized that Sylvester was not his name at all, but only one he gave her, to use as a marker. She felt silly, exposed, to have given him her actual name; in a way, she hoped he believed she'd given him a false one, too—in another way, she hoped he knew the truth.

They climbed from the bed, together, and went to the hole in the wall. Bending down, they took turns peering through. The room on the other side was the same as the one they stood in, only more broken-down and empty, littered with sticks of broken furniture.

~~

It's late, the streetlights blending into each other, the pedestrians harder to see. Lily circles through traffic, around the blocks of the city, in spirals, in figure eights. Where could he be? Is he looking for her? She drives slowly, aimlessly, choosing the narrowest alleyways, waiting patiently as people attempt to parallel park.

Once they'd broken that rule, they couldn't stop. The scratch of Sylvester's beard left its mark, a kind of rash beneath her clothes; at work, she'd look down the neck of her blouse and shiver at the sight—a sign from another world—as she anticipated the next time. Only once did he call her, and then only to say he was thinking of her, that he liked the smell of her. He will never meet her, not outside of the hotel, not without Dr. Bender calling first, and he'll never talk of how they met, their connection to each other. He won't discuss Dr. Bender at all, what they do for him, or why—as if the language on the outside cannot describe it, as if they can only come together inside that staged scene.

She will find him. She'll see him waving from the dark sidewalk, and she'll pull over; he'll open the door, and ask if he can drive. The driver's door is broken, so she'll slide across and climb out. They'll kiss, their bodies brushing against each other as they switch places, and then they'll begin to move through the city, out Kelly Drive, along boathouse row, the Schuylkill dark and frozen on the left.

It's just so nice to finally see him outside of room 418, she'll say. She'll tell him that she feels like she can breathe. The dashboard light will flicker, as it does; Sylvester's expression will stay the same. Calm. When he turns his head to check his blindspot, he'll look at Lily for a dangerously long time before returning his attention to the road.

She'll ask if he's taking her somewhere, if he's going to do things to her, and he'll only smile. They'll swoop across the Strawberry Mansion Bridge, toward the gates of the zoo, the dark shapes of fences and cages. In the parking lot, they'll fold down the Pinto's back seat and do it all—they'll say whatever they like, and take things in any order, and leave their clothes on or take them all off. Afterward, Sylvester will hold her; he will talk to her, like he always does.

Sometimes he tells her that he is not married, that he runs a small business; he never says exactly what kind. He talks about things she can't quite follow, and his voice rises with a kind of pride. He says there's a different kind of economy in the city—one that is about scores being settled, one that is not only about money. For him, though, it *is* about money, because of the things he can do, the things he can make happen. Sometimes it has to seem like a random accident, a strange coincidence, and other times it has to seem like a prank. The more powerful people are, he says, the more petty they are. Motivations are subtle, difficult to figure.

Sylvester can do all this, and more. And it means that whenever someone crosses *him,* whenever he feels someone taking advantage, he knows how to handle the situation—he takes pleasure in doing so. *I won't stand being disrespected*, he said, once, lying back with his hand on his forehead, staring at the hotel room's cracked ceiling. *I can get behind anyone, no matter what they're doing and who they are, how quick—I'll be behind them and they won't even know it.* He tells Lily to let him know if anyone makes her feel afraid. He says he can straighten anything.

She needs him here, on the outside; to have him only in room 418 is worse than not at all. It tears at her now, remembering how he'll turn over, how he'll hold her so gently with his soft voice spilling all around her.

~~

Now she drives past the zoo parking lot, down the other bank of the Schuylkill. She heads back into the city, into the narrow streets. Her eyes want to close; her legs are cramped. She parks, opens the passenger door, then slides across and stretches in the cold air. Reaching across the lighted cab, she kills the ignition, pockets the keys. She locks the passenger door and starts off. She feels the need to walk.

There's only the sound of her arms against her sides, the sick whisper of nylon. She mistakes squirrels for rats, before she sees their tails—one tries to bite the other's ass, they spiral up a tree. The streets are empty. Still, she feels as if she's being followed; she looks behind her, but she can't see far. What time is it? She doesn't have her watch. She lingers in dark, narrow alleys, pauses to stamp snow from her boots. She cannot feel her fingers or toes. Paper and plastic bags circle in the cold wind, caught in an empty intersection. She wants to be at its center, spun there, her arms wide. Three men in hard-hats, one half-submerged in a manhole, watch her pass; next to them, a metal heater shaped like a torpedo blows steam into the night. The men disappear and surface in the cloud.

When Lily sees the diner, she's thinking of coffee, of chicken noodle soup. The neon is faint through the steam-covered windows. She leans into the door and, overhead, bells ring.

There are only a few tables, booths along the windows, and a horseshoe-shaped counter ringed with stools. The Formica is dull, worn in round spots where many elbows have rested. The air smells of burnt coffee, of hamburgers.

Lily is not certain if she senses him before she sees him. Dr. Bender. He absolutely fills one side of a booth; no one could fit next to him. His back faces her, and he has not seen her, but she cannot walk away. Instead, she is drawn closer, until she could reach out and touch his shoulder. Loose papers cover the table, and he is writing in a notebook. He hums, murmurs to himself. His pen does not stop or slow; it trails a line of black, crooked letters, words impossible for her to read.

Turning suddenly, Dr. Bender smiles, as if he is hardly surprised, as if he is happy to see her. She's embarrassed of her clothes—the red nylon jacket, the striped hat—but he doesn't seem to take offense or even notice.

"Lily," he says. "Are you unhappy?" He gently closes the notebook, then begins shuffling and stacking the papers.

"Sit down." He grips the edges of the table in his huge hands and pulls it toward him, making space on the other side. "Where are my manners?"

"I don't know," she says. "It's late, I mean. I don't know if I can sit down."

"Sit down," he says again. "It can't get much later."

She sits, only half facing him. There's no room for her legs beneath the table. Over the doorway, she sees there's plastic mistletoe. Strings of popcorn and cranberries hang from the ceiling above the counter. She feels Dr. Bender watching her, even as he continues to straighten his papers. Is this meeting a coincidence? Does it matter? Suddenly, she's sweating, as if warmth radiates from the doctor's huge body. She unzips her jacket, shrugs it off behind her.

"It can always get later," she says.

"I suppose you're right," he says. "Until it becomes early again."

She has not seen him up close for months; he seems older now, more tired. His hands, loose on the table, look wide and dangerous; his head is enormous, heavy, and his small eyes are fixed on her. The loose skin on his face and neck suggests that he was once even larger, that he is shrinking.

"I'm surprised you'd ask me to sit here," she says. "I thought it was against the rules—seeing each other outside, I mean."

"It's late," he says.

Lily cannot tell if he means more than just the hour. A silence settles between them. She wonders if they can now talk about what was forbidden before; she wonders what else they would have to discuss. Away from room 418, he seems less overwhelming—frail, somehow, despite his size. She feels suddenly unfettered, facing him.

"Are you really a doctor?" she says.

"Yes," he says. "A kind of doctor."

"A kind?"

"I am an examiner." He gestures to the papers at his elbow. "I investigate murders. I find clues in the bodies of the deceased."

She kicks him under the table, by mistake. The cups of coffee—when did the waitress bring them?—quiver and spill into their saucers before settling. Dr. Bender waves off her apology.

"What brings you out this late at night?" he says.

"Driving." She shrugs, to show that speaking of herself does not interest her, that this is not where she wants to take the conversation. "So," she says, "all these papers have to do with a murder?"

"I've been involved in an investigation this evening, yes."

"Well," Lily says.

Dr. Bender takes his pipe from a pocket, but the waitress stops him before he can light it. He thanks her, and sets it carefully on the table. Time passes very slowly, as if the air has thickened around them.

"I think we know who's responsible," he says to Lily, his voice lower. "I think you do." He looks into her eyes. "The man we know as Sylvester," he says.

Lily is surrounded by the smell of old pipe smoke, of chemicals and cologne. The surface of her skin tightens, winding cold and then loosening, her muscles finally relaxing. She imagines Sylvester's face, his smile. A murderer. She finds it hard, if not impossible to believe.

"By your reaction," Dr. Bender says, "I can see that you did not know about it. I'm thankful to find that's the case. Still, it would interest me to be put in touch with him. Sylvester."

"You could call him," Lily says. "Set up a meeting in room 418."

"We will get to that. We will discuss the hotel." Dr. Bender rakes his hair back from his forehead, mops his face with a handkerchief, smoothes his mustache. "Now, though, I'd like to ask your help in contacting this man. Tonight's events may impair my ability to do so, and I believe you might have more direct means. I'd be willing to pay."

"This was never about money," she says, her mouth dry, her voice uneven.

"Of course not," he says. "I apologize for my presumption. You've already done so much for me."

Lily watches drops of water roll down the inside of the window, making long rips in the steam, collecting in puddles around the dead flies on the sill. She remembers Dr. Bender in her wig, his huge body moving in slow motion, teaching her all the pieces of the scene. She tests a fork's tines against her fingertips.

"You told us never to contact each other," she says. "I never even tried."

"On the contrary." Shifting the papers, he takes out a microcassette player; it looks like a domino against his huge hand. "This tape," he says, "was in the answering

machine, at the scene of the crime I am investigating."
Dr. Bender pushes the Play button. At first, through the
static, there's his own voice:

*"Thursday, November nineteenth, five-thirty PM. The
location remains the same as always."*

Lily recognizes the message—it's identical to the
ones he leaves for her. Then there's a click, and a beep,
and then a woman's voice; it takes a moment for her to
realize it's her own. The message is from today, earlier,
while she stood in her kitchen. Her voice is strained,
insistent. Dr. Bender lets the message play to its end, and
then he stops the tape.

"'Jackass elephant man,'" he says, almost smiling.
"That's pretty good." He puts the tape player away.
"Now," he says, "there's no reason we can't be honest
with each other."

"I don't know," Lily says. She feels caught, found
out, and she cannot tell why Dr. Bender is not more
upset with her. "I only have the phone number you do,"
she says. "Obviously."

"I believe," Dr. Bender says, "that our friend
Sylvester misunderstood my intentions. My motivations. I know he's followed me, that he's collected information. None of that matters. I want to find him, to tell
him that. This is no competition; I do not want to challenge or hurt him."

"What about me?" Lily says. "What if I was hurt?"

Dr. Bender closes his eyes, opens them, closes them

again. The sharp hands of the clock above the counter are about to meet at 12.

"I was hurt," she says. "I think everything's changed and I don't know why, except now you have to tell me, now I'm going to ask. Don't interrupt." Lily struggles to keep her voice down. She stares across at him until he turns his eyes away. "I used to think it was simple," she says, "that you liked to watch, and while your eye was watching us your hands were on yourself, on the other side of that wall. Now I think it was something else, something more complicated. I don't know what."

Dr. Bender opens his eyes. He does not seem to see her. He licks his lips, then begins to speak.

"At first," he says, "I just wanted to see it, to see something like that. Between people, you understand. It was never so crass as you suggest."

"At first?" she says.

He takes out his handkerchief and wipes his face. His lips tremble, but no words come out. Finally, he waves to the waitress, then orders a bowl of soup.

"Who did he kill?" Lily says.

Dr. Bender looks at her as if what she's said makes no sense at all. On the stools at the counter, two men turn to stare.

"I apologize," he says. "I understand how you could have reached that conclusion. However, while this evening's investigation appeared to be a murder, it turned out to be no such thing. I don't believe our friend is in fact capable of such a crime."

Lily's coffee is gone; she can still feel it on her teeth, sour in her stomach. With one hand, she squeezes the napkin dispenser. The spring inside squeaks. Her other hand tests the chewing gum, dried and hard, stuck along the bottom of the table.

"I wanted," Dr. Bender says, the words coming slowly, "I wanted it to be pure. Does that sound ridiculous?"

Lily tries to shake the sympathy rising in her. She wants to comfort him, but she has to fight for herself, as well. Is it ridiculous, what he is saying?

"Only because it was fake," she says. "It was set up and artificial from the beginning."

"Yes, he says. "In the beginning. Let me ask you this—it took about three months, didn't it? Before you started breaking rules? I could tell. Just the way your movements changed, the slight adjustment in how you reacted to each other. A different tension between you. A new familiarity."

"You expected too much," she says. "We're just people."

"Exactly," he says. "It was never meant to be perfect. I saw the attraction, it was necessary, and I expected you would eventually consummate it. Once you had that secret, you moved differently; the lights shone on you in a new way."

"You watched us?"

"No," he says. "Not beyond what we'd rehearsed. I

was happy to recognize it, though, that you two had dared. I wanted the feelings to become real. I wanted you to forget me and how everything began."

"That was the point?" Lily says. "How could we forget?"

"You couldn't," he says. "And I couldn't. That could not be overcome. I did not know that at first. I had to learn it. I had to learn that the person who had to see it was someone else entirely, someone who didn't know the beginning."

"What are you talking about?"

"This was the final night," he says. "Tonight. I won't be calling you again."

"Just like that," Lily says, her voice soft. It is a statement, not a question. Her hands are in fists, and she straightens her fingers; she has failed to hold on to anything. The news does not come as a surprise, she tells herself, since she has already sensed that it's over.

Dr. Bender straightens his stack of papers, his gaze turned down. He looks less tired, now. His eyes shine, his thick fingers unfold. Shifting his weight, he slides his two leather suitcases out from under the table. He opens one, and feeds his papers into it. He holds up the microcassette player for a moment, as if it's a joke between them.

"If you'll excuse me," he says, standing. "It has been my pleasure."

"Your soup," she says.

It rests in the middle of the table, yellow and steaming.

"I ordered it for you," he says.

As he walks away, the heavy suitcases, one in each hand, seem necessary to hold his feet to the floor. He is already at the door, too far away to hear, when Lily calls out to thank him.

~~

The waitress takes away the bowl once the soup is gone. Lily sits, summoning the energy to rise, trying to remember where her car is parked. She is thinking of all she gave up, all she hoped for—that world has collapsed in on itself and cannot be found again, can never be understood from here. This saddens her; at the same time, she feels a kind of relief.

Then a movement startles her. Someone is outside, on the other side of the window, a hand only inches from her face, trying to scrub away the steam. The steam is on the inside, so it cannot be cleared. Next, a white face, blurred and strange, leans close, trying to see her. Lily feels her heart accelerate, her fingers go cold.

Then the bells ring, and a man enters. He's slight—a boy, actually. A teenager. He doesn't hesitate; he walks straight for her. There's something eerie about him, not quite right. The white lining, like cotton, pushes through holes in his jacket. His long blond hair is parted straight down the middle, that line a bright arrow, pointing at her.

He stands next to the table. She tries not to meet his eyes. He reaches out, picks up the glass of water Dr. Bender left behind. When she looks at the boy, she realizes that the shining on the smooth skin of his face, and his hands, is not reflected from the light above. It's coming from within, radiating outward.

"I almost didn't recognize you," he whispers, his lips hardly moving. "I like your hair this way."

Lily does not answer, and he does not seem to mind. He begins to drink, and she watches. She has never seen him before. His fingers on the glass are almost translucent; they disappear, they multiply. She senses that something is about to happen, that this is no coincidence, no mistake. The boy does not set the glass down until the ice rattles against his teeth. He still does not sit, but remains standing close, watching her.

"No one told me to find you," he says.

"What?" she says, her voice even lower than his.

"Is it all right if I touch you?" he says.

Lily doesn't answer, doesn't really nod.

His fingers are cold, electric, working beneath the hair at the nape of her neck, then pressing her skin. A delicious warmth pours down her spine, along her nerves that branch like trees, like fingers—feathers of heat roll down her arms, her legs, to the tip of each finger and toe and circling darkly back. She gasps. Warm filaments snake around her bones, loose in her skull, and settle everywhere, rooted and tight.

Then the boy withdraws his hand. Turning, he walks slowly away, through the door.

Lily watches him go. She sees him outside, along the steamy window, the shape of him fading and then no longer there. The warmth remains; it resides in her. She knows that she will carry this change out into the night, that she will rise with it in the morning. Days and weeks, months and years. She will find love, here and in other places, with other people. Hope will overflow and spread out before her.

Acknowledgments

These are for my friend Handsome Craig Smith, who in his short life always appreciated a good story; I trust you can read them, Craig, wherever you are, and hope you find them entertaining.

So many of these stories arose from my fortunate life with the champion, Ella Vining, who continues to help and improve me, every single day. Thanks to all Vinings, Rocks, and family traveling under other names. My editor Kate Nitze understands and believes, shines like a steady light. Deep gratitude for help with this project to David Poindexter, Julie Burton, Dorothy Carico Smith and Ira Silverberg. Thanks to all the magazine editors who, often at great risk and danger, first published these stories. Stories require friends. Two editors who became important friends, and who encouraged me at hard times when no one else would: Michael Koch and Adrienne Brodeur. I won't forget.